The Price of

Loss

Stuart Allison

To Rebecca
I hope you enjoy the story –
Best wishes.
S. All

The risk of love is loss, and the price of loss is grief. - Hilary Stanton Zunin

Chapter 1

The car carried on gathering pace as it left the road and bounced across the grass verge towards the tree. At the last minute I wrenched the wheel to the right as the left wing of the vehicle collided with the trunk in a rending screech of tortured metal. I had just enough time to see my passenger fly forward before the airbag exploded in my face and everything turned black.

I awoke screaming in my own bed, sitting up sweating. I reached out for my wife only to encounter an empty space, Jane was gone. It was just as well I slept alone, as the dream was a frequent companion since the events of last summer. I had survived the crash, my passenger had not, mostly because I had released his seatbelt an instant before the collision with the tree. So the racist politician who had held me captive and threatened the life of my friend and my daughter had died. I had been left with the dream and I could talk to no-one about it, as I had told no-one the full story. Perhaps I would have told my wife Jane, but she had walked out of our thirty year marriage a few weeks earlier and now, eight months later was happily living in Southampton with Simon, the boyfriend she had before we met. I was alone with the dream.

Life goes on and I had begun to rebuild some sort of existence, except for the recurring dream I looked at the alarm and cursed as I made out the digits 3:30. Switching on the light with a shaking hand, I pulled a book off the bedside table. I tried to read, hoping that it would relax me, but it was too difficult to concentrate. I gave up and turned off the light, tossing and turning for the next hour until eventually sleep reclaimed me.

The alarm roused me at 7:15 and I as I rolled out of bed to shower and shave. Dressed and breakfasted, I set out for school and stepped into my office bleary eyed and tired even before the day began. Thank God the holidays were nearly upon us. At least I could catch up on some sleep, though the solitary days of the holidays tended to drag.

'Good morning, Ian.' Graham Price, the head of modern languages, greeted me cheerily. 'You look rough, still not sleeping?'

'No, I suppose I just can't get used to sleeping alone,' I lied.

'Time heals all, you'll get used to it.'

'Thanks Graham.' I was spared further well-meaning platitudes by the ringing of the office phone. I picked up the receiver.

'Ian.' I said.

'Ah Mr West, could you come down to reception, you have a visitor.'

'I wasn't expecting anyone, who is it?'

'It's an ex-student; she says you'll be glad to see her.'

'Okay, I'll be right there.'

As I turned the corner and the reception area came into view, I caught sight of my visitor and my heart began to beat a little faster. Standing at five feet six in her high-heeled boots, my visitor was dressed in a leather jacket, tight jeans rolled up to mid-calf. Her long blonde hair tumbled over her shoulders. I recognised her at once, my accomplice from the events of last summer.

'Hi Lisa,' I called.

She turned. Her dark blue eyes sparkled with pleasure and her even white teeth showed in a broad smile. She enveloped me in a hug and kissed my cheek. Students in the vicinity turned to look. I froze; being a red-blooded male, I had no objection to being hugged by Lisa Mann. In fact, had I been thirty years younger it

6

would have been my aim in life. To love Lisa Mann would be easy, but as a middle aged teacher, I doubted the propriety of being seen hugging a twenty-five year old ex-student in the middle of the corridor at school; particularly one that looked like Lisa. She noticed my discomfort.

'Oops, sorry Ian, I didn't mean to embarrass you, it's just so good to see you again.'

'No problem. How are things? '

We chatted as I escorted her to my office. I was amused to see the head of almost every boy we passed turn to follow Lisa's progress. In my office, Lisa settled into a chair and crossed her legs.

'When do you break up?'

'Tomorrow, thank God! It can't come too soon. Even the younger members of staff are complaining of being tired, so an old fart like me is really knackered.'

'Still putting yourself down, I see. I've told you before; you're the youngest fifty-five year old I know.'

'I'm fifty-six and probably the only one you know!'

She laughed. 'Got any plans for the holiday?'

'Nothing firm. Rob and Lucy will be home for some of the holiday, not much beyond that.'

Lucy was my daughter, now researching her PhD in politics at Birmingham. Rob, my son, was approaching the end of his first year at Nottingham University, reading history and politics.

'Well, if you're free, I'd like to ask you a favour.'

'Will this favour lead to me nearly being killed like last year?'

'Hopefully not, that was enough excitement for a lifetime.'

'Ask away then.'

'I've inherited this old house down near the Essex border from my Mum's Aunt and it's apparently full of old stuff that needs cleaning out. You know... possible

7

antiques and lots of old papers. I haven't been down yet myself yet, but Dan gave it the once over last week. I wondered if you'd take a look for me.'

'The house, the antiques or the papers?'

'The papers mostly, I know you've always had an interest in the First World War and there's supposed to be a whole pile of letters from my great-great uncle to his sister. I thought you might be interested; they cover the whole of the war. You'd know if they were worth anything historically. You know I can't depend on Dan for anything to do with history.'

That was true, Lisa's brother Dan was not my greatest success as a history teacher. If it hadn't involved sport, then Dan had deemed it unworthy of his full attention.

'I'll look them over for you. When do you need me?'

'It can wait until the weekend. I'm staying at Dad's for a couple of weeks to start sorting things out, whilst James is away. Why don't we drive down together Saturday about midday and I'll buy you lunch in the pub.'

'Oh, you're a lady of means now, eh?'

'I will be, if I decide to sell. But it seems a pity; the place has been in the family for nearly two hundred years.'

'Maybe you'll have a better idea of what to do once you've seen the place for yourself.'

'Yeah, that's what I'm hoping.'

'Look, I'm sorry to rush you out, but I've got to take assembly in five minutes. Why don't you come over this evening and we'll talk about it all then. That's if you're not busy.'

'No, not at all; I went out with the girls last night when I arrived from London. So I'm free tonight.'

'Okay, come over about seven thirty and I'll cook dinner; if you're prepared to risk my cooking, that is.'

8

She smiled. 'It's a date, I'll see you then. No need to show me out, I still remember the way.' She pecked me on the cheek and left.

Lisa arrived at my house at 7.45. Settled on the sofa, she took advantage of the hiatus until the meal was ready to fill me in on her inheritance.

'The house is an old timber framed place, it's been in my mother's family forever. It belonged to my great, great grandparents. It passed from them to a son who died in the 1930s; we don't know much about him, except that he left it to his sister Elizabeth. She never married and when she died in the nineties, she left it to my Mum's maiden aunt. Great aunt Emily never approved of Mum getting divorced from Dad and wanted to keep up the principle of it passing down the female line, so I got it. Dan is seriously pissed. All he inherited was a couple of grand. Since the last two owners never married, I just hope it isn't a sign.'

'You'll be fine. When is the wedding?'

'We'd like to go for next summer, but we've been having trouble finding a suitable date; James is away so much it's difficult. I'm sure we'll work it out eventually. Dan picked up this.'

She reached into her bag and pulled out a book and handed it to me. It was about five inches by seven and a full inch thick, bound in red leather with the gold title '1914-5' impressed on it. I opened the book to find it was a collection of handwritten sheets bound into a volume. A quick flick showed that they were a series of letters written from the Western Front sent by Lieutenant Thomas Etherington to his sister Elizabeth, who had clearly saved and bound all the correspondence.

'Dan says there are volumes for 1916, 17 and 18 too. There are also old diaries and other letters from the time. It looks like multi-great aunt Elizabeth was a great hoarder.'

9

We were interrupted by the bleeping of the oven timer, warning me that the food was cooked. We sat at the table eating baked ziti, served with focaccia and we split a large bottle of Peroni beer.

'This is amazing Ian, you never told me you could cook.'

'I used to dabble. I had a few signature dishes, but since Jane left, I've been on a steep learning curve.'

'How are things with Jane?'

'I still hear from her every now and then. The divorce came through last month.'

'You okay with it now?'

'No, I never will be, but I've got a simple choice — I can sit and dwell on it or get on with my life - which is no choice really.'

'Any ladies on the scene?'

'No. I'm embarrassed to admit I tried internet dating, I even went so far as to meet one lady in Cambridge.'

'And..?'

'She was a nice lady, but not my type. It just made me realise that I'm not ready. I don't know if I ever will be. After Jane, I've got more baggage than Heathrow and to be honest, I don't know if I could ever trust a woman again.'

'Thanks.'

'Present company excepted. What I mean is that I've got commitment issues; I've no problem with women as friends. I still find it difficult to understand how Jane could move on so quickly. She tells me our marriage is over and within a few weeks is in a new relationship.' I shook my head sadly.

'You will get over it, Ian, it just takes time. I told you last year that it took Dad two years, but he's happily remarried now.'

'I know, things are getting easier, but I feel so alone sometimes... I'm getting maudlin here, let's change

10

the subject. Can I hang on to the letters until the weekend? I'd like to read through them to see what's there.'

'Sure, help yourself.'

We talked on about her new job and her plans and I filled her in on the progress of Lucy and Rob at university.

Soon it was time for her to leave. She kissed me on the cheek and said, 'Thanks for the meal, Ian, it was yummy. I'll pick you up at 11.30 on Saturday, if that's okay. Then I'll show you the house.'

'I'll look forward to it.'

After Lisa had left, I sat with a scotch. I found myself smiling. It felt good to have Lisa back in my life, everything somehow seemed brighter. I picked up the book from the coffee table and began to read.

Belgium
15th October 1914
Dear Libby,

Thanks for your last letter; it is always good to hear how things are at home. It is such vestiges of normality that help us to keep our equilibrium out here.

The Battalion has been in action for the first time in the past few days but I cannot say where. Whilst officers' letters are not censored, we are honour bound not to divulge anything that might be of use to the enemy, should the letter go astray. I am perfectly fine, although first contact with the enemy leaves a man changed. Seeing wave after wave of German troops, many hardly more than schoolboys, falling before our fire, leaves one strangely sickened. I understand from a prisoner that the event is already being called the 'Slaughter of the Innocents' in the German army. I'm sorry to say that one fellow in my company did not behave too well under fire and is currently under arrest, awaiting court martial and I fear the worst for him – that he will be made an example of and pay the ultimate penalty.

How is Edwin faring? Have you heard anything from him recently? It is such a pity that he too did not join up with the regiment, but opted to accept the invitation to join that one-legged oddity from the Admiralty. Though this war is not turning out to be the honourable affair I expected, there is something about Edwin's employment that seems rather distasteful for a gentleman.

If you have the opportunity to send me more supplies like your recent parcel, they would be gratefully received, as we are somewhat short of luxuries (and sometimes basics) here.

Your loving brother
Thomas

I read another few letters until the fatigue of a long term, added to the beer and scotch, took its toll and I fell into bed. Thankfully, the dream was noticeable by its absence and I slept through until morning.

Chapter 2

Friday at school dragged, the promise of seeing Lisa the next day made the wait difficult. It's not that the teaching was a problem; I have always said that the day I don't get a buzz from the classroom is the day I'll walk away, because I'll be doing no good for anyone. No, the lessons flew by, but strangely, the day still seemed interminable. That night I read on with Thomas's letters to Libby, they were good stuff, the whole of the first two years of the war seen through the eyes of a young officer, as he changed from being the innocent subaltern in charge of a platoon to a rather jaded veteran company commander. There was no doubting it - if the next three volumes were as good, then with a bit of careful editing, they would be well worth publishing.

I was up early Saturday morning and was reading the papers over coffee, when a car horn sounded from the drive. I looked through the window to see Lisa, hair tied back in a ponytail and wearing the same leather jacket, sitting in a new blue Mazda sports car with the roof down. I went out to join her, pulling on my own leather jacket, the early spring day was bright, but rather chilly for driving in an open-topped car.

'Nice wheels. When did you get the car?'

'Just last week, I decided to invest some of the royalties I got from the book we wrote about our discoveries last summer. I'd always wanted an MX5 convertible and this was my chance. What did you do with your share?'

'You had dinner in it the other night. I used the cash to help buy out Jane's share of the house; it's thanks to the book that I've still got a roof over my head.'

'Right, good move, now belt up and we'll get going.'

I fastened the seat belt and was pressed back into my seat as Lisa accelerated off down the road. We left town and hurtled south along the country lanes, the proximity of the sports car to the road only augmenting the feeling of speed. I had been right about the roof, it was freezing.

'Jeez, do you always drive like this?'

'Sorry, I only got the car last week and I still haven't got over the way it handles, I love the acceleration.' Nevertheless she slowed, making me feel slightly safer.

'How are you really coping alone? I saw the brave face you put on the other night, but I know you, Ian, especially after what we went through together last summer.'

'Yeah, it's harder than I like to admit, even to myself. I still miss Jane every day. I wake up each morning expecting to see her in bed beside me. I guess the habits of thirty odd years of marriage are difficult to break. It'll always be my deepest regret that I couldn't be the husband she deserved.'

'You're too hard on yourself, Ian, it takes two to make a marriage, I'm just beginning to realise how true that is now that I've got James. You never cheated on her and I know first-hand how kind and thoughtful you are, so Jane has to take her share of the responsibility for the breakdown of your marriage; stop beating yourself up.'

'You might be right, but this is the hardest thing I've ever had to do. Sometimes I feel very alone. I know, I try to put on a brave face, I figure if I can convince everyone else I'm fine, I might convince myself. Let's change the subject, I don't care what people say, talking about it doesn't help.'

'Okay, you're wrong, but I'll humour you. Did you have the chance to read any of those letters I left you?'

'Yeah, I've read most of the first volume, they're really interesting. Tell me again how you're related to this.'

'I know this, I've researched it all. See, I did learn a thing or two from you,' she said.

'I never doubted it. Go on.'

'Okay, the family tree goes like this. My great-great grandparents owned the house before the First World War. They had four children; the eldest was Edwin, he's the one we don't know much about. Then there was Thomas, he's the one who wrote the letters and he was about nineteen when the war began. Elizabeth, the Libby of the letters, was about sixteen in 1914, then there was Daisy, my great grandmother, who seems to have been an afterthought, she was only six at the time. Their parents were killed in a zeppelin raid on London in 1916 and the house passed to Edwin. Elizabeth lived there and brought up Daisy, but she never married. She was an amazing woman. Elizabeth went to Girton College, Cambridge and studied history when she was in her thirties. She ended up as a lecturer there. Edwin died in the 1930s, but I couldn't find out much about it, just that he left the house to Elizabeth. Anyway, to finish the story, Daisy married and had two daughters, of which, Elizabeth, the youngest, is my Nan. Emily, the eldest, inherited the house from her aunt and left it to me.'

'Right, I think I get it. The house, after Elizabeth, passes down the female unmarried line,' I said.

The blue two-seater roared down the country roads, slowing only to heed the speed limit when passing through picture-postcard villages full of pink-painted timber framed housing. I was pleasantly surprised at how

15

comfortable the car was, having been expecting the worst when I had squeezed myself in to it. After forty minutes or so, Lisa slowed the car and turned off into a narrow lane. A mile further on we drove up a hill and, near the crest, entered the village. The road turned sharply and we were looking down the steep high street lined with high street lined with even more rose-coloured buildings, but this time, dotted among them, we saw the occasional traditional white-plastered house with exposed black beams, tall brick chimneys abounded. It occurred to me that there was not a single building that was more recent than 1700. A ford ran at the foot of the slope then the road climbed up the other side of the valley. I examined the Tudor housing as Lisa's Mazda descended the slope and slowed to a crawl as we approached the ford. I wondered whether attempting the ford in the low-riding sports car was a good idea, but the water was no more than five or six inches deep and we passed through it without a problem.

'Nearly there,' Lisa said. 'The house is just at the top of the hill here near the church.'

We ascended the slope and followed the road as it twisted in a hairpin bend amidst the budding trees. Suddenly, Lisa signalled and turned into a gravelled driveway on the right. The drive curved through the trees for twenty yards, then we saw the house. Set in about an acre of land, the house was laid out like a hollow letter E. Three levels of windows pierced the front faces of the wings, rising to a smaller window nestled in the steep eves. The central range had only two levels, crowned by the two small dormer set into the roof. The house was covered in decorated pink plaster rendering and capped by a russet-brown tiled roof covered in a patina of lichen.

'At least it doesn't have a thatched roof, they have to be replaced at intervals and it would be just my luck to inherit a house that needed reroofing.'

'Oh yeah, your luck is so bad. Good job, sports car, a handsome, high-achieving fiancé and now this house. I'd swap my luck for yours any day. I'll pass on the fiancé though, he's not my type.'

Lisa laughed. 'I don't care if he is your type; he's mine and staying that way!'

'You're quite safe, just because I've got issues with women, doesn't mean …'

'Yeah, yeah. Come on, let's go explore the place.' She got out of the Mazda and, pulling a key from the pocket of her tight blue jeans, marched up the steps to the white painted front door.

The door opened into a sizable hall with an oak staircase running from the left hand side. The furniture was sparse, but clearly antique. A long oak table, which from its distressed surface was contemporary with the house, stood surrounded by several chairs of a similar age in the centre of the hall; along the right wall stood an oak dresser.

'That's where Dan found the books of letters,' said Lisa, crossing to the dresser and pulling open the right hand door of its base. 'Yeah, look, there are three more books here.' She pulled out the three red leather-bound books bearing the gold titles 1916, 1917 and 1918 and placed them on the table. 'We can take these with us when we go.'

'Homework! What's this, payback for your schooldays?' I scowled.

'I'm sorry Ian, you don't mind, do you? It's not a problem if you do.'

I laughed. 'No, I'm just yanking your chain. I got quite interested in the first volume and I'm looking forward to reading the rest.'

'Sure?'

'I'd tell you if I wasn't. Come on, show me round.'

'Well, I haven't been here since I was small, but I think that's the sitting room over there,' she said, pointing to the left. 'This way.'

She led the way into the room in the front wing of the house. Pushing open the oak door, she ushered me into a comfortable room. A leather three piece suite encircled a low table in the centre of the room, facing a surprisingly modern large flat screen TV.

'Great-aunt Emily loved her soaps and had the money to watch them on the best TV available.'

'Looks comfy in here, what's the rest of the layout?'

'I think the study's there,' she pointed towards the back wall of the room. I went back into the hall and poked my head through the door on the left at the foot of the stairs. A roll-top desk stood under the window and the rest of the walls were lined with shelves of books, mostly leather bound.

'I should think these books would be worth a few quid, especially if there are any first editions amongst them. Go on. What's over there?' I asked, nodding to the opposite wing of the house.

'Kitchen at the back and dining room in the front.'

'Upstairs? How many bedrooms?'

'I've never been upstairs, or at least I don't remember, if I have. According to Dan, there are four bedrooms and a bathroom on the first floor and two more bedrooms and another bathroom at the top of the house.'

I raised my eyebrows, the house must be worth a bomb. I doubted there would be much change from three quarters of a million, if you wanted to buy it. I knew Lisa came from a privileged background, I remembered her telling me her mother had gone to a good private school, but I had not realised until now just how wealthy her family was.

18

'If you decide to sell this place, you'd be able to get a reasonable place in London for you and James, when you get married.'

'I really hadn't thought of that, I didn't remember the house as being this big.'

We ascended the wooden staircase and briefly looked round the bedrooms, before making our way to the top floor. There the layout was strange. Two bedrooms at the top of each wing, linked by a corridor that ran along the front of the central range, with an attic space walled off in the rear. Behind one bedroom a second bathroom was located.

'It's going to take me quite a while to work my way through all of this isn't it?' she said.

'Oh yes! Do you want a hand?'

'I can't ask you to give up your holiday.'

'It's not like I've got anything planned. You never know, if Lucy and Rob are home for a few days, they might even lend a hand,' I replied.

'I couldn't ask them, it wouldn't be fair.'

'I could, I'm the guy keeping them at Uni, the least they could do is give us a few hours' work clearing out here.'

'Lucy did seem interested when I told her about the place.'

'I didn't know you two were that close.'

'We've spoken quite often on the phone after the events of last summer and we're always on Facebook. So she might not mind, but I don't know about Rob.'

'Are you kidding? Rob might not like work too much, but he'd be in his element here. I'll bet you that within ten minutes he'll be tapping on the walls looking for priest holes.'

'We'll see, when they're back, but I'd be really grateful for your help.'

'You've got it. Where do we start?' I asked.

'Downstairs with a cup of coffee. You go through to the sitting room and I'll make coffee. I brought a few essentials like tea, coffee, milk and sugar with me in the boot.'

At the bottom of the stairs, I picked up the 1917 volume of letters off the table and took it into the sitting room with me, whilst Lisa went out to the car. I switched on the electric fire as the room was chilly and sat on the sofa and began to browse through the book.

Chapter 3

Flanders
Friday 31ˢᵗ August 1917
   Dear Libby,
      It is hard to believe that it was a few short weeks ago that I was home on leave with you and Daisy. The dichotomy between life at home and conditions here is incredible. I know that it is against regulations to describe what is going on here, but I feel that in the light of blind, unthinking patriotism of those at home (not you, my dear sister, but idiots like Major Formby), I have a higher duty to the men suffering in these atrocious conditions to let the real truth be known.

      Our attack took place at a time when the rain had stopped for the first time since I arrived here, but the ground was utterly impossible to cross. For twenty yards at a time the land was covered in cloying mud and water-filled shell holes were everywhere. What a time for me to lead a new company for the first time. The attack was set for midday; I had to rush forward at zero minus ten as the barrage opened. I was in the centre of the company as, with a mighty crash, every gun opened up, supported by machine guns and mortars. The Germans must have known of our attack, for as I stood the company up to advance, the enemy barrage opened up. With shells pouring into the area around us, we advanced through clouds of smoke and eruptions of mud and water. Ahead, I could just make out lines of men making their way forward. With sinking heart I saw the lines waver and break, then disappear from sight. Streams of machine gun bullets poured overhead and the crackle of enemy fire from our front marked their frontline. Coming up to the road, I saw Morris, frozen with fear.

21

'Are you going to let your mates go forward, while you stay here?' I asked.

'No, Sir!' he replied and ran across the road, falling dead before he had taken three steps.

Our artillery now lifted on to the ridge and our attack was completely hung up, with heavy casualties. The C.O. sent me forward to see if there was anything I could do. Dodging and weaving, I dashed across the road into the morass of mud and water, followed by my servant, Holmes, and eight runners. With bullets spitting around us we threw ourselves from shell hole to shell hole. One of the men in front of us was hit, happy to have got a blighty wound that would send him home; he leapt from cover to make his way back, but was immediately struck by a machine gun burst and collapsed soundlessly. All the time, my mind seemed to be working on two planes, part in the present, assessing the dangers and making decisions; the other half of my brain seemed to be trying to protect me from the horrors I was seeing and the terror I was feeling. Images of a happier time flashed through my mind, I could see the sights of Ragusa, during our tour, with Edwin standing on the city walls and the clear azure of the Mediterranean behind him, I could even smell the dry heat and herbs in the air. I had to force myself to focus, or I would be the death of us all.

Exhausted by my efforts, I halted in a shell hole, only to find I was sinking. Struggle as I might, I could not extricate myself and was dragged deeper and deeper into the mud. I tried to pull myself out by grabbing the arm of a corpse sticking out from the side of the hole, but it came away in my hands. I was fortunate that Holmes had seen my peril and he and two other men linked their rifle slings to toss to me and haul me free. So many of our men were casualties and the rest had gone to ground, that it was difficult to round up more than a few. Moving forward I found about fifteen men sheltering from the shrapnel in two mired tanks.

As we advanced on Enfield, stranded and wounded men from our regiment and the Warwicks joined us. It was getting dark and the flash of grenades could be seen around the German pillbox, when suddenly the garrison came out with their hands up, having been outflanked by another party of Tommies. We sent the prisoners back towards the rear, but within a hundred yards, they had been cut down by a German machine gun. We set up our HQ in the Enfield pillbox and awaited reinforcements. It was more than an hour and two German counterattacks before relief arrived. By the time we were withdrawn from the line, my company had been reduced from two hundred and ten men and five officers to one hundred and thirty men and I was the only surviving officer.

These experiences defy belief, could it be just a few short years ago that Edwin and I were home from school, convincing you that the addition of 'us' to the end of a word was speaking Latin? It all seems as if it was a hundred years ago. I know I have criticised Edwin for going to serve with Cumming instead of active service, but in all truth, whatever he is doing in Russia has to be an improvement on this.

I am sorry to sound so pessimistic; perhaps it is because I am so exhausted and upset over our losses. I know that you see this terrible war for what it is and that I can trust you with the truth of that which we have to endure here. I think of you and Daisy, and indeed Edwin, every day and I cannot wait for the day that this dreadful war ends and we can again be together.

Your loving brother
Thomas

Lisa entered carrying a tray of china cups and saucers and a plate of biscuits. She put it down on the low table and handed me a cup.

'Sorry, no mugs, we'll have to make do with a bit of formality.'

'Did you know that you had a spook in the family?' I asked.

'Eh? A ghost?'

'No, a spy.'

'What do you mean?'

'I think that Elizabeth's elder brother might have been working for MI6 in the First World War.'

'I know I said we didn't know a lot about him, but that's a pretty big jump.'

'Well, in one of the first letters, Thomas is concerned that Edwin had not joined his regiment and was engaged in work unsuitable for a gentleman. He also mentions him working for 'that one-legged oddity from the Admiralty'. In the letter I've just read, he mentions him serving with Cumming and being in Russia. Captain Mansfield Smith-Cumming was the first head of MI6 or the Secret Intelligence Service if you prefer. He was the first 'C'. Today it stands for Chief; originally Cumming signed all documents with a C for Cumming. He also had a wooden leg, having had part of his right leg amputated after a motor accident in France. It all fits,' I informed her.

'Multi-great uncle Edwin was a spy, that's cool. Do you think we could find out more?'

'I don't really know; I presume all the existing records are available, they couldn't still be classified, but I'm buggered if I'd know where to start looking.'

'That's a pity, I'd love to know more about it, not many people are related to one of the earliest spies.'

'I think you'll find that spying started well before that, but I know what you mean. You might even find more here, after all this was his house and has stayed in the family, so it's quite possible that some of Edwin's documents are still around. If you think about it, Elizabeth's papers are still here, so why not Edwin's?'

24

'I hadn't thought of that,' she said, 'we'll have to keep our eyes open as we sort through the stuff.'

Whilst we were talking, Lisa was leafing through the book of letters, when a puzzled expression crossed her face.

'That's funny.'

'What?'

'This letter's in a different hand.'

'Let me see.'

I leant over so that Lisa too could read the letter.

16ᵗʰ January 1918

Dearest Libby,

I must, of necessity, be brief, but I have to let you know how I may be contacted in an emergency. As you are aware, my responsibilities cause me to travel extensively and again, I find I must leave you and Daisy to answer the call of duty and I do not know when I will return. This is not a task I happily accept and I cannot go into detail for security reasons, let it be enough to say that thanks to what we learned at matushka's knee, I am ideally qualified for the task in hand. If you should need to contact me, you can send a message through Robert Bruce Lockhart at the Moscow Consulate; tell him the message is for Yakovlev, it should reach me quickly.

If you could let Thomas know that I will be incommunicado for the near future, then worrying about me will not be an extra burden that he will have to bear. I pray daily for his safety and for you and little Daisy.

Your loving brother

Edwin

'Do you know anything about Elizabeth's parentage?'

'A little, her father was Edward who was 46 when he died and her mother was Helen who was twelve years younger. Why?'

'Well, matushka sounds rather Russian, as does the name Yakovlev... Yakovlev... I know that name from somewhere...No, I can't remember it. You know how these things flash across your mind and you can't quite grasp them. It'll come back to me,' I said.

'I don't think so; the name Helen doesn't sound especially Russian.'

'The name Bruce Lockhart rings a bell too, it's going to bug me all night now. I suppose it will come back to me, let's get on with the sorting out.'

'Fair enough. I've had an idea. I brought bread, cheese etc. Why don't we have lunch here and I'll take you to the pub tonight for dinner. We could go back home then, or we could make up a couple of rooms here, I've checked and there's plenty of clean sheets and so on.'

'Fine by me. I'll start in the study while you get lunch. I suggest we divide things into three heaps, one for stuff relating to Elizabeth's generation, one for your great aunt Emily and one for anything before Elizabeth.'

'Sounds like you've got it sorted.'

Lisa left the room for the kitchen and I wandered into the study and began to search through the contents of the roll top desk. In the main part of the desk all of the documents related to Emily; bills, bank statements and other mundane papers. I pulled open one of the drawers and amongst the papers inside was a genealogy - clearly Aunt Emily had been keen on tracing her roots. I was about to put it aside as something Lisa might be interested to see when my eyes alighted on the entry for the generation we had been discussing. At that moment Lisa came into the room with the sandwiches.

26

'Have you seen this?' I asked indicating the family tree.

'What?'

'It's your family tree going back into the eighteenth century. It's quite interesting, Elizabeth's mother is listed here as Helena rather than Helen. It doesn't sound quite so English.'

'Yeah, but we can't check it now. Come on, eat.'

'It's a pity we've got no internet, we could check up and see what we could find out about Helen or Helena.'

Lisa laughed and threw me her phone.

'Welcome to the twenty-first century. My iPhone can access the internet. Go on, give it a go.'

I looked at the phone for a few minutes, perplexed, 'I know it's a touch screen, but how do you turn the damn thing on?'

Lisa's laughter rang through the empty house.

'Come on Ian, even my Dad can work it.'

'Just turn the bloody thing on and get on the net and I'll do the rest.'

Still laughing at my incompetence, Lisa started tapping her fingers across the screen, then handed it back to me. I saw it was on the Google homepage and tapped in instructions to get me to the 1891 census. Retrieving the page, I tapped in the name Etherington and scrolled through to the Hs. There were several Helens, but no Helenas. To make matters worse, none were remotely near East Anglia.

'I can't find her, what did you say her husband was called?'

'Edward, Edward Peter.'

I typed in the name and came up with eight. Only one was in Suffolk. Fortunately, I already had credits from researching my own family and was able to quickly call up the full entry.

'Here it is, Edward Peter Etherington, age 31, born in Colchester, occupation solicitor. Ahh.'

'What?'

'That explains your cheekbones and blonde hair.'

'WHAT?'

I smiled at her impatience, then gave in and read the entry aloud, 'His wife, Yelena Ekaterina Etherington, age 20, born St Petersburg, Russia.

Chapter 4

We carried on sorting papers until it got dark, then Lisa kept her promise of dinner at the local pub, where the steak pie was exceptional.

'Have you thought about my offer for you to stay tonight?'

'Yeah, the problem is neither of us have got anything with us, no change of clothes, toothbrush or even deodorants.'

'Good point; I'd hate to start smelling,' she declared.

'Why don't we go back tonight, pick up some clothes and a laptop, then come back tomorrow and stay?'

'That sounds like a plan.'

Lisa dropped me off at home at 10 p.m. and accelerated away into the night. I settled in an armchair and mulled over the day in my mind. The names Bruce Lockhart and Yakovlev definitely meant something to me, but would not come back to me. I fetched my laptop from the dining room table and started it up. I began a search for Bruce Lockhart and found him immediately. The British Vice Consul in Moscow during the First World War, he was actually a member of the Secret Intelligence Service. Now it came back to me and I could see how multi-great Uncle Edwin might be involved with him. Satisfied, I retired for the night.

Lisa picked me up early the following day and as the blue Mazda sped south, I described what I had found the previous night.

'So you're saying that this Robert Bruce Lockhart was a spy?' she said.

'He was what we'd call the head of station in Moscow, which had become the capital after the October Revolution.'

'Yeah, I remember that.'

'Bruce Lockhart was involved with the infamous Reilly, the so-called Ace of Spies. They were both involved up to their eyes in the Ambassador's Plot to assassinate Lenin.'

'I don't recall that. Perhaps I was dozing that day,' she confessed.

'Flirting is more likely! But you're in the clear; it's not something we usually teach.'

'So this Reilly was like James Bond?'

'More true than you may have thought, it's believed that Fleming based James Bond on Reilly. Bruce Lockhart seems to have been involved in a plot with Reilly to allegedly use Latvian guards at the Kremlin to overthrow the Bolsheviks in August/September 1918.'

'But it didn't happen?'

'Right, just before the plot was to happen, Fanny Kaplan shot Lenin in a botched assassination attempt.'

'I remember that. Wasn't she almost blind?'

'Quite. An unlikely assassin. Anyway, the Head of the Petrograd Cheka was assassinated the same day and, fearing a plot, the Bolsheviks launched the Red Terror, in which all of those involved in the coup were arrested. Bruce Lockhart was arrested and eventually swapped for a soviet agent. Reilly escaped but both he and Bruce Lockhart were sentenced to death *in absentia,*' I went on.

'And Edwin was involved in all this?' She asked. 'Possibly, but I don't think so; I've never come across his name.'

'What about Yako…Yakovlev?'

'I still can't remember and a quick internet search this morning turned nothing.'

'Well, I've got mobile internet on my laptop, so you might get the chance to have a deeper search later.'

We soon arrived at the house and spent the next hour sorting papers. The growing pile of papers belonging to great aunt Emily was of little interest, but the smaller pile of Elizabeth's documents had one or two nuggets of gold.

'Come and look at this,' Lisa called from a first floor bedroom. I went up to see her waving another letter. 'It's another one from Thomas and it's about Edwin.' She handed me the letter.

17ʰ October 1924

> *Dearest Libby,*
>
> *Just a quick note to thank you for your hospitality last week. Both Mary and little Wilfred really enjoyed their time with you. Wilfred always loves to visit "the old house", as he calls it. It is always good to visit my childhood home and it is strange how the feeling of belonging is still there, even though I now have a family of my own.*
>
> *Having spent time with Edwin, I fully understand the concerns that you expressed to me. He is not the man I knew before the War. There is something missing in him that has become increasingly apparent since his return from the war. I know that our experiences in the Great War have changed our whole generation, but Edwin seems to be especially affected, which is strange as he did not see action in the way that the rest of us did. The more I see of Edwin, the more obvious it becomes that he left part of himself in Russia in 1918. I don't know what happened; he has never talked about it and resents my mentioning the topic. The brother we knew is lost somewhere in his past and I am not sure that we will be able to rescue him from whatever it is that holds him prisoner, there is a sadness about him that was never there before.*

'What do you think it was that affected him?' Lisa asked.

'Who knows? If he had fought in the war I'd suggest shell-shock, but being a spy in Russia during the Revolution and possibly the Civil War that followed could have left him with post-traumatic stress.'

'I suppose it could be, but I feel that there's something else. PTSD wouldn't make him sad; it's almost as if he suffered a loss.'

'It's possible; there were a hell of a lot of people killed in the Red Terror and the Civil War,' I reminded her.

'I wish we could know what happened, but I don't suppose we'll ever know. If he couldn't talk about it to his family, I don't see how we can find out. It's such a pity.'

'That's you all over Lisa, a romantic at heart. It must be love!' Lisa coloured fetchingly.

'If I wasn't in love I wouldn't be getting married. You're just a grumpy old so-and-so. It's jealousy.'

This brought my teasing to a rapid halt. I realised how much I still missed Jane and how empty my life had become without her. Lisa must have seen my face fall.

'Oh Ian, I'm so sorry. I didn't mean to upset you. I didn't think. You still miss her, don't you?' I nodded, too choked to answer. 'You really need to get someone in your life to replace her.'

'There never will be anyone to replace her.'

'There will be one day; you're just not ready yet. I told you when it first happened, it took my Dad years before he got it together after he and Mum broke up. Look at him now, he's perfectly happy.'

'I don't see it happening to me, but let's change the subject. This one's too painful, to be honest. If it was a person that Edwin lost, I can empathise with him.'

'Okay, we'll change the subject. There is one thing that I thought you might be able to explain, it's been bugging me ever since I first saw the inside of the house.'

'And that is...?'

'Those roman numerals carved on the beam there,' she pointed, 'and there and over there. What are they?'

I looked at the beams, each of the uprights had a small roman numeral cut into it and the horizontal beams in the ceiling were the same.

'Actually I can explain, a friend of mine had a timber framed house and there were similar inscriptions there. He told me that it was because the building was prefabricated and it told the builders which part fitted where, a bit like an Ikea wardrobe.'

'That's fascinating and it makes sense, all of the numbers are in sequence.'

'That's me; a veritable font of useless information!' I laughed.

'Well, since you're on a roll, can you think of any way we could find out more about Edwin in Russia?' she asked.

'I'd say your best bet would be to see if there's anything else that relates to his time in Russia. We best get back to work and see what we can find.'

'I've got a better idea. Here,' she said, handing me a laptop bag, 'see if you can refine your search on Mr Yakovlev while I unpack the stuff from the car and make some coffee.'

Obediently I took the bag and set up the laptop's mobile connection and got on the internet. I began to search for the name Yakovlev. Most references were related to an Alexander Yakovlev, an aircraft designer. I had heard of him, but that was not what I was looking for. Another Alexander Yakovlev was a soviet politician and an Anton Yakovlev, an actor, I had never heard of either of them. I tried a second page of hits, still no joy, they all related to the aeroplane designer, so I omitted aircraft from the search. There were a lot of Yakovlevs.

'How's it going?' Lisa called from the hall.

'Yakovlev seems to be the Russian equivalent of Smith to judge by the number of Yakovlevs on Google.' Lisa's laughter came through the door.

I had a hunch about Yakovlev. I typed in Yakovlev and Tsar Nicholas II. My intuition was correct, the third hit mentioned Commissar Vasily Yakovlev and it all came back to me. I called Lisa in.

'I've got it! Yakovlev was a 'Special Commissar' sent by the Bolshevik government in Moscow to move the Russian Royal Family from Tobolsk and possibly move them to Moscow, but they were intercepted at Ekaterinburg.'

'I remember this, they were all murdered there, weren't they?'

'Yes, the Tsar, the Tsarina, their son the Tsarevitch Alexei and their four daughters, Olga, Tatiana, Maria and of course, Anastasia.'

'I thought Anastasia survived.'

'Only in the Disney version. It was always rumoured that one of the younger daughters escaped, and that was encouraged by the claims of Anna Anderson to be the Grand Duchess Anastasia, but it was all untrue. The skeletons of the Tsar and his family were discovered in 1998 and identified by DNA.'

'Weren't some of the bodies missing?'

'Yes, Alexei's body and one of the younger Grand Duchesses were found to be missing. Russian forensic scientists claimed it was Maria, American forensic anthropologists claimed it was Anastasia.'

'So Anastasia could have survived?' she asked.

'No, the remains of the other two bodies were found and identified by DNA in 2007.'

'Was it Anastasia or Maria?'

'It's never been proved one way or the other. There were aspects of the first skeleton that led scientists to contradictory conclusions and the second was too badly damaged to settle the argument.'

'And somehow, Great-uncle Edwin was part of this?'

'I don't know; all we can say for sure is that was the name he gave as a contact and from the internet search, Yakovlev is not an uncommon name. Edwin might have been using the alias Yakovlev, but it doesn't mean he was the Yakovlev involved in the Ekaterinburg massacre. Except....'

'Except what?'

'Well from what I remember Vasily Yakovlev, the Special Commissar, was an enigmatic character. I once read a book in the eighties about the Ekaterinburg Massacre, written by two reporters and his role seems shrouded in mystery. After the murders, he fought for the Whites, the anti-communists, which seems a bit strange. Perhaps we need to investigate him more deeply when we have a minute to spare.'

'Do it now.'

'But I thought we were here to clear the house.'

'Boring! This is far more interesting, we can spare half an hour anyway.'

'Okaaay. Let's see what we've got here then.' I began to tap at the keyboard. 'Right. I was right, Vasily Yakovlev was sent from Moscow by Sverdlov seemingly to move the Romanovs back to Moscow.'

'Sverdlov? I've never heard of him.'

'He was a close ally of Lenin, Head of the All-Russian Central Executive Committee, effectively the Head of State.'

'I thought that was Lenin.'

'Sverdlov was the titular head of state; Lenin was Chairman of the Council of Peoples' Commissars, the government. Sverdlov was also the head of the Party secretariat, a post that was known as General Secretary when it was occupied by Stalin a bit later on.'

'How come I've never heard of him?'

'You had a crap teacher,' I smiled. 'He died in 1919, probably of flu. He would almost certainly have been Lenin's heir apparent, had he lived.'

'And he sent Yakovlev to move the Tsar?'

'Yes, it's never been clear whether he was under pressure from the British or the Germans to protect the Tsar from the extremists in the Urals, or whether he wanted to put the Tsar on trial. There are even those who think Sverdlov was involved in facilitating the murders and Yakovlev was his way of distancing himself from the murder to avoid repercussions from the Germans. Remember the Tsarina was German. Anyway, it seems that Yakovlev took his orders from him.'

'What is it that makes people think he was a spy?'

'Look here,' I indicated the screen. 'This shows the way Yakovlev behaved when he first met the Tsar, bowing to him and addressing him as "Your Majesty". It says he was kind and attentive, ordering an extra coat to be procured for him when they travelled by sledge from Tobolsk to Tyumen. I've also seen this elsewhere, the way that he insisted on being alone in the telegraph office and using the telegraph key personally. None of that quite fits with the image of him as a loyal, convinced Bolshevik. Then there's the evidence of him joining the White counter-revolutionary army shortly after the Ekaterinburg murders.'

'Mmm, I see what you mean about him being enigmatic.'

'Yes, but none of that proves, or even hints that he was the alter ego of Edwin.'

'No, I suppose not, but it would be great if we could show that he was involved,' she said.

'History's about evidence, not guess work or supposition. We've got no evidence to go on, so I suggest we get on with clearing the house.'

'I suppose you're right,' Lisa sighed, 'but it still would have been cool.'

'Well there is one outside possibility...'

'Go on.'

'Josh Ryan, from the year below you, Lucy's year, is researching a PhD on the topic of British involvement in Russia after the Revolution. He emailed me a few months ago.'

'Yeah, I remember him, he had a reputation for being manipulative, especially with the girls. I can't say I liked him, though I didn't know him well,' Lisa commented.

'He wasn't the easiest student, he was always polite to the point obsequiousness, but he was very bright and a first class historian. I could contact him to see if he's heard of your relative, or what else he knows about Yakovlev.'

'The computer's there, email him.'

I sent the email and included my mobile number for any information he might find. Not that I held out much hope.

Chapter 5

We spent the next two days clearing out and sorting papers. We were joined by my daughter Lucy, who had offered to help for a couple of days. At five feet four, Lucy had her mother's dark hair and olive skin, she was attractive and intelligent. The latter accounted for her researching some obscure facet of post-Cold War politics for her PhD. She had arrived home and had driven my Saab over to the house to help with the clearing. Lisa had told her about the mysterious Uncle Edwin and Lucy, like Lisa, had been caught up with the romantic notion of him as the enigmatic Yakovlev, despite my protests.

'The trouble is you've got no romance in your soul, Dad.'

'Yeah, that's why your mother left, I'm sure Simon is far more romantic.' Simon was the former boyfriend that my ex-wife, Jane, had moved in with after leaving me.

'No, Simon's a total dickhead!'

'You're just saying that to suck up to me.' I have to admit to still being rather bitter about the end of my marriage. Though I never encouraged it, hearing my children disparage the new man in my ex-wife's life gave me a certain petty satisfaction.

'No, I mean it. I just hope Mum wakes up to reality before she marries him…'

I recoiled in shock. Jane was getting married again! I knew our marriage was over, but I had never contemplated her getting remarried. I had always thought that, like me, she would be too deeply scarred by our break up to want seconds. Deep inside me, I still loved

38

Jane, and I always would. She had moved on whist I could not. I was locked-in, trapped in time like a prehistoric insect in amber. Now there was a sinking feeling in the pit of my stomach and my world began to spin. I did not hear the rest of Lucy's sentence. Suddenly she saw my reaction.

'Shit, Dad, I'm sorry, I thought you knew. Mum hasn't told you, has she?'

'We haven't spoken for a few weeks; I guess there's no reason why she should tell me. I'm not really part of her life any more, just part of her past.'

'I don't think she meant to hurt you Dad, she's probably trying to avoid hurting you.'

My vision was clouded by tears and there was a thickness in my mouth and nose. I fought to hold back the tears.

'Yeah, I'm sure that's the case.' My voice sounded strangled even to me.

'Would you like a look round the house Lucy?' Lisa changed the subject and led Lucy out of the room for the grand tour, deliberately giving me time to pull myself together.

Lucy returned ten minutes later.

'Lisa has asked me if I want to stay tonight, to save me having to travel home. She's making up a bed for me now.'

'Which room? I'm in the front room above us and Lisa's on the other side.'

'You don't have to go to all the trouble of moving into separate rooms, Dad,' she said with an amused look.

'What do you mean?…Oh…There's nothing like that…'

Lucy smiled at me and gave me a knowing look, affectionately shaking her head. 'But Dad, it's clear that…never mind.'

I looked at my daughter, she clearly saw what I was unwilling to admit even to myself. I was in love with

Lisa, an emotion I could never express or act on, not only because of the inappropriate age difference, but because to do so would be futile and ruin the relationship I had with her. I knew I would have to settle for that relationship, any other choice would be no choice because I would lose her from my life and I did not want that. With my cheeks burning, I changed the subject.

'Errm…it would be a good idea if you started sorting the papers in the study.'

'Okay Dad, if that's what you want.' She turned and left.

An hour or so later, Lisa came hurrying in to where I was sorting a mountain of paper.

'Hey Ian, look at this.' She handed me a small wooden chest about a foot long and eight inches high.

'What's this, a treasure chest?'

'Right first time. Open it.'

I unclipped the hasp and opened the lid; inside, the base of the box was covered with green and black coins. I picked one out and examined it in detail.

'It's Roman.' I peered at it. 'Emperor Diocletian, late third century. I don't know what the denomination is, but it's bronze.' I picked up another. 'This one's silver, Emperor Vespasian, first century.' I picked up a third. 'Silver penny, Edward II, medieval. That's a fair collection. There's no way they could all have come from the same place, they're some sort of collection; maybe someone with a metal detector. They could be worth a bit, we can try to identify and value them on the net later on.'

The sorting of papers went on all day. Once it got dark, I offered to cook whilst the girls finished off. Retreating to the kitchen I prepared pasta with a tomato and mascarpone sauce and Italian bread. As we sat eating around the kitchen table, Lucy produced a letter and handed it to me.

'What do you make of this Dad?'

40

I looked at the envelope she handed me. I instantly recognised Edwin's handwriting. It was simply addressed "Libby". I extracted the single sheet of paper from the envelope.

'Have you seen this?' I asked Lisa.

'Yeah,' she nodded, 'but it doesn't mean much to me. If you can decipher it, it could be an important part of the story.' I began to read.

15th March 1928

Dearest Libby,

I don't quite know how to say this, but I am leaving England and returning to Russia. I know I have not been myself these past years and I cannot go into too much detail here. I can only apologise, dearest sister, for my distractedness, I deeply regret the way I have held you, Thomas and Daisy at a distance. I could not explain, it would have been too dangerous and to be honest, too painful.

Nevertheless, as I am leaving, it is necessary to ensure that you are properly cared for and, to that end, some explanation is necessary. There is still some danger involved, so I will have to take precautions. I have left insurance in our childhood hiding place. If you desire to understand, the way to knowledge lies in Atticus between XVIII and XX. The Lacrymae Christi will be your salvation.

It is unlikely I will return from Russia, but I have unfinished business that can no longer be put aside. Please give my love to Thomas and Daisy.

Your loving brother

Edwin

'Well?' Lisa asked.

'Yeah, come on Dad, enlighten us,' Lucy added.

'Very cryptic; I don't follow all of it, but Atticus was a Greek philosopher, a contemporary of Plato. Maybe the clue is in his writings. We could check to see if there is a copy on the shelves in the study. If Edwin was leaving a clue like this, I would have thought he would be referring to a text Elizabeth could easily access. As for the Lacrymae Christi, it means tears of Christ, but apart from being a wine, I haven't got a clue.'

'Let's go check the study,' said Lucy, leaping up from the table.

'Hey, I've just spent a whole fifteen minutes slaving over a hot stove; it'll wait until we've finished eating.' Lucy reluctantly sat down and even Lisa looked disappointed.

'Spoilsport!' she pouted.

'Brains need food, we'll go look as soon as we've eaten. It's quite possible that the book isn't there anymore, if it ever was.'

Whilst eating, I idly turned over the letter, there was something written on the back of the page in pencil, it was faded with age to the point of being virtually illegible. I peered at it, moving the page so that the light caught it at different angles in an attempt to read it, but my eyesight was not good enough - all I could read was one or two faint words, though I did recognise Elizabeth's handwriting.

'Didn't you two notice that Elizabeth had written something on the back?'

'No,' Lisa replied. 'What does it say?'

'It's too faded for me to make out more than a couple of words.'

'Let me see,' Lisa and Lucy said in chorus.

I handed over the letter and they huddled over it, squinting in an attempt to decipher the faint squiggles.

'I can read a bit,' Lisa said at length. 'It says – 'Oh Edwin, now I understand why you have not been the same since your return....' I can't make out the next bit,

42

then it goes on – 'I cannot even imagine how you must have felt to lose her in such a way. If only you had told me.....' See, I told you it was a tragic love story! I can't read any more though, it's too faded.'

'Hang on.' Lucy took the letter. 'This bit at the end says –'I have returned everything to where you left it, where it will stay until your return. Only you can decide what to do about the gift entrusted to you, so that too will remain where you left it.' That's all I can read.'

'So whatever it was that Edwin left is still there!' said Lisa excitedly. 'We have to find that book.'

As soon as the meal was over we withdrew to the study and began a feverish search of the bookshelves, but after an hour it was clear that there was no Atticus to be found amongst the volumes there.

'Any ideas?' Lisa asked.

'Not really, it was a bit of a longshot at best,' I said.

'What about trying the internet Dad?'

'Okay, there might be something.' My quick search proved unfruitful. 'It says here that Atticus' book did not survive, we only know about his work from fragments preserved in Eusabius' Preparatio Evangelica. Anyone remember that from the bookshelves?'

No-one did, we had met a dead end for now. In the light of our lack of progress we did the washing up and retired for the night.

At breakfast the next day, Lucy announced that she had texted a friend at the university to see if she could find a copy of Eusabius in the library and to email her a copy of what he said about Atticus, especially chapters or sections 18 to 20. Her friend had promised to get back to her by midday, so we could get some answers after all. The mundane sorting of Elizabeth and Emily's papers became more boring whilst we waited for the reply that could lead us further into an enigma that was far more fascinating. All three of us shuffled papers lethargically with only half of our minds on the task. At about 11.00 Lucy's phone chirped, indicating she had a text. She pulled out her phone and read.

'Sorry, that was Charlotte; she found a copy of the book, but there are no direct quotes from Atticus, only paraphrases of his work and summaries and a critique of his ideas. There's nothing like sections or chapters and no reference to 18 to 20. It's a total bust.'

We were all disappointed at this, I knew we were there to help Lisa sort out the house, but the mystery surrounding Edwin and what happened to him as a spy in Russia had fired the curiosity of all three of us. Nevertheless, with three people energetically engaged in the sorting of papers, by evening there was light at the end of the tunnel - only a few papers remained to be sifted.

A horn sounded outside and we looked out to see Rob, my son, on the drive in the old Ford that the children used as a runabout when they were home. He walked to the door with his arms loaded with boxes of pizza.

'Hi Dad, I dropped in at home for the night on my way to Michelle's. When I found no-one there I phoned Lucy, who told me where you were. I thought you guys could do with some food.'

I grinned at my son. At five feet ten, he was slightly shorter than me. With dark good looks, he was the image of his sister, but in a male way. Michelle was his long term girlfriend who was in London with her mother. I hugged him.

'Good to see you Rob, why didn't you tell me you were coming?'

'Bit of a spur of the moment thing, Dad, I thought I'd surprise you. Hi Sis!' He hugged Lucy as she appeared in the doorway. 'Oh...er...Hi Lisa, I hope you don't mind me dropping in.'

Faced with Lisa, my grown up son became a gauche schoolboy again. He had been several years behind Lisa at school and had secretly worshipped her from afar. Now, despite having a long standing girlfriend, he always found himself under her spell when in Lisa's presence. I knew how he felt.

'No problem, Rob, you're welcome, especially if you bring pizza.' She too gave him a hug and a kiss on the cheek, making his day. Like father, like son. I was glad that Rob did not share his sister's perspicacity when it came to my feelings for Lisa.

After consuming the pizza around the kitchen table, Lisa showed Rob round the house. As I had predicted, he was fascinated, tapping and poking at the panelling and peering up the chimneys.

'I don't think you'll be finding any priests' holes,' I told him. 'This house isn't really big enough and this area was a hotbed of Puritanism in the Elizabethan period, so it's unlikely to have places to hide a catholic priest.'

'I know that, Dad. You don't find many secret rooms in Suffolk, but there were often hidden recesses and cupboards for hiding valuables.' He rocked back and forth on the stair on which he was standing. With a smile, he knelt on the stair below and began to fiddle with the stair's riser. When he stood, a section of the stair was in his hand and he was pointing to a dark recess that was exposed. 'Like that,' he said smugly. 'Anyone got a torch?'

Chapter 6

Lisa pulled out her iPhone and using it as a torch, we all peered into the hole. The space was almost the full width of the stair, went back two feet and was about two feet deep. From behind Rob, nothing could be seen except for a wall of cobwebs. Rob cleared the webs away with his hand, causing Lisa to shudder. He reached in and lifted out a rusted metal box, a little bigger than a biscuit tin. It was so covered in cobwebs that little could be seen of it.

'It's heavy,' he said.

He carried it into the kitchen, wiping away the webs that stuck to the surface of the box as he put it down on the table. It was indeed an old biscuit tin, hinged along the back, measuring about sixteen inches by nine and three inches deep, the lid had the painted remains of what looked like a hunting scene. The seam between the lid and the rest of the box had been sealed with wax, even along the hinged section. I picked up a kitchen knife and ran the point along the seam to free the lid. As I picked up the box, I was surprised by its weight. It must have weighed about three pounds. Using my fingernails I pried off the lid to expose a layer of newspaper that had been used as packing. I lifted the paper out to uncover a roughly triangular oilskin-wrapped package tied with string. Cutting the string I opened the package to uncover a brown leather holster containing a large revolver. I unbuttoned the flap and cautiously drew the revolver. About eleven inches long and weighing as much as a bag of sugar, it felt oddly uncomfortable in my hand. I depressed the lever by my right thumb causing the barrel and cylinder to drop forward from the frame. The pistol was unloaded. Examining it in more detail, I found that the gun, despite its age was in perfect condition, with no signs of damage or rust, having been protected by the oilskin. Closing the gun I pulled the trigger and saw the hammer rise then snap forward with a satisfying click.

'It's a Webley .445 Mk VI,' I said, reading the name stamped on frame. 'Standard issue officer's revolver from the First World War. The GR stamped here would be George V.'

'Can I see?' asked Lisa.

'I suppose it's yours, so why not?' I handed it over. She took it gingerly.

'Is it safe?'

'It's okay, it's not loaded.'

'It's heavy. It makes you wonder how they used them.' Then a thought struck her. 'Isn't possession of a gun illegal? What are we going to do?'

'When we've finished clearing the house, we'll take it into the police and explain.' While speaking I picked up the leather pouch that accompanied the holster and opened it to discover six bullets, also apparently in perfect condition. 'This must be the insurance that Edwin left. He must have been expecting trouble.'

'I wonder if Elizabeth ever opened the box,' Lucy mused.

'I think she did,' said Lisa who had picked up the newspaper packing, 'the date on here is December 1928, Edwin's letter was dated March wasn't it?'

I nodded, then collected the gun, holster and ammunition pouch and locked them in the top drawer of the desk in the study.

'We'll hand that in when we've finished, who knows what else we could find.'

'Yeah, I read about a place where they found a heap of live grenades,' said Rob.

'Thanks for that,' Lisa said, 'now every time I open a cupboard or drawer, I'll be worried I'll be blown to pieces.'

'You'll be alright as long as you don't pull the pin out,' answered Rob cheerfully.

After that excitement the rest of the evening was a little flat, despite my pleasure at being with my son and daughter. Rob offered to give Lucy a lift home, so that I could have the Saab there. They bade goodbye and promised to visit again when they got back from their planned trip to Corfu with their respective partners. Lisa had been looking at the tin and its remaining contents, to give me chance say goodbye. When I returned to the kitchen she showed me what she had found.

'This was at the bottom of the box. It's a note from Edwin to Elizabeth and as cryptic as ever. It says "Libby, There are those who wish to possess the Lachrymae Christi. To embark on the quest could be perilous, so I have left you my old service revolver for protection, if you need it." It's signed Edwin.'

'I don't see how a search for wine could be dangerous enough to need a gun. I wish we knew what he's referring to,' I mused.

'Have you had any more thoughts about Atticus?'

'No, I think it must be something that had a meaning just for Elizabeth, I don't think it refers to the Atticus I knew about. I really don't have a clue.....Hang on....can you get that letter from Thomas about Passchendaele.'

'Why?' Lisa asked.

'Just an idea, get the book and if I'm right, I'll explain.'

She fetched the 1917 volume and I riffled through the bound letters until I came to the right one. I scanned the letter and there was the clue.

'Look,' I said indicating the relevant section.

'Go on, explain.'

'Edwin and Thomas played a prank on Elizabeth, coming home from school and telling her they were teaching her Latin, when all they did was add "us" or "um" to English words. Atticus may simply mean the attic.'

'But where, there's a lot of attic up there to search for something we don't know what it is. Can't you be more precise?'

'Do me a favour, what am I supposed to be, psychic?' I complained.

'I'm just disappointed, every time we seem to be getting somewhere, we hit another brick wall.'

'Let's sleep on it, maybe we'll come up with something in the morning, or have a bit of luck if we just search the attic.'

As we were about to turn out the lights, my mobile chirped to indicate the arrival of a text message.

'It's from Josh, he doesn't know anything off the top of his head, but he's meeting with someone this afternoon who might know more.'

'Ask him about the Lachrymae Christi too.'

'We've got no evidence that's related to Russia.'

'I've just got a feeling, humour me and text him, please.'

I gave in and sent the text and went to bed.

I was in a deep sleep, dreaming that I was being shaken in an earthquake, when I awoke to find Lisa shaking me.

'Whaaat?' I opened my eyes and saw Lisa clad in her nightdress standing over me. 'Lisa? What's going on?'

'Ian, I think I've worked it out.'

'Worked out what?' I was still dazed.

'Ian, wake up!' The sight of Lisa in her nightwear of a long T-shirt and little else suddenly brought me to my senses.

'Sorry, what is it?'

'I've worked it out, the Atticus XVIII to XX.'

'Go on.'

'The markings on the beams, you know, the roman numerals, look in the attic between beams eighteen and twenty, i.e. around beam nineteen.'

'You could be right, but we won't be able to find out until the morning.'

'It is morning, it's seven o'clock. I've been waiting for the past two hours to tell you,' she complained.

'Okay, I'll get up and we'll go look as soon as we get dressed, and the sooner you leave the room, the sooner I can get dressed.'

I dressed hurriedly and found Lisa waiting impatiently on the landing between the second storey bedrooms, where the access into the attic space was located. She was holding a large torch and peering through the low doorway into the darkness beyond, in what was the roof space to the rear of the house.

'Well?' I asked.

She looked round at me.

'I think it'll be easier said than done, the attic seems to have been a dumping ground for all sorts of junk. It's covered with spider webs too,' she said with a shudder.

'That means I get to go first, I suppose'

'If you would Ian, I really hate spiders.'

'As long as they're small enough for me to tread on, there's no problem, but if they're big enough to tread on me, I'm going to hide behind you.'

'Here, take this.' She held out a smaller LED torch.

Picking our way across the cluttered roof space was anything but easy. It was the equivalent of attempting an obstacle course whilst playing hopscotch, as we avoided the debris scattered around the attic, whilst stepping from beam to beam in the torchlight. We discovered that beams numbered in the late teens and twenties were rafters that were typically in the farthest corner from where we had come in. I swore as I caught my toe on the edge of an old fashioned treadle sewing machine that rested across a beam and nearly stumbled and put my foot through the ceiling of the bedroom below. I shone the torch across the attic.

'Christ, there's everything up here. That bloody sewing machine is probably an antique on its own.' I swung the torch round to illuminate a pair of chairs. 'They look pretty old, it wouldn't surprise me if they're antique. Hey look there.' I picked out a relatively modern metal detector, with its own battery charger. 'I told you those coins were the result of metal detecting. We've got the lot here, ancient and modern. I'm glad I don't have to sort this lot out. You might be advised to get some reputable auctioneer or antiques dealer to have a look.'

It was a struggle, but finally we reached the farthest corner of the attic. Unlike the rest of the space, the area beneath the last rafters was strangely uncluttered.

'Thank God for that, at last I've got the chance to look around without the possibility of tripping over junk. Shine the torch up here, Lisa'

She shone the light along the beam with XIX carved on it. I scrutinised first one side then the other. There was nothing to be seen. We tried the intervening space between the neighbouring beams, still nothing.

'What about a look at beams XVIII and XX?' Lisa asked.

'We could take a look, but it distinctly said between them, which is XIX. Let's have another look.'

Holding the small torch between my teeth, I began to run my hands along both sides of the beam. Something brushed against my index finger on the far side of the beam. I ducked under and saw sticking out between the beam and the roof, the corner of an envelope that stuck out about a quarter of an inch beyond the beam. I tried to grasp it, but it resisted all my attempts to get a strong enough grip to pull it out.

'There's an envelope or something here, but I can't get hold of it, I need tweezers or something.'

'Let me have a go, my nails are longer.'

She took my place and reached up, fiddling for a minute, then pulled from its hiding place an age-stained envelope.

'Got it!' she said. 'Now let's see what we've got, there's certainly something solid in here.'

'Better to wait until we get out of here, if you drop anything, we'll never find it again.'

'Spoilsport! But I suppose you're right. Come on let's get out of here, so we can see what we've got.'

She led the way, navigating around the detritus stored in the attic and safely back to the door to the landing. I spluttered and rubbed cobwebs from my face and hair.

'It's alright for you, you were short enough to avoid the worst of the cobwebs, I'm covered.'

'At last, being short has an advantage! Who said it was a tall person's world?'

'Whoever it was had never been in your attic!' I grunted.

Lisa laughed at me.

'Come on Mr Grumpy, let's go downstairs and see what we've got.'

Chapter 7

Downstairs in the light, Lisa set the envelope down on the kitchen table and we examined it.

'It's been opened before,' Lisa said. 'You can see where it has been sealed again with tape.'

'I suspect it's been opened more than once, that tape must date from the late twentieth century, they certainly didn't have it in the 1920s. Then there's the broken seal.' I pointed to where a red wax seal on the flap had been separated from the envelope below. 'Then it's been resealed with adhesive. That means it has been opened at least twice.'

Lisa peeled back the tape and opened the envelope, extracting a folded piece of paper.

'There's something here, wrapped in the paper,' she said, tipping out the contents. A sturdy brass key, two inches long, fell on to the table. Lisa picked it up and inspected it, turning it over in her hand.

'There's a number stamped into the key, 0473, nothing else. Any ideas?'

'Try reading the document that came with it.'

Lisa unfolded the paper and spread it out on the table. It was written in a familiar hand.

Dearest Libby,

You have followed my clues so far, but there is still further to travel. I am sorry to be so cryptic, but when you use the key to discover the full story of my wartime experiences, then my demeanour and the danger attached to them will all become clear. I have written a full account for you and left it safely deposited with father's bank in Colchester. The choice of whether to continue or not is yours, for with knowledge comes risk.

By now you will have realised that I have returned to Russia; my business there is unfinished, though I fear that I will not return, regardless of whether I am successful or not.

I do not want to leave you, especially with the responsibility of raising Daisy, but if you read my story, you will at least understand why I have made this choice.

Farewell, my beloved sister

Edwin

'It's more cryptic than ever. How are we supposed to make sense of this?' Lisa asked.

'I don't know, let me see the note.' I peered at the paper, angling it to catch the light. 'There's an imprint here, it looks as if something has been written on a sheet of paper on top of this, but I can't make it out.'

Lisa took the paper, but had no greater success.

'There's one thing we can try, but it'll be make or break; if it fails, it will destroy whatever imprint is there,' I said.

'Well, we're not going to get anything from it any other way. Go for it.'

I picked a pencil off the table and began to rub the lead lightly over the indentations on the page. Holding it to catch the light, three words were just about visible "Hendy Brothers Bank".

'There you go then, you're looking for a safety deposit box from the 1920s at Hendy's Bank, Colchester.'

'I've never heard of Hendy Brothers Bank. Do you think they have been taken over since then by one of the big high street banks? Because if they were, I doubt if they'll still have the safety deposit box now,' Lisa replied.

'I don't know. There were a lot of private banks around in the late nineteenth and early twentieth centuries. A lot of them went under in the Great Depression, but some did survive. You might be lucky.'

'The internet?' she enquired.

'Give it a go!'

Twenty minutes on the internet produced no trace of a Hendy Brothers Bank and Lisa gave up in frustration.

'What now?' she asked.

'I suggest we carry on with the clearing out until we get some inspiration.'

We spent the rest of the morning clearing out papers, before breaking for lunch. Whilst Lisa was cutting up bread, I idly picked up her iPhone and began browsing for private banks in Colchester. There were three. I called up the website of the first, but it contained nothing useful. On the second, however I struck pay dirt.

'Got it,' I said. 'Gilbert's Bank, a private bank in Colchester, which incorporated Hendy's in 1952. It lists two addresses in Colchester, but I don't know which one we want.'

'Have you got the phone number? I'll ring them and see what I can find out.'

I gave Lisa one of the numbers. She dialled it.

'Oh, hello, I wonder if you can help me. I've been clearing out the effects of my late aunt and have come across a key to a safe deposit box from Hendy Brothers Bank. I understand that you assumed the assets of Hendy's...Yes, the deposit seems to date from the 1920s, would you still have...Yes, 0473...Uhuh. The deposit was originally made by Edwin Etherington sometime in 1928... Yes, I am both the executor and the heir...Okay, thank you, I'll do that,' she turned to me. 'They've still got it; it's at the branch in Axton Street which used to be Hendy Brothers. I have to go in with the probate papers, ID and the key, then I can open the box.'

'We go to Colchester then?'

'Yep, we go to Colchester. I've all the papers in a file in my room. My driving licence will do for id. Do you mind eating as we go? We won't have time to get there before they close otherwise.'

'A picnic en route is fine by me.'

We wrapped the bread in kitchen roll and put the food in a bag, then set off for Colchester.

We were just turning out of the drive when my mobile rang.

'Hello,' I answered.

'Hi Ian, it's Josh, Josh Ryan.'

'Hi Josh, How are things?'

'Fine. I'm just phoning about the query you sent me. My friend's ears really picked up at the mention of the Lachrimae Christi, but I think he's holding back and not telling me much. Have you found anything else?'

'We might have. We've just found that there's a safe deposit box in Colchester which might contain some useful information. We're on our way there now.'

'Sounds interesting. Let me know what you find.'

Will do, Josh. Speak to you later.'

With the speed at which Lisa drove, we made it to Colchester in just over an hour; a journey that had me clinging to my seatbelt and biting my tongue to avoid comment. I drive reasonably fast when the conditions allow, but an excited Lisa in a hurry would give an F1 driver a run for his money. I was glad of the distraction when my mobile chirped a text alert. It was from Josh, reiterating his interest in what we might find in the safe deposit box.

'Josh seems almost as keen on this as we are,' I commented casually to Lisa.

'I'm not surprised, it's a fascinating mystery,' she replied and accelerated even harder.

Lisa knew Colchester well as she had attended university there and wasted no time in locating the right street. It was a fairly broad, tree-lined street flanked by two terraces of large, rather select Edwardian buildings. She succeeded in parking the Mazda at one end of the road, but there were no obvious signs of any of the buildings being a bank. We began to walk down the road, looking up the stone steps to each door, searching for some sign that one gave entry to a bank. Most had entry-phones which indicated that they had been converted into flats. We had covered two thirds of the road before we saw a discrete brass plaque beside a polished hardwood door which read "Gilbert's Bank Ltd".

With Lisa leading the way we ascended the steps to the door, where she hesitated.

'Do we knock, ring the bell or go straight in?' she asked.

'It's a business, I don't suppose you need to ask permission to go in, try the door.'

She pushed the door that opened easily into a large, expensively decorated and furnished entrance hall. A young man in a well cut suit and striped tie was sitting behind the desk to the right of the room.

'May I help you?' he enquired, with an icy politeness.

Lisa gave him her most winning smile, the one that would guarantee co-operation from any red blooded heterosexual male and would even make some non-heterosexual ones reconsider their life choices.

'Hello. I phoned earlier and spoke to a Mr Cottrell about a safety deposit box that is part of an estate that I have just inherited.'

The smile worked, as there was an immediate thaw in the young man's demeanour. He smiled at Lisa.

'I'm James Cottrell.' He consulted some notes on the desk in front of him. 'Yes, deposit box number 0473, original depositor Mr Edwin Etherington, subsequently held by Miss Elizabeth Etherington and then Miss Emily Ruston. Do you have the documents I requested?'

Lisa handed over her licence and a folder of documents that Cottrell perused.

'That all seems to be in order. Do you have the key?' Lisa held it up for him to see. 'Right then, if you would just take a seat for a moment.'

Lisa and I sat on a comfortable leather sofa whilst he spoke quietly into a telephone. Two minutes later an attractive young woman arrived to take his place at the desk and he ushered us into a small well-appointed room that lay beyond the hall.

'If you would wait here for a moment, then I'll have the box brought in. Please feel free to take as long as you want; when you have finished your business, if you press that bell, I'll have someone collect the box and I'll show you out. Are you aware of the contents of the box?'

'No,' Lisa replied. 'We only just found out about its existence. Are you?'

'Oh no Miss Mann, the contents of deposit boxes are strictly confidential. We pride ourselves on our discretion, even after this long. That's what our customers pay for. Please have a seat.'

We sat at the simple teak table in the centre of the room and within a minute, the door opened and a uniformed messenger placed a black pressed steel box on the table. The box was about fifteen inches square and three inches deep, the top was hinged about a third of the way along and there was a keyhole in the front face of the box. Shaking with excitement, Lisa thrust the key into the lock and turned it. The lid opened easily to reveal a sheaf of slightly yellowed paper. She extracted it and we both recognised the handwriting instantly. Lisa placed them on the table between us and we began to read.

Chapter 8

This is the memoir of me, Edwin David Etherington, relating to my experiences in Russia during and after the Great War.

In August 1914, on the recommendation from a friend from my days at Oxford, I met with Captain Mansfield Smith-Cumming, the head of what was soon to become known as MI 1c. at my London club. He recruited me to join his section, persuading me that the war was to be a long term struggle that would not be 'over by Christmas'. I realised at once that I could be of greater use to the war effort working for C, as I came to know him, than as an expendable junior officer on the Western Front.

I will pass over my wartime service, much of which was less than glorious, despite my having been promoted to the honorific rank of major. The real story starts on a crisp winter's day, 2nd December 1917, when I was summoned to C's office. I knocked and, on hearing C's growled 'Come in,' I turned the doorknob and entered. As the door swung open I froze, for in front of me stood George V, King of the United Kingdom of Great Britain and Ireland and Emperor of India. The King stood five feet six inches in height and was dressed in the uniform of a field marshal. His full brown beard was flecked with grey. As I hauled myself to attention and saluted he fixed me with his piercing blue eyes.

'Stand easy Major,' he commanded. 'Captain Smith-Cumming tells me that you are his Russian expert.'

'I'm hardly an expert, Your Majesty. I had a Russian mother and I speak Russian, but I had only ever been there twice in my life, before C sent me there last spring.'

'We understand that you could pass as a Russian, is that true?'

'I am informed so, Your Majesty. I have a Muscovite accent, or so I have been told.'

'Major Etherington, We have a favour to ask of you.'

'I'm yours to command, Your Highness.'

'I am not commanding Major, I am asking, and do drop the protocol.'

'Yes, sir.'

The King looked over to C.

'Would you mind giving us a moment, Captain?'

C stood up, saluted and, leaning on his cane, limped out of the office. The King sat down and waved me into a chair.

'Major, I am going to be totally frank with you and I would appreciate your discretion.'

'Of course, Sir.'

'Sixth months ago I made a grievous error of judgement. My government was offering my cousin, the Tsar and his family, asylum here in England. My advisors convinced me that his presence and expressly that of his wife would be detrimental to the country and especially the position of the monarchy. As King, I have become the figurehead behind whom the nation has united in this time of trial; I could not allow private or family considerations to affect that. Consequently, I had Stamfordham persuade the Prime Minister to withdraw the offer of asylum. At the time I had no reason to believe that my cousin and his family were in any danger. With the subsequent events in Russia and the bloody Bolsheviks coming to power, it appears that I have inadvertently put their lives in jeopardy. That is where you come in.'

'How can I help, Sir?'

'I want you to go to Russia and bring Nicky, Aliky and the children to safety.'

'I assume that there is a plan, sir?'

'Yes. My government cannot be seen to be involved in this, but Lloyd George has given his blessing to an unofficial rescue mission and will do what he can to assist. Through covert diplomatic channels, Lenin has been persuaded that it would be in his interests for him to be relieved of the problem of the Imperial Family. I have been talking to Captain Cumming, who is developing a plan, but I need you to go to Russia to execute that plan. Will you go, Major?'

I thought for a moment before replying.

'If C's plan has a chance of success, I would be honoured to go. The Bolsheviks are a ruthless bunch and I would not feel right if I left the Tsar and his family at their mercy, when I could do something about it.'

The King looked at me and I saw tears in his eyes.

'Thank you, Major, you do not know how much this means to me. Living with the decision I made about Nicky and his family, especially those lovely girls, has not been easy. A bad conscience is a terrible thing. Of course, it would still be ill-advised for them to come to Britain; the considerations that led to my initial decision still apply. However, King Christian of Denmark, who is also the Tsar's cousin, has offered them a home. As Denmark is not involved in this damned war, Aliky's German connections do not present him with the same problems. Even the Kaiser has given his blessing and has, through neutral intermediaries agreed to allow the family safe passage to Denmark.'

The King stood and I respectfully jumped to my feet. He held out his hand to me.

'I am really very grateful to you.' He reached inside his jacket and withdrew an envelope and handed it to me. 'That is a personal letter from me to the Tsar, telling him that you are my representative and he can trust you. Smith-Cumming will brief you fully. Good luck, Major Etherington, and thank you.'

With that he left the office and I found myself alone. I turned over the envelope that simply had the word 'Nicky' written on it. I thrust it inside my jacket and awaited the return of C.

Lisa looked up from the text.

'I can't believe that a relative of mine was involved in a secret mission for the King to rescue the Tsar. I mean, you taught me about what happened and all the time one of my ancestors was closely involved. It sort of brings it all to life.'

'Don't get too carried away, you don't know what role he really plays yet.'

'Okay, let's read on for a bit.'

Within a few minutes, C limped back into the office. He gave me an appraising look.

'I understand you have agreed to take part in this damned fool mission. I thought you'd have more sense. Good God, we're fighting a war here; all the evidence points to Russia making peace with the Bosche in the next few weeks. Then they'll turn to the Western Front with their full attention and their whole army. We will be hard pressed to hold them in those circumstances – we cannot depend on too much American support just yet and the Frogs are next to bloody useless after the mutinies of last summer. But you try convincing that bloody fool Haig of that, the man's an idiot! All this and we have to go charging into Russia like some knight errant looking to save princesses from the Bolshevik dragon.'

'But sir, the King put up a good argument and seemed genuinely concerned about the safety of the Imperial Family...'

'Put not your trust in Princes, Etherington. If he wanted to save the Romanovs, he shouldn't have pulled the rug from under the asylum offer last year.'

'You know about that?'

'It's my business to know. I am aware that his majesty is concerned about the safety of the Romanov family, but mark my words, if it was a choice between them and the position of the monarchy here, it would be no contest, he would drop the Tsar as quickly as a whore's drawers.'

'Sir, I feel you are being a bit unfair...'

'I'm not criticising his majesty, I'm sure his heart is in the right place and he genuinely wants to see the Imperial Family safe, but at the same time he knows he has a duty to the future of the monarchy and particularly to the country. The king is a good man, but he knows that duty takes precedence over personal desires.'

'What is the plan then, sir.?'

'Your ship, HMS Lancaster, sails from Portsmouth tomorrow and will take you to Norway. From there, you will travel through Sweden, Finland and on to Moscow. The Consul-General there, Bruce-Lockhart, is one of ours and he will provide you with a detailed briefing on the plan, when it is complete. For the record, you are to be attached to the Consulate in Moscow, until you are to carry out the extraction. You will be on the Consular staff as Major Etherington, deputy military attaché. For all

63

your dealings with the Bolsheviks, you will adopt the mantle of one Vasily Yakovlev. Bruce-Lockhart and the Russians will provide you with all of the necessary documentation.'

The journey to Moscow and the hardships endured were terrible, but nothing compared with what was to come. On March 10th, Lenin moved the government to Moscow and the consulate there became a hive of activity. Two days later I was summoned into the office of the Consul-General Robert Bruce-Lockhart, my immediate superior both in the consulate and in MI 1c in Moscow. Lockhart was seated at his desk, a slight figure in his early forties, with a centre parting and slightly protuberant ears. He was attended by a ferret-face man with bulbous eyes and slicked-back hair.

'You wanted to see me, Sir?' I nodded in greeting to the man accompanying him. 'Reilly.'

'Ah, Etherington. I'm glad you could join us. We finally have things ready for your mission to get the former Tsar and his family to a place of safety. The Imperial Family is currently held in Tobolsk; we want you to go there and escort them back to Moscow and then onwards to Riga, from whence the Germans will arrange for them to be transported to Denmark.'

'What is the attitude of the Bolshevik government?'

'There have been high level talks,' Reilly answered. 'Lenin has agreed. The Imperial family presents him with something of a dilemma. He would be only too happy to put Nicholas on trial, but the Tsarina, the Tsarevich and the Grand Duchesses are a different matter. He has no wish to be seen as a Russian Robespierre, should anything happen to them and he is all too aware of the danger presented to them by the wild men of the Urals. In short, he has decided that he would

64

be better off to get the whole family out of Russia, especially if it helps to reduce the threat of allied intervention. The government has unofficially agreed to respect Russian sovereign territory, if the Imperial family are released.'

'So the Bolshevik government is in agreement?' I asked.

'Not quite, Lenin and Trotsky certainly favour it, but it has not been widely discussed. Lenin knows it will be unpopular with some elements of the Central Committee, so he plans to present them with a fait accompli. Sverdlov is going to be our liaison with the government, though I suspect he is somewhat ambivalent,' Bruce-Lockhart added. 'You have to realise that Lloyd George and the government do not want to be seen to be involved, but there is great pressure coming from the Palace.'

'I understand that, Sir.'

'Your problem is going to be to get the Family past Ekaterinburg. The Soviet there is very extreme and the Romanovs would certainly be in great peril if they were to fall into their hands,' Reilly said.

'If you cannot get by Ekaterinburg, you could take the Family east towards Vladivostok. We would have to make new plans about where they then go on to. If there is a change of plans, you will get a message from me addressed to your real name and containing the code word Matushka,' Bruce-Lockhart informed me.

There was a discrete tap on the door and Cottrell's voice came from outside. 'May I come in?' When he received an affirmative answer, he put his head around the door.

'I am sorry to disturb you, but the bank is closing in a quarter of an hour. Of course, if you need longer, we can remain open for you.'

'It's quite alright,' Lisa smiled, 'we've almost finished, another few minutes and we'll be ready to leave.'

Cottrell left and Lisa picked up the manuscript, sliding it into the file in which she had brought her documentation. She then locked the safety deposit box and stood up.

'Come on, we can read the rest later.

Chapter 9

Lisa insisted that I drive the Mazda whilst she continued to read the Etherington papers. The small sports car handled like a dream, but that was not enough to make up for missing out on the next instalment of the narrative.

'Hey, not fair! If I'm going to drive, the least you can do is to read out loud.'

'Okay,' Lisa smiled and then picked up the story.

The next morning Bruce-Lockhart drove me through the frozen streets of Moscow to drop me outside St Basil's Cathedral, whose ornate onion-domed turrets were wreathed in snow. I pulled up the collar of my greatcoat against the bitter cold that struck like a blow. I silently thanked Bruce-Lockhart for the fur shapka that prevented my head from turning to a block of ice. I turned towards the Kremlin and began to trudge through the frozen snow that covered the Red Square, aiming for the entrance that had been pointed out to me. At the doorway I was stopped by two Red Army soldiers armed with rifles and fixed bayonets.

'State your business,' the older of the soldiers, a sergeant, who must have been at least sixty, demanded curtly. They both looked half frozen from having to stand sentry outside of the door and relished the opportunity to take out their icy discomfort on someone.

'Yakovlev, I have an appointment with Comrade Sverdlov,' I replied equally formally.

'Papers.' The word was less a request than a command. I handed him the papers that Bruce-Lockhart had provided. The guard took them.

'Wait.' He turned and entered the building, leaving me to be watched by his young colleague. This second guard was much younger, about eighteen I guessed, his smooth cheeks were flushed with the cold.

'Your sergeant's a talkative one.' I smiled at him, trying to draw him into conversation. He regarded me impassively and said nothing.

The sergeant reappeared with an officer in tow. He wore a well cut uniform, but I was unfamiliar with the badges of rank on his shoulder boards.

'Comrade Yakovlev?' I nodded. 'I'm Zhukov, one of Comrade Sverlov's aides. If you would follow me, Comrade.' He led me into the building. 'Please leave your coat here.' I took off the greatcoat. 'If you would please raise your arms, Comrade.' Another guard ran his hands quickly over my uniform jacket, then nodded to Zhukov.

'I'm sorry about that, but no weapons are allowed beyond here. There have been a number of attempts on the lives of members of the Council of People's Commissars by counter-revolutionary elements. We take no chances.'

He led me through a series of service corridors, then up a broad staircase and waved me into an anteroom.

'Please have a seat. I will come for you when Comrade Sverdlov is ready to see you.'

I was waiting for about twenty minutes. I spent the time examining my surroundings. Living in what was formerly a royal residence, it was clear that these Bolshevik leaders did not shy away from their creature comforts. Eventually Zhukov reappeared and ushered me into the palatial office beyond. Sverdlov was seated at his

68

desk. He was a slender man in his thirties with a fine head of wavy dark hair; he had a thin beard that lined his jaw and a moustache. Cold eyes regarded me with distaste from behind his round wire-framed glasses.

'Comrade Yakovlev?' The voice made me turn to a man on my left who was looking out of the window with his hands clasped behind his back. Vladimir Ilych Lenin turned to face me. He stood five feet five inches and was dressed in a rumpled suit and waistcoat. He was balding and what remained of his reddish hair was cropped short, his goatee beard and moustache were also auburn and flecked with grey. He regarded me with intelligent and knowing eyes.

'Yes, sir,' I replied.

'And what is your real name?'

'Edwin Etherington, sir.'

'Your Russian is good, I would have believed you were a Muscovite had I not known otherwise.'

'Thank you, sir. My mother was Russian, her family came from Moscow.'

He looked at me with curiosity. 'Was your father Edward Etherington and your mother Yelena?'

I looked at him in surprise.

'You are very well informed.'

'No, I met your mother and father once in London, only a brief meeting, but your mother made an indelible impression on me, she was a very beautiful woman. Now, Edon Edvardovitch,' he used the Russian version of my name, including the more familiar patronymic, 'how can we assist you?'

'I thought that was all arranged sir.'

'In principle, yes, but we need to know what material help you might need.'

'A letter of introduction and authorisation to remove the Tsar and his family would be a great help.'

69

'You mean Comrade Romanov!' Sverdlov spat.

'Forgive Yakob Mihailovich, he understands the necessity for us to rid ourselves of the former Tsar and his family, but he does not like it.' He addressed Sverdlov, 'We have discussed this, Yakob Mihailovich. You know it is the best of our alternatives. We have spent hours going through this with Trotsky.'

'I understand, Vladimir Ilych, but the Central Committee should not be kept in the dark. You know that we have many comrades who believe Nicholas Romanov and his family should be put on trial and executed for their crimes against the Russian people.'

Lenin looked sharply at Sverdlov.

'The matter has been decided, Comrade. Romanov presents a greater threat to us dead than he does alive and we do not wage war on women and children. Do you want us to be invaded by the Germans? Do you want Britain and France to aid our counter-revolutionary enemies against us? You agreed to help in the matter; if you cannot perform your part in this transaction, then I will find someone who can.'

Sverdlov looked abashed

'I will do as we agreed, Vladimir Ilych. I'm just uncomfortable at doing it behind the backs of our comrades. You know that you can depend on me for anything. I will ensure that Comrade Yakovlev has the necessary documentation and support.'

'Very well then.' He turned to me. 'Good luck Edon Edvardovitch. Comrade Sverlov will now liaise and assist you in this matter. All I would ask is that you get on with this quickly and get it over. The sooner this matter is resolved, the better for everyone.'

Lenin then stalked out of the room. Sverdlov regarded me with barely concealed hostility. He got up and crossed to a door that led into a sitting room. I could see through the open door and noted the bedroom that lay beyond. Sverdlov picked up a wallet of papers and returned to the office.

'Here.' He thrust the letters across the desk at me. 'A letter introducing Extraordinary Commissar Yakovlev, commanding local civil military authorities to render any assistance that you may request. There is also authorisation signed by myself and Comrade Lenin for you to remove the Romanov family from Tobolsk and transport them on to Moscow. These papers grant you wide-ranging powers. Should you have any difficulties with the Urals soviets, I will ensure that they are smoothed over so that you can complete your mission. Comrade Trotsky has arranged for a handpicked troop of cavalry to meet at Ufa and escort you on to Tobolsk. I have also arranged for you to meet with Bykov from the Ural Soviet and Goloshchekin, the regional Military Commissar. That should help to ease your passage. Now if there is nothing else, I have work to do.'

I took my cue to leave and Zhukov escorted me back to my greatcoat and the exit.

Back at the consulate after a long cold walk, I met with Bruce-Lockhart in his cluttered office.

'How did the meeting go?'

'Lenin was there, he seemed to have a genuine desire to get the former Tsar and his family out of Russia. I'm less sure about Sverdlov. He does not seem to like being the middle man and I got the distinct impression that he had been coerced into helping by Lenin. I doubt his motives and do not trust him,' I declared.

'I am afraid he is the most help you are going to get in this. You will have to make the best of a bad job, be circumspect in your dealings with him. My advice would be to rely on him as little as possible. The situation

71

in the Urals is very volatile. Whatever you do, you must keep the Imperial Family out of the hands of the lunatics in Ekaterinburg.'

'I'll do my best. I leave tomorrow for Ufa, then onwards to Tobolsk.'

'If getting through Ekaterinburg is impossible, you are to take the Family north towards Archangel or Murmansk. We will have to make new plans about how they then proceed, but facilities are being constructed there where they can stay in safety until the Royal Navy can transport then to their final destination.'

'Right, so now I have a back-up plan. That at least allows me more flexibility when I come to transport them out of the Urals.'

'Do you have a gun, Etherington?'

'No.'

'Here.' He reached into a draw and extracted an army issue Webley .455 that he slid across the desk to me. I picked up the heavy weapon and checked its cylinder. It was unloaded.

'I'm not keeping a loaded pistol in my desk.' He smiled and pushed a box of fat .455 cartridges across to me. 'Good luck Etherington. I wish you success. Nicholas is a good man; he was a poor Tsar, but he's well-meaning and cares deeply about his family.'

I will pass over the perils of the journey to Ufa, first by train crowded with troops, then by horse over the snow covered steppes. It was more than two weeks later that I arrived in Ufa, to meet with Krasnov, the commander of the troops who were to accompany me to Tobolsk. He was a tough man of about forty, with a huge grizzled beard and fierce grin. He greeted me with a salute.

'At your orders, Comrade. Commissar Trotsky himself has placed me and my men at your disposal.'

'Thank you, Captain. Our mission is of the utmost importance, I will brief you later this evening. I understand that Comrades Bykov and Goloshchekin are awaiting me.'

'Over there.' He nodded towards the town hall. 'My advice is not to stand any nonsense from them and above all, don't trust them, Comrade. They're a pair of horses' arses, all puffed up with their own importance. Give 'em half a chance and they'll screw up your mission just to show how important they are.'

With Krasnov I crossed to the town hall and we were taken in to meet Goloshchekin. Surprisingly, Goloshchekin was alone.

'Comrade Bykov could wait no longer for you Comrade, he is a busy man,' he said.

I looked him up and down; he was a slight man of about thirty with wavy hair and a goatee beard

'Sverdlov ordered you both to meet me here,' I said coldly. 'Or do you think you are so important that orders from the Chairman of the Council of Peoples' Commissars are treated as mere guidelines?' Goloshchekin began to bridle, but I continued, 'I am a member of the Central Committee and I have been sent on a mission of special importance. These mandates confirm my authority to transport the former Tsar from Tobolsk and to have anyone shot if they interfere or hinder my mission.'

'You cannot seriously...'

I threw the two documents on to the desk beside him.

'I suggest you look at the signature on the second document,' I said flatly.

Goloshchekin unfolded the paper and stared.

'Yes, that is Comrade Lenin's signature, so please do not doubt my authority or my determination. If you or

73

anyone else gets in my way, I will have you shot without hesitation.'

'Yes, Comrade, you can count on my complete co-operation.'

'I'm sure I can, Comrade. You are dismissed.' Goloshchekin left hurriedly to the delight of Krasnov.

'That showed the little shit,' he said, with a broad grin. 'Are we really to move Romanov?'

'Yes, along with his whole family. Our job is to see them safely back to Moscow, or failing that, Archangel, if they cut up rough in Ekaterinburg.'

'But with your powers, surely...'

'Not everyone is as loyal and obedient to Moscow as you and your men, Captain. If the rabble in Ekaterinburg do get difficult, we'd be outnumbered and outgunned; you may as well wipe your arse with those papers then. No, that bluster was to cower Goloshchekin, in the hope of avoiding difficulty, but I suspect intelligence and cunning will have more effect than force...'

Chapter 10

'Fuck!' I interrupted Lisa's reading as I swerved and braked hard to avoid a grey Ford that cut in front of the Mazda.

The brake lights on the Ford flared as it rapidly slowed in front of us, attempting to drive us on to the grass verge.

'What the fuck is this cretin playing at?' I cursed.

I looked into the car and noted the two shaven-headed, thuggish young men inside, as the Ford slewed across the road in front of us and the men began to get out.

'I don't like the look of this,' Lisa commented. 'Don't stop, Ian.'

'I wasn't going to,' I said slamming the sports car into reverse and flooring the accelerator.

The engine screamed as the car sped backwards. I spun the steering wheel to the left and rammed the car into gear as the car spun through a hundred and eighty degrees and accelerated away.

In the rear-view mirror I saw the two men running back to their car and turn it to follow us.

We had a reasonable lead and I kept the accelerator pressed flat to the floor. The Ford pursuing us struggled to keep in contact with the speeding Mazda. The speedometer hovered around the hundred miles an hour mark as we flew down the road.

'Bloody typical,' I grunted. 'Where the police with a radar gun when you want them?'

'Ian, take the next left,' Lisa instructed, 'it will take us into Sudbury, I think there's a police station there.'

I stood on the brakes and changed down as I swung the wheel to the left. With the tyres squealing the car made the turn and I struggled to stop the rear end from swinging us into a spin. I hit the throttle again and the car straightened. In my mirror I saw the Ford attempt the same manoeuver, only to fail and spin out, leaving the vehicle stationary facing the wrong way.

In minutes we were in the town and there was no sign of our pursuers.

'What the hell was that about?' I asked, wiping my sweaty palms one-by-one on my jeans and trying hard not to let Lisa see how much they were shaking.

'I haven't got a clue.' Lisa was pale in the seat beside me. 'Did they plan to rob us?'

'I don't know, but they've gone now. Do you still want to go to the police?' I asked.

'They can't do much, so there's no point, let's just go home, but keep your eyes open in case they reappear.'

We reached the house without further incident, by which time I felt exhausted as the rush of adrenaline subsided.

Ensconced in the lounge we continued to read the manuscript together.

There was little to note of our journey on from Ufa to Tobolsk, save that we were joined by Alexander Avdeyev, a member of the Ural Soviet and a hard-line Bolshevik. From the beginning, it was clear that he mistrusted me and had been sent to keep an eye on me. He was Ekaterinburg's man on the scene and I would have to manage his presence carefully. To make matters worse, I learned that a group of heavily armed Bolshevik guards under a certain Commissar Brusyatsky had been sent out to intercept us and capture the Tsar dead or alive. They outnumbered and were better armed than Krasnov's men, though I doubted they possessed the same level of professionalism.

The ring tone of my mobile interrupted the reading.

'Hi Ian, it's Josh,' came the reply to my greeting. 'I just wondered how you had got on Colchester? Discover anything useful?'

'Possibly, we found a manuscript written by Lisa's relative. We haven't got that far yet, but he seems to be heavily involved in a British attempt to rescue the Tsar and his family. It seems that he might have been the Vasily Yakovlev who tried to take them back to Moscow from Tobolsk.'

'Really? That sounds fascinating; I'd love to read it sometime. Have you found out about the Lachrymae Christi yet? I'm afraid I've had no luck in that respect.'

'Not yet, but we're only part of the way through. I'll keep you informed.' I told him.

'Please do, this sounds right up my street and could help with my PhD.'

'Josh.' I told Lisa as I ended the call.

'He seems very keen,' Lisa commented.

'Yeah, he reckons it could help with his PhD. It might be useful to have an expert at our disposal later on.'

'Maybe, but let's get back to the story.'

It was late April when we finally rode into Tobolsk. Having cleaned myself up, I presented myself at the Governor's House where the Imperial Family were being held, guarded by the Special Detachment under Colonel Kobylinsky. I met with Kobylinsky in his office and showed him my orders. After examining them thoroughly, he agreed to lead me on an inspection of the

House, accompanied by Avdeyev and Krasnov. As we crossed a corridor on the upper floor, a door opened and we were faced by the Tsar and three of the grand duchesses. Although I should have been concentrating on the Tsar, I was immediately captivated by the beauty of the youngest of the three women.

Standing 5 feet 7 inches, she was as tall as her father, thick strawberry blonde hair cascaded to her shoulders and large, startlingly blue eyes looked at me from beneath straight brows. A small regular nose presided over a perfectly shaped mouth. This was the Tsar's third daughter, the eighteen year old Grand Duchess Maria Nikolaevna, and she took my breath away. The young women with her bore a strong sisterly resemblance, but were slimmer and no comparison to their younger sister. It was with difficulty that I dragged my attention away and focused on the Tsar. Still somewhat flustered, I bowed.

'Are you satisfied with the guard, Your Majesty? Do you have any complaints to make?' I asked him.

'No, I am very pleased and have no complaints.'

For the first time, I looked at the Tsar. His hair and beard were turning grey and his eyes were kind and gentle. He bore a remarkable resemblance to his cousin, King George, and I estimated him to be about 50. He was dressed in a simple soldier's khaki shirt and trousers and an officer's belt and worn boots. I noticed that he wore no badges of rank.

'I would like to see the Tsarevich Alexei please, Your Highness,' I asked.

'I am afraid Alexei Nikolaevich is quite ill.'

'I'm sorry, Sir. I must insist, it is very important.'

'Very well, but only you alone.'

78

The Tsar led me into a nearby bedroom. The Tsarevich, a frail boy of 14, lay in bed, clearly very ill. His complexion was yellow and his face was beaded with sweat, he looked very close to death.

'What happened?' I asked.

The Tsar gave a wan smile.

'He tried to toboggan down the stairs. He complained of pain in his leg, which simply got worse. He is a haemophiliac; this is the worst attack I can remember in years. I fear he might...' At this point, the Tsar's voice was curtailed by a strangled sob. It was clear that the Tsarevich's condition was going to present a severe obstacle to my plans.

'Could I see the Tsaritsa, Sir?'

'I am afraid she is not yet dressed.'

'Then I will return later, Sir.'

I completed a cursory inspection of the rest of the rooms, apologising for the interruption, especially to the youngest grand duchess, who was engaged in an English lesson. I hurried to the telegraph office, where I sent coded messages to both Sverdlov and Bruce-Lockhart outlining the Tsarevich's condition and the problems it presented. At eleven o'clock I returned to meet with the Tsar and Tsaritsa. There, I discussed the Tsarevich's condition and began to assess the situation. The Tsaritsa, despite her reputation, did not give the appearance of either haughtiness or arrogance. She seemed older than her years and worn down by the situation she found herself in. Her face was drawn and slightly haggard and her hair was greying. She spoke to me politely, without the iciness I had expected her to show to a Bolshevik commissar. Present too was Pierre Gilliard, the Swiss tutor to the Imperial children.

'Do their majesties have much baggage Monsieur Gilliard?' I asked in French. He looked at me in surprise before replying.

'Not too much, most of their belongings were left at Tsarskoe Selo when we moved. Does that mean we are leaving here?'

'Just an enquiry,' I smiled.

When I left the Governor's House and returned to the telegraph office, I had my reply.

BL agrees that plan to remove only the principle baggage is the only option. Proceed on your own initiative.
Sverdlov

I returned to the Governor's House the next day to tell Kobylinsky that I was moving the Imperial Family from Tobolsk.

'How?' he asked. 'Alexei is sick, he cannot travel.'

'I know, that's why I delayed until today, my instructions are to take just the Emperor and leave the family if necessary. I need to speak to the Emperor privately.'

However, the Tsaritsa had other ideas and refused to leave her husband.

'I never leave him alone to speak to anyone,' she said, in a tone that implied he could not be trusted to do so. Rather than cause a scene, I gave in and allowed her to stay.

'Sir, I am instructed to remove you from here; you must be ready to go tomorrow.'

'Where am I to be taken?'

'I cannot disclose that at present, sir.'

'Then I decline to go with you.'

80

'Please, sir, I beg you not to refuse. I have orders I must carry out. I would be compelled to take you by force or resign. In which case, I believe I would be replaced by a less scrupulous man. Sir, I am responsible with my life for your safety. If it helps, you may take with you whoever you desire. We leave tomorrow at 04.00.'

It was the Tsaritsa who replied.

'What are you going to do with him? You cannot tear him away from his family. His son is sick. He must stay with us!' She had tears in her eyes.

'I'm sorry, Your Highness, but the Tsar must come with me. I assure you that I act in his best interests.'

The Tsaritsa paced up and down the room like a captive tigress.

'This is too cruel. I cannot believe you could do this.' As she continued to pace I heard her muttering to herself. 'If he goes alone, he'll do something stupid again. Without me they can force him to agree to anything.'

'I imagine they want me to sign the treaty with Germany. But I won't, I'd rather cut my hand off,' Nicholas declared.

Alexandra looked close to tears. I understood that she was struggling to decide whether to go with her husband or stay with her sick son. Nicholas looked distraught and left to check on Alexei.

'I can't let the Emperor go alone,' Alexandra declared to Gilliard. 'They want to separate him from his family, again… I should be at his side in times of trouble, but the boy is still so ill…Oh, God, this is torture. For the first time ever, I don't know what to do… I can't think.' She fled the room on the verge of tears and I followed reluctantly to find her in Alexei's room with tears coursing down her cheeks.

'Your Highness...' I started.

'Don't, please don't add to my grief.'

The Grand Duchess Tatiana took her hand.

'Mama, you cannot torment yourself like this; if Papa has to go, something must be decided.'

Alexandra looked at her daughter. 'I will go with the Emperor, that will be best,' she declared.

'It looks like the Grand Duchess Maria had a big impact on him.'

'She was reputed to have been very attractive, both physically and her personality.'

'It's getting late; shall we leave the rest until morning?' Lisa asked.

'Okay. I'll see you in the morning, goodnight.'

I double checked the lock on the doors and windows and made my way to bed.

Chapter 11

We both slept in the next day and only picked up Edwin's story after a late breakfast.

At 10.30 I joined the Imperial Family and members of the household in the drawing room. Alexandra sat on the sofa, her eyes still red and puffy from tears. The Grand Duchesses Olga and Anastasia sat beside her. Tatiana sat on a chair alongside the Tsar, with the luminous Maria standing behind him. Olga, who understood the import of the decision, wept silently.

'Tatiana, you must stay to look after Alexei. Take care of your brother. Anastasia, you must stay with your sister, you are too young to undertake such a journey.'

Maria stepped forward, her beautiful face set with determination.

'Mama, I will accompany you and Papa, Olga and Tatiana don't need me as well to look after Alexei. You need someone to be with you.'

'Thank you Marie,' the Empress smiled wanly. 'Your Papa and I would welcome your support, but you will have to be prepared for a hard journey. Demidova, Chemodurov, Sednev and you, Prince Dolgursky, will accompany us. Is that acceptable Commissar Yakovlev?'

'Of course, Your Majesty, I will make arrangements. If you would excuse me.'

I turned and walked to the door, to be intercepted by Maria.

'You are destroying my family, can't you see that? I hate you, you heartless beast!' she hissed at me, her blue eyes flashing with anger.

I'm sorry, My Lady, I know it is hard, but I can assure you that I am trying to help your father.'

She gave me a look of utter contempt and turned away. I don't know why, but her disapproval disturbed me more than it should have.

'He's got it bad,' Lisa said with a smile. 'Do you think anything could have come of it?'

'Not in those days. The class system, particularly in Court circles was rigid. Anyway, she doesn't seem to have liked your Uncle Edwin.'

Lisa called a halt to the reading in early the afternoon as she had appointment in town with her great-aunt's bank. I accompanied her, seizing the opportunity to pick up some clean clothes, before meeting her outside the bank at the end of her meeting and travelling back together.

Lisa pulled the car on to the gravelled drive of the house and came to a sudden halt. The front door of the house was standing open.

'Did you lock the door when we left?' I asked.

'Of course I did, we must have been burgled. Do you think they might still be in there?'

'I don't know. There's no vehicle on the road or here on the drive and I'd have thought they would have some sort of getaway car; so most likely there's no-one in there.'

'I'm going to call the police anyway.'

'Good idea. You phone and I'll have a look round.'

'No, Ian, don't you dare go in there alone.'

'I've no intention. I'm going to have a look from outside.'

I got out of the car as she picked up her phone. I warily approached the front door, it had been forced. The edge of the door jamb was splintered where the lock had engaged. There was no-one to be seen inside. I crossed to the hall window, then the sitting room window, there was no-one to be seen. Behind me, I heard Lisa get out of the car.

'The bloody police are on their way, but they're going to be at least half an hour, there's been a big accident on the main road.'

'Okay…'

'Well, I'm not going to sit on the drive outside my own house while I wait for the police to put in an appearance. Come on.'

'Whoah, Tiger.' I grabbed her arm. 'You are not going in there.'

'Yes I am.' She pulled away and marched in through the front door. I sighed and looked around me. On the edge of the flower bed was a broken broom handle about three feet long. I grabbed it and followed Lisa.

'I like the caveman thing you've got going on there,' she remarked nodding to my makeshift club.

I grunted in response. We went from room to room. There was no-one there, but the house had been searched, and none too carefully. In each room drawers had been pulled out and rummaged through, wardrobe and cupboards had been left open. Nothing, however, seemed to be missing. The television, stereo and everything else were still there. Lisa looked round in confusion.

'What the fuck is going on? The place has been ransacked, but everything of value seems to be here,' she said.

There was the sound of a car on the drive and we looked out the window to see a police panda car on the drive. A young-looking policeman was getting out and pulling on his cap.

'There's been a break-in reported at this address,' he stated in a tone that was almost a question.

85

'Yes, I reported it, but there's no-one here now,' Lisa told him.

'You shouldn't have gone in until I arrived, Miss, it could have been dangerous.'

'It was safe, whoever broke in was long gone.'

'Have you checked to see if anything is missing?'

'Nothing appears to have been taken. Things just seem to have been turfed around.'

The policeman looked around the house and confirmed that there was no-one there.

'It seems a bit peculiar, Miss. Is there any reason that someone might have done this?'

'Absolutely none that I can think of. What do I do about getting the house made secure? I'm not going to sleep in a house with the front door wide open.'

'I can recommend a locksmith who will come straight out and secure your premises,' he said handing her a card. 'You'll also need to have a crime report number in case you have to claim on your insurance.' He wrote a number on a form that he handed to her. 'I'm sorry, Miss, but that's about all I can do. If it will make you feel better, I'll make sure I drive by and keep an eye on the place when I'm on duty.'

'Thank you, Officer. I would appreciate that,' Lisa said giving him her most winning smile. The policeman left, reluctantly, after his encounter with Lisa's smile.

Lisa phoned the number on the card and the locksmith agreed to come out immediately. By the time we had got a meal together the locksmith had arrived. Within an hour he had repaired the damage and fitted a new lock.

'That will keep you safe,' he said. 'I've fitted you a new lock that's far more secure than your old one. No-one will be getting through that one in a hurry.'

I went to pay him, but he preferred to submit his bill formally, which would probably be taken care of by Lisa's insurance.

'What do you think they were after?' Lisa asked me.

'I'm not sure, but it's strange that nothing was taken.'

'All this seems to have started once we found the manuscript. Do you think that someone wants that?'

'It's possible. Where is it, I haven't seen it.'

'Somewhere safe,' she smiled and went to the secret compartment in the stairs that Rob had found. She opened the stair and took out the sheaf of hand-written papers. 'I don't know why, but some instinct told me to hide them and this was the safest place I could think of.'

'Well, if that was what they were after, it was pretty smart thinking,' I told her.

Chapter 12

There was no time to continue with our reading, so it wasn't until after breakfast the next day that we began with the memoirs again.

The transportation I had commandeered arrived at the Governor's House as ordered at two o'clock the next morning; a mixture of peasant carts, a tantarass, a covered long-wheelbase cart pulled by three horses and a sleigh. I arrived shortly before four, as dawn was breaking. There had been frequent heavy snow flurries during the night and there was a good covering of fresh snow on the ground. It was bitterly cold. I saluted the Tsar as he came out.

'Are you ready, Sir?'

'I am, Yakovlev and here are the ladies.'

The Tsaritsa and Maria appeared wearing long coats of Persian lamb and swaddling themselves in furs. Still unsure that they would be enough I approached Dr Botkin.

'Doctor, will you give me your greatcoat, I think the ladies might have need of it before our journey is done.'

I gave the coat to the Tsaritsa whilst Botkin fetched himself another coat.

'Please take this madam, it is a long way and you might have need of it.'

Alexandra took it graciously, whilst Maria glared icily at me. Clearly, her hostility had not abated overnight. I was about to say something to her to try to melt her icy demeanour when the Tsar came out again, dressed in his usual army officer's greatcoat.

'Sir, you're only wearing an overcoat!'

'It's all I ever wear.'

I collected a second coat from the house.

'It is particularly cold and a long way, please take this as well, sir.'

The Tsar took the coat then began to help his wife into the tantarass. Gilliard had placed a mattress in the cart to try to cushion the occupants from the bumps of what was going to be a rough journey. I offered my hand to Maria, who pointedly ignored me and climbed up under her own steam. The Tsar was about to follow them, when I laid a hand on his arm to prevent him.

'If you would travel with me in the first vehicle, sir.'

'Very well, Commissar.'

I stood stiffly to attention and saluted as the Tsar climbed in, then swung myself into the sleigh. Botkin and Prince Dolguruky rode in the third cart and the servants in the fourth. Krasnov and his hundred and fifty men escorted us as we sped away down the street.

An hour passed and the Tsar still sat silently, deep in his own thoughts. I judged this was the time to tell him what was going on.

'Sir, we need to talk,' I said in English. The Tsar looked at me with surprise. 'I am not a Bolshevik commissar, I am a British officer. I have been sent on the orders of your cousin, the King, to see you and your family safely out of Russia. The Bolshevik government has agreed to this and this is the first stage of our journey to liberty.' I reached beneath my coat and handed him the envelope the King had entrusted to me. The Tsar extracted the letter and read it carefully. When he had finished there were tears in his eyes.

'God bless cousin Georgie. I thought he had abandoned us, but now he has come through. It appears that even cousin Willi is in agreement. What is the plan?'

I outlined the plan to extract the Imperial Family and the fall-back plan Bruce-Lockhart had briefed me on. For twenty minutes the Tsar questioned me on various details of the plan, including how I now intended to achieve the removal of his remaining children to safety. Nicholas nodded.

'And what is your name young man, if you are not Commissar Yakovlev?'

'My name is Edwin Etherington, sir.'

'Your Russian is immaculate, I would have never have guessed that you are English.'

'My mother was Russian, sir, that's why I was chosen for this mission.'

'I saw Marie was giving you a difficult time, she's a fiery one, but she has a good heart. I will explain to her and the Empress when we stop, I'm sure she will be more civil once she knows what is going on.'

'Sir, it might be safer if only you and I knew the true purpose of my mission.'

The Tsar regarded me levelly.

'My wife and daughter are totally trustworthy and discrete, Mr Etherington.'

'I didn't mean to suggest otherwise, sir. I simply thought that the fewer people who knew, the safer it would be, but I will accede to whatever you consider best. But it would be best if you told them tonight, somewhere there is little chance of being overheard.'

The Tsar sank back into his own thoughts as the sleigh bumped and bounced over the frozen rutted road. Hour after hour the horses pulled us over the bone-jarring frozen terrain. Young as I was, I ached and was tired long before we completed our day's journey. Never once did the Tsar complain. When we stopped to change horses at a staging post, he took himself off, walking to stretch his legs and get some exercise. After one such halt, I accompanied the former emperor whilst he checked on the comfort of his wife and daughter. He offered his hand to the Tsaritsa to help her mount the cart. I made a similar gesture to the Grand Duchess, only to be met once more by a withering glare from those stony blue eyes.

'I can manage perfectly well, thank you, Commissar. I can think of no situation when I would either need or want your assistance,' she said in a voice that was colder than the frozen landscape across which we were travelling, ignoring my hand and hauling herself into the cart. I had clearly made a big impression on her and I did not know why the opinion of this pampered, spoiled girl concerned me so much.

'Look, it's nearly lunchtime, why don't I take you to the local pub for lunch?

'Fine by me, thanks.'

'You drive,' she said throwing me the keys. 'You seemed to enjoy driving the Mazda the other day, at least until we ran into that trouble.'

'Yes, it was fun up to then. I'd never driven a sports car before and I was really enjoying it. It must be my mid-life crisis. I'll have to sell the Saab and buy a Porsche.'

Lisa laughed.

Lunch in the pub with Lisa was very pleasant and made me realised how much I missed company. My life had become a predictable round of work and solitary evenings. I really did need to get a life, I decided.

I swung the car on to Lisa's gravelled drive, only to have to brake sharply to avoid colliding with a dark sedan parked there. The Mazda slewed to a halt in a hailstorm of gravel.

'Bloody hell! What idiot parked there?'

I looked at the car, it was a black Mercedes, new and shiny and as I walked to the back of it, I noticed that it had diplomatic plates.

'Do you know any diplomats?' I asked Lisa.

'Diplomats? What sort of diplomat would want to see me?'

We soon found out. From around the side of the house came a tall, well-built man in an expensive suit. He was taller than my six feet, in his mid-twenties and his light brown hair was well-cut. He walked briskly towards us.

'Nadya!' he called out.

From the other side of the house a woman appeared, and what a woman. She was jaw-droppingly stunning. Lisa was a beautiful young woman, but this woman was something else. She was probably thirty; her platinum blonde hair was tied back in a ponytail away from a face that would stop traffic. High cheek bones and startling green eyes highlighted a face that no red blooded man would forget in a hurry. She was dressed in a conservative business suit that could not hide the curves beneath. She walked over to us with a smile that could melt a glacier.

'Miss Mann and Mr West?' She offered her hand. 'May I introduce myself? I am Nadezhda Kuznetsova. I am a member of the Cultural attaché's office at the Russian Embassy. This is my colleague Pavel Timoshenko.'

Her English was near perfect, only by concentrating could I detect the slightest hint of an Eastern European accent.

'What is a Russian diplomat doing here?' Lisa asked.

'We have come to see you, or rather you and Mr West.'

'Why on earth would you want to see us?' I asked

'Perhaps I could explain inside?'

Lisa reluctantly opened the door and showed the Russians through to the sitting room.

'Please sit down. Would you like a coffee?' she asked.

'No, thank you. Allow me to explain, but first a question. What do you know about the Tears of Christ or the Lachrymae Christi as they are sometimes known?'

'Not much. We've found some cryptic references in a text we've been looking at. Hang on…how did you know that?' I asked.

Nadya smiled.

'It's not rocket science, Mr West. A British historical researcher, a Joshua Ryan, was making enquiries at the Embassy. When we asked him what his interest was, he said that he was making enquiries on your behalves. It really was not difficult to find you after that. So what is your interest?'

'We don't have an interest,' Lisa stated. 'As Ian said, we came upon a cryptic reference in some old documents. We don't even know what the Tears of Christ are. But why are you so interested?'

'Look Ms Kuznetsova, it might help if you explained what the Tears of Christ are,' I put in.

'The Tears are a pair of perfectly matched blue diamonds that belonged to the Tsars. They disappeared during the Revolution and have not been seen since.'

'Diamonds?' Lisa and I exclaimed together.

'Yes, diamonds. Ever since Communist times, our government has been seeking to recover this treasure for the Russian people. Let me explain, I am not talking about engagement ring diamonds here. These diamonds weighed nearly 30 carats. Each was the size of a pigeon's egg. Individually, each would be valued close to twenty million pounds today. As a matched pair, their value would probably exceed fifty million.'

'A not inconsiderable sum for an individual, but peanuts to the Russian government,' I remarked.

'Its monetary value is not important, but the diamonds do have a great historical and cultural significance. But there is more to it. There are groups other than our government who would very much like to possess the Tears, how can I phrase it…less legitimate groups, who would stop at nothing and I am sure that if we have heard of your interest, then they most certainly have.'

'You're talking the Russian mafia, Miss Kuznetsova?' I asked.

'Please, call me Nadya, you will find it easier. To answer your question, there are certainly criminal enterprises involved. That is where Pavel and I come in. Whilst our government would like to possess the Tears of Christ, we have a much bigger concern. My country and yours are about to sign a commercial agreement whose value is in the billions, not millions, to both countries. If these illegal elements thought you knew anything that could lead them to the Tears, there could be an incident that would cause serious embarrassment to my country and could endanger the trade agreement. It is our job to ensure that does not happen.'

'You must realise that these are very bad people.' Pavel spoke for the first time; his English was more heavily accented than his colleague's.

'Cultural attaché be damned. What are you SVR? FSB?' I asked, referring to the Russian counterparts of MI6 and MI5, the successors of the KGB.

'We…' Pavel started, but was halted by Nadya who help up her hand.

'If I admitted it, I would be a fool; if I denied it, I would be a liar; to borrow a quotation. Do you recognise it Mr West?' she said with a smile.

'Yeah, Karl Ernst, Berlin Nazi leader, when he was asked if he was involved in the Reichstag fire. You've clearly done your homework about our historical research last year.'

'Was it you who broke in here yesterday and made that bloody mess?' Lisa demanded.

A look of concern crossed Nadya's face.

'You were broken into yesterday? That is worrying.'

'And you really expect me to believe it wasn't your lot who broke in and searched my house?' Lisa retorted with hostility.

'Miss Mann, if my lot, as you put it, had broken into your house, you would never have known.'

'She's got a point Lisa. Yesterday's break-in was anything but professional. I can't imagine that it was done by Nadya's people,' I said, and was rewarded by a smile from Nadya.

'Look, we don't care if you are looking for the Tears; in fact I am sure that if you located them, my government would be interested in purchasing them from you. I do care if your quest provokes an incident that endangers the treaty. Are you actively seeking the diamonds?'

Lisa opened her mouth to reply, I could see from her face that she would be confrontational and I did not think that would be productive.

'We have not been searching for the diamonds,' I jumped in. 'We really did find references to the Lachrymae Christi in a letter from an ancestor of Lisa's who was in Russia in 1917. We didn't know what the Lachrymae were and couldn't make sense of what he was saying.'

'Who was this gentleman?'

'His name was Edwin Etherington,' Lisa answered.

'Edwin Etherington...' Nadya mused. 'I have never heard the name in connection with the Tears. And it is a subject I know a little about. The Tears of Christ

95

have a long and unfortunate history. They have brought sorrow and bad luck to all who possessed them.'

'We think he might have used another name,' Lisa said vaguely.

'So he was a spy? Does he say anything about the location of the diamonds?'

'We suspect he might have been,' I confirmed. 'He was using the name Yakovlev.' I saw Lisa glaring daggers a me. 'He does talk cryptically about something he calls the Lachrymae Christi, but we haven't decoded his meaning.'

'Those diamonds belong to Russia and should be returned!' Pavel interjected menacingly.

'Pavel!' Nadya reproved him sharply. Then turning to Lisa she said, 'I am sorry, Lisa - may I call you Lisa? Pavel is out of line, but there is a bit of a nationalist agenda here. If you pursue the Tears, you run a genuine risk, but that is your choice. It is not up to me or my government to interfere. All I ask is that you take care not to create too much fuss and if you find yourselves out of your depth or in a situation that could lead to embarrassment for my country, then you give me the opportunity to help avoid such difficulties. If you find the Tears, please contact me and allow us to make you an offer for them. Or if you simply locate where they are, there would be a considerable finder's fee. I will leave you my card, if you need anything, call me.' She put an embossed card on the mantelpiece. 'Come, Pavel, we must not impose on Mr West and Miss Mann any further. Goodbye, I wish you luck, please take care.'

With that the two Russians left and drove off in the Mercedes.

'What do you make of that?' Lisa asked.

'I think she was genuine. I've read in the papers about this trade treaty with Moscow. She clearly had the big picture in mind, but Pavel struck me as an old style

KGB thug. Maybe we should have told her about the attempt to run us off the road as well.'

'Do you really think that it's diamonds that Edwin is talking about in his letters to Libby?'

'It must be; that's why all his references were so cryptic. Fifty million quid, phew!' I whistled.

'Do you think that Edwin knows what happened to the diamonds?'

'His letters imply that, but we don't know where or how he came across them or what happened to them,' I replied.

'There's only one place where we're likely to find out – the memoirs!'

'Agreed, so it's back to them I think.'

Chapter 12

Lisa made coffee and we settled once more to the reading.

The freezing journey seemed interminable. By the time we reached our lodgings for the night, everyone was exhausted.

A simple but wholesome meal was provided for us. The Tsar and his family sat at a table near the fire, I stood in by the door balancing my plate in my hand. The Tsar came over to me.

'Please, join us at the table.'

I looked across, only to meet the challenging eyes of the Grand Duchess Maria, daring me to join the royal family in their meal.

'Thank you for the offer, Sir, but I wouldn't want to spoil your daughter's meal,' I said loudly enough for her to hear. I was treated to another icy glare from those amazing blue eyes.

'I have to check the guards anyway. Good night, Sir.'

By the time I had returned from checking the guard with Krasnov, the Romanovs had retired to their room for the night. I spread out my bedroll and stretched out on it. I was asleep within seconds.

Well before dawn the next day, our party set off on its journey across the frigid landscape. Once more the Tsar travelled with me in the sleigh.

'I did not have the opportunity to tell my wife and daughter about your mission, Etherington. Alicky was

just too tired and needed to rest, Marie too. They were so exhausted that I doubted they could have comprehended what I was saying. If you could arrange for us to have some privacy when we halt, I will tell them then.'

At 8.00 a.m. we halted and prepared to cross the Irtysh River. I ordered the guards to man the perimeter, giving Nicholas the privacy he had requested. The Tsar took his wife and daughter aside and I heard him explaining to them in English. As we were about to start off again, the Grand Duchess approached me.

'I believe I owe you an apology. My father has explained your mission. I'm sorry for the way I treated you before.' She looked up at me earnestly.

'You have nothing to apologise for, Madam. You were not to know what was going on.'

She smiled at me and for a moment I was lost in the warmth of her smile.

'Please, don't refer to me as madam, it makes me feel like Mama. My friends and family call me Marie or occasionally Mashka.'

'I would be honoured to be considered your friend, Marie.'

'It is time we were moving again Commissar,' Krasnov's bass tones interrupted us.

I climbed back into the sleigh and took the reins and was surprised when Marie joined me.

'I thought your father was travelling with me.'

'Mama wanted Papa to travel with her, she had many questions to ask about your plans, so I volunteered to accompany you. Don't you want me to join you?' She pouted prettily and I realised that Marie was not simply a grand duchess and daughter of an emperor; she was also an eighteen year old young woman and a very attractive one at that.

99

The crossing of the river was not easy. Although the river was not wide, it was fast flowing due to the spring thaw and ice floes sailed past us at speed. The horses dragged our sleigh into the river and as the current hit us, the sleigh gave a sudden lurch. For a moment I thought the sleigh was going to overturn and I grabbed Marie to stop her from being thrown from the seat beside me. At the last minute the sleigh righted itself, throwing Marie into my arms. I was still holding her as the sleigh bounced up the opposite bank. Marie made no attempt to pull out of my embrace. From the depths of her fur lined hood, she looked up at me with her eyes laughing.

'Thank you, Edwin, but you can let go of me now,' she said coquettishly and then giggled as I coloured and hurriedly released her. 'I shouldn't tease you, but you make it so easy; besides which, Mama and Papa are watching and this is not the time or place.' Her eyes seemed to promise that there would be another time and place.

The carts crossed the river with even greater difficulty. Although more stable and resistant to the current due to their weight, the wheels sank into the mud and it was only with the an enormous effort that the horses managed to drag the wheels from its cloying embrace. All in all, the crossing took nearly an hour. Once on the road again, we soon had to stop to change horses at a staging post I had arranged.

For mile after mile the sleigh bounced and swayed along the frozen rutted road. Flurries of snow whipped our faces, making our eyes water and skin sore. Never once did Marie complain. She spoke animatedly about her life before the revolution and experiences since the fall of the monarchy.

I was brought up to be a princess, a decoration, to marry into royalty, now…well now it feels more as if I can be me. I'm sorry for Papa and what he has lost, but for me it feels…liberating. Now I can be anything I like, anyone I like, not tied by convention and protocol.'

'What do you want to do when you leave Russia?'

'Leave Russia? Do you know, I've never really thought of that? I would like to be an artist. Everyone tells me I have a talent, but as an Imperial Grand Duchess, no-one would ever take me seriously. I'd like to draw and paint and have my work judged as Maria, not the Grand Duchess Maria Nikolaevna.'

The sleigh continued to bounce along the frozen tracks as Marie asked endless questions about my life in England before the war, my siblings, way of life and my late parents.

'I am sorry to ask so many questions. I have been to England several times,' she said, 'but I have never met real people, only cousin George and the Royal Family and the court. I so want to know about the life of people there, it is so different and so much better than in Russia. I think that I would like to live in England, when this is all over.'

'That may be possible, once this damned war is over. But I don't think it would be possible before that, your mother's German connections would make things very difficult.'

'Why would that be? Cousin George has similar German ancestry to me and he is King.'

'Yes, I know, but your mother's connections to Germany are more immediate, your uncle the Duke of Hesse is a general in the German army. Even for the King, his German connections are a severe embarrassment. That is why the King changed his name to Windsor last year, to rid himself of the overt German links. Look at the way your cousin, Louis of Battenberg, was hounded out of the Royal Navy at the start of the war. When it is all over, you would be free to settle in England, but for the duration, it will be Denmark that will be your home.'

'Is that because of Grandmama?'

'Yes, the King has offered you refuge and as it's a neutral country, you will be able to wait out the war in safety. You will be able to go wherever you want afterwards.'

Marie looked sadly at me with tears in her eyes.

'I am afraid I will never be able to go where I like, my future will be mapped out for me by my family. They will choose what I do, who with and who I will marry. My part in such decisions will be a small one.'

'Not if you stand up for what you want. This war has turned the whole world on its head and things will never quite be the same again. You've seen the changes here, well they're not as extreme elsewhere, but there is a new spirit of equality, the old system is breaking down. I believe England will even give women the vote. The old ways are broken beyond repair and you could take advantage of it, if you are strong enough.'

'Do you really think that Edwin?' She hesitated. 'Edwin...if I did live in England...would you visit me?'

'Gladly Marie, I can think of nothing that I would rather do.'

She turned her big, innocent blue eyes to me.

'Edwin, perhaps in this brave new world of yours, we could be more than friends.'

I looked down into her amazing eyes and saw an indefinable something that made my heart leap. Could it really be true that Marie had the same feelings for me that I had for her? I had always believed that love at first sight was romantic poppycock, now I was not so sure.

With a smile, Marie snuggled down close beside me, in a way that did nothing to dispel my hopes.

The journey continued as it grew dark and still we travelled on as the cold grew more intense. We had stopped twice to change horses, giving us the opportunity to stretch our legs, but it was little relief, even the indestructible Krasnov was slumped tiredly in his saddle. In the sleigh I held the reins, bone weary, exhausted by the bone-jarring transit of the Siberian waste. Marie was huddled close beside me, she was quiet now and her beautiful face was red with cold and drawn with fatigue.

'How much further is it, Edwin?' she asked. 'Mama is not as strong as she would have you believe, nor is Papa, though he would never let anyone see.'

I pulled off a glove and drew my watch from beneath my coat. It was half past seven.

'It can't be too much further, Marie. We planned to be there by now, but we lost a lot of time crossing the river this morning. I'm sure we'll be there within the next hour.'

Marie fell silent again. Within half an hour we saw the lights of the post house at Yevlevo, where we planned to spend the night. Once in the warmth of the house, I arranged food and accommodation for our party. Once more everyone was glad of the opportunity to get warm and after a quick meal we all retired for the night.

Early next morning I went over to speak to Krasnov, while he and his men were mounting up. As I turned back towards the carts, I could see the Tsar helping the Tsaritsa into her cart. I pulled myself up into the sleigh and was surprised to find Marie already seated there.

'I told Papa that I wanted to know more about how you are to get us out of Russia and what you plan to do to get Alexei and my sisters to catch up with us.

103

Mama was not keen on me travelling with you again without a chaperone, but Papa said it would be alright. I told you, he likes you.'

'I am flattered that you wanted to travel with me, Marie, but today will be a hard trek and this sleigh will give you little shelter. You should go back to your parents.'

'Do not tell me what to do, Edwin! All my life I have been told what to do and how to behave. I thought better of you,' she blazed.

'I am sorry, Marie, I was only concerned for your welfare.'

She smiled at me apologetically.

'No Edwin, it is I who am sorry. I am a little tired and irritable and I should not have taken it out on you. You do not deserve that.'

Despite the gruelling journey, that day I spent in the sleigh with Marie will always be one of the best in my life. We talked of anything and everything. Just a man and a woman enthralled with each other's company. Despite the cold and the gathering gloom, the journey came to an end all too soon. We reached the next post house and disembarked and went into the inn.

Krasnov's men camped in the barn and would guard the perimeter. The rest of the party would have to make do with the warmth of the main room, though I got two camp beds in a private room for the Tsar and Tsaritsa and pulled a mattress in there for Marie. As soon as they had eaten, the Tsar and Tsaritsa retired to their beds. I pulled on my coat and went out on to the porch to check the guards that Krasnov had posted. As I huddled to light a cigarette, I heard the door behind me open and close. I turned to find Marie.

'Mama and Papa are asleep,' she said. 'I cannot settle. I can still feel the bumping of the sleigh, it's almost as if I am still in it.'

'I would have thought you would have been as tired as your parents, it's been a long and tiring day. I don't expect tomorrow will be any different, you will need your rest.'

'Are you trying to get rid of me?' she asked. 'Have you had enough of me today?'

'Erm...no, of course not.' I stammered. The last thing I wanted was for Marie to think I didn't enjoy her company.

Marie laughed at my discomfort.

'I was teasing,' she said, looking up at me. 'I think you feel as I do.'

Then she was in my arms and she kissed me, a long lingering kiss. In that moment, she got her wish, she was not the Grand Duchess Maria Nikolaevna Romanova, the daughter of the Tsar, she was simply Marie, my Marie. She broke away from me, flushed and breathless.

'I'm sorry,' she said. 'I've never behaved so improperly before, it's just that...' her voice tailed off.

'Don't apologise, Marie, if you hadn't kissed me, I don't know if I would have been brave enough to have kissed you.'

'You are the man who is brave enough to travel all the way to Russia to rescue my family and you are frightened to kiss me?' she smiled.

'I was frightened it wouldn't be welcome.'

She looked up at me. 'Edwin, you will always be welcome.'

I held her close, unwilling to let the moment end and felt her shiver with the cold.

'Marie, you should go in, you're freezing. Besides which, the servants will notice and I don't think your

105

parents would approve of you being out here alone with me.' She pulled away reluctantly.

'You are right, Edwin, I have never been alone with a man, not without a chaperone, though you might be surprised by Papa; he seems to like you. But you are right, Mama would not approve of my wanton behaviour. I should go.'

She smiled, pecked me on the cheek and was gone.

I followed her in a few minutes later. Marie was the last thought I had as I rolled in my blanket and fell asleep on the floor.

'Now we're getting to the good bits,' said Lisa with a smile. 'I love a bit of romance.'

'Doesn't every young woman?'

'Cynic!'

Chapter 14

After dinner we gave up on the memoirs and sat chatting. Lisa was excited to be planning her wedding, but there was still something there that did not ring true.

'What's the problem? I can sense that there's something not quite right.'

'You know me too well. I love him to bits, but he's away so often, it's hard to be apart, but that's his job and he loves it.'

'More than you? Have you talked to him about it?'

'No. I don't want to be that kind of fiancée. He might think that I don't trust him, but it's not that, it's just that I miss him so much. I don't want to have a part-time marriage. I think that's where mum and dad went wrong.'

'You've got to talk to him. Believe me avoiding the issue will only make it worse, that's what I did and look how my marriage ended up.'

'Don't be so hard on yourself, you managed 30 years, that's a lot more than some marriages.'

'It still broke down in the end.'

'Still hurts, huh?'

'Yes, I still miss her, I think I always will.'

'You must have some new women on the scene.'

'Naah. I've tried, I even met up with one or two, but nothing lasted beyond the first date. There was something missing, something that I can't describe.'

'That spark?'

'Yeah, I think so; but it's no use moping, Jane's getting remarried. We've been divorced for a while now, but it's still not easy.'

She looked at me with sympathy.

'There will be someone Ian, I'm sure. It's just going to take time that's all. Look, it's getting late, why don't we call it a night and start on the memoirs again in the morning. We could do with a break.'

The next morning after breakfast we started anew on the memoirs.

I was shaken awake by Krasnov just before 4.00 a.m.

'Sir, we have a problem. I had some of my men keeping an eye on the town. They report that a detachment from Ekaterinburg arrived late last night. They're well-armed, they even have machine guns. Their leader is an arsehole called Zaslavsky; Kobylisky told me he had led an armed attempt to seize the Romanovs in Tobolsk.'

'And you think he intends to try the same here,' I stated.

'That's what it looks like. I suggest we get going as soon as we can.'

'I'm not so sure. If they ambush us once we're out in the open, they'll shred us with those machine guns. We should have arrested that bastard in Tobolsk. Get the transport ready to leave, but post your men ready to repel an attack. I'll see if I can get the dogs called off.'

At that moment the Tsar and Tsarita came down, accompanied by Marie, who looked radiant.

'We are ready to leave, Commissar,' Nicholas said.

'Erm... We'll be a little delayed Sir, we're missing some baggage,' I lied, believing that there was nothing to be gained by panicking the royal party. 'I'll be back as soon as we locate it.' I turned to Krasnov and muttered, 'Take charge here, nothing must happen to them. I won't be gone long.'

I left and hurried to the telegraph office, from where I sent an urgent telegram to Goloshchekin in Ekaterinburg.

"I have just received information that your people commanded by Zaslavsky want to take the baggage by force. If you do not act at once, bloodshed will be inevitable. I am leaving Yevlevo immediately."

I then sent a second telegram to Tyumen, asking for a strong well-armed detachment to be sent to meet us en route.

I returned to the post house and pulled Krasnov aside.

'We're leaving, but we need to proceed cautiously. I want you to send your best scouts out ahead to watch for an ambush.'

'I will do,' Krasnov replied. 'We need to be more vigilant than ever, Zaslavsky's been joined by another heavily armed detachment. We're outgunned and outnumbered.'

'Woah, this doesn't look good. Is this how they were taken to Ekaterinburg?' Lisa asked.

'Spoiler alert! Are you sure you want me to answer?'

'Go on, just don't go too far ahead. Are they captured?'

'No, to the best of my recall, it was later when they were intercepted, but I don't want to spoil the story for you. So I'll shut up now.'

We read on.

'We're ready to leave, Sir,' I informed the Tsar and escorted him out to the tantarass and helped Alexandra up into her seat. When I got to the sleigh, I found Marie ensconced there yet again.

'Mama thought it was improper for me to ride with you again and wanted me to travel with her and Papa; but I persuaded Papa that it would reflect badly if we left our rescuer to travel alone. Besides, I enjoyed your company, Edwin. It was so refreshing to be able to talk to someone as an equal, without all of that stuffy protocol...And then there was last night...' she blushed.

'Marie, I am delighted to have your company too. I have only known you a few days, but I feel as if I have known you for ever...' my voice tailed off.

I flicked the reins to get the horses into action to cover my embarrassment. As the sleigh lurched off into its bumpy motion, Marie wriggled herself under my arm and snuggled beside me. Her mother would most definitely not have approved.

When we reached the river which was awash with ice floes I took no chances, remembering the difficulties of the day before and sent for planks to be put across the shifting ice. Even then I was worried about the ice bearing the weight of the carts and I ordered that the passengers get out and cross by foot. The Tsarrisa looked unimpressed by my decision, but bore it stoically and accompanied her husband without complaint, leaning on his arm as she made her way across the rough-hewed planking. Marie crossed the ice on my arm. Somehow, having Marie on my arm felt like the most natural thing in the world.

Once on our way again Marie turned to me.

'There are problems ahead aren't there, Edwin?' she stated. 'I can tell. You are tense and more watchful than yesterday. Please, Edwin, be honest with me.'

'I'll always be honest with you, Marie. You're right. I received information that there is an armed contingent from Ekaterinburg that has been sent to intercept us. They don't want your father going to

110

Moscow, they want him to remain a prisoner in the Urals.'

'Does Papa know?'

'No. I didn't want to alarm him or your mother. We left well ahead of them and because I have arranged for frequent changes of horses, we'll be moving faster than them. I've also sent for reinforcements from Tyumen to meet us en route. We'll be safe enough as long as we keep moving.'

'If you are sure, Edwin, I will say nothing to Mama and Papa. Tell me more about your life in England.'

We carried on talking through two more halts to change horses until we approached Pokrovskoye. Marie had been fascinated by even the most mundane details of everyday life in England.

'You are so lucky, Edwin, you have no idea how much I would like to live such an ordinary life away from the claustrophobia of court and the expectations of being Maria Romanova. I want nothing more than to spend my life with a man I love and be nothing more than his wife and the mother to his children. But alas, that can never be.' She looked at me sadly.'

'I told you before, Marie, times are changing, this damned war is altering the very fabric of the world we live in. I doubt your family will ever be the Tsars of Russia again, which will make you freer than you would have been. There will be no courtly life in the way that you know it, once I get you out of Russia. You will have the chance to meet a man you will fall in love with and marry.'

'And if I have already met him?' she asked, looking up and smiling at me and my heart skipped a beat.

'Marie, I am very flattered, but I am sure that you will meet better, more aristocratic men than me.'

'More aristocratic? Yes. Better? I do not think so. You are one of the kindest, bravest men I have ever met. Edwin, I think I am in love you.'

My head swam and my heart leapt with elation.

'Marie, I think I am in love with you too. I never believed in love at first sight, but...'

The rest of my sentence was cut off as she turned her head up to me and kissed me passionately. Fortunately our sleigh was the first in the convoy and her parents could not see. Krasnov, however, had noticed. He grinned and gave me a knowing wink.

As we entered the village I felt Marie shiver, despite the mild spring weather.

'This is where Rasputin lived. He scared me. I know Mama thought he was a holy man and he did help Alexei, but there was something in the way he used to look at me that frightened me. I should not say it, but I was relieved when he died.'

As we changed horses, Marie nodded to one house where a peasant woman held back the curtain and looked down on us.

'That is Rasputin's wife.'

I looked up at the window and the woman very deliberately crossed herself then disappeared behind the curtain. As I looked away I caught sight of the Tsaritsa, who was standing silently apart from everyone and had also seen Rasputin's wife. She beckoned me over.

'Commissar Yakovlev, could I please send a message to find out how Alexei and my daughters are.'

'Certainly, Your Highness, tell me what you want to say and I will send the telegram personally.'

I was making my way to the telegraph office when an old peasant approached me. His face was wrinkled and his hair and beard were snow white.

'Is that the former Emperor?' His lack of teeth made it difficult to understand him. 'Where are you taking him?'

'To Moscow, father.'

'Thank the Lord. Moscow. Now Russia will have order again!'

He turned and ambled off and I crossed to the telegraph office where I showed the telegrapher my warrant.

'I need to send some messages, but they are confidential, I will send them personally. Would you mind taking a walk for a few minutes?'

He nodded and left and I settled myself at the telegraph key. First I tapped out a telegram to Kobylinsky.

"Proceeding safely. How is the little one? Yakovlev."

I then tapped out the Tsaritsa's personal messages to her children, though for security I signed them with my name.

Then it was back to join the others and soon we were on the road again. Once we were under way and her parents could not see, Marie snuggled close to me again. There was something about her intimate proximity that simply felt natural and right. I settled myself to enjoy the moment.

By late afternoon we reached the village of Borki, where our last change of horses was due to take place. I pulled up the sleigh and helped Marie down. A sudden

113

commotion made me turn. Dr Botkin had fallen to the ground groaning in pain.

'What's wrong, Doctor?' I asked.

'It's my kidneys...sharp pain....' he gasped.

I got two of Krasnov's men to help him to a nearby house. We put him to bed and left him to rest.

'Is he going to be alright?' Nicholas asked with concern.

'I think so, Sir. If we let him rest for a while, I hope he will be able to complete the journey.'

The former Tsar turned away to convey the news to his wife and Marie came up beside me.

'This delay, is it dangerous? Will our pursuers catch up with us?'

'I think we will be fine, Marie, just as long as we do not remain here too long. We've got a good lead over them. If it's going to last more than a couple of hours, we'll have to leave Dr Botkin behind. I'm not going to take any chances. We'll get you and your parents safely to Tyumen'

'This is just like our very own thriller,' Lisa said.

'More like a tragedy, remember we know how this all ends.'

'Oh I forgot. That makes it all the more sad. Poor Marie, poor Edwin.'

'Yeah, but we've yet to get them to that part. There's a way to go yet and the whole thing about the Tears of Christ still to go.'

Chapter 15

'Look Lisa, I've been thinking we're taking all of this on face value. We haven't looked for any supporting evidence. That makes us piss poor historians. Everything I've read fits with the historical facts I know, but I don't have a detailed knowledge of what happened to the Romanovs. Before we go any further with the memoirs we need to confirm their accuracy and authenticity,' I said, as we sat down to lunch.

'Correct historical method, eh? It's a bit by-the-book but I suppose you are right. We can't go off on some manic treasure hunt based on what might be fiction. Where are we going to check, this isn't London after all.'

'Let's go into town and start at the local library. We could then try the bookshops and see if they have anything.'

It took us forty minutes to get into town and Lisa headed to the library whilst I headed to the local bookshop. My search came up with two books specifically on the fate of the Romanovs, one paperback, the other a detailed hardback tome. The latter was rather expensive, but would serve to check the memoirs. My mobile phone rang, it was Lisa.

'Library's no use at all, all they've got is very general histories, nothing detailed enough to authenticate the memoir. You had any luck?'

'I've found a couple of texts on Ekaterinburg, they should suit our needs.'

'Wait there and I'll pick you up outside.'

Within five minutes the blue Mazda pulled up and I got in. We hurtled our way south, taking one particular bend a bit too wide for my liking.

'Hey slow down a bit, we nearly took that bend on the wrong side.'

The sports car fishtailed as she braked.

'Sorry. There's something not right, the car's not holding the road like it usually does.'

'Pull in over there.' I said indicating a lay-by.

I got out and checked the tyres; sure enough the rear offside tyre was punctured.

'Your tyre's flat, there's a bloody great nail sticking out of it. Just as well they're run-on-flats or we'd have been in real trouble back there. Where's your spare?'

She unstowed the spare wheel whilst I jacked up the car and removed the wheel.

'Hang on, what's that?' I asked pointing to a small square protrusion hidden inside the wheel arch. I gripped it and pulled; the magnetic underside gave way as it came off in my hand.

'What is it?'

'I'm not sure, but my guess would be some kind of tracking device.'

'Tracking device? Who would put that there?' she asked.

'I don't know, but if Nadya is to be believed there are a host of people interested in what they think we might have a lead on.'

'But a tracking device?'

'Mmm. It doesn't really sound like the Russian mafia, I'd have expected something more direct like a tail.'

'More official then. Perhaps a present left by Nadya herself.'

'I don't know why, but my instinct is we can trust her.'

'You're just a sucker for a pretty face.'

'No seriously, I think she has bigger fish to fry. But you're right, this is at least semi-official, someone is

116

trying to keep tabs on us in the hope that we'll find the jewels.'

I finished replacing the wheel and got back into the car still holding the tracker.

'Leave that behind.' Lisa instructed.

'No. It doesn't matter if we're tracked at the moment, we have no idea where the Tears are. As long as this remains in the car, whoever planted it thinks they know where we are or where we're going. So let them. Then if we need to go off the grid, we can just ditch the tracker.'

'Devious, I like it!'

Back at the house Lisa seized the paperback, leaving me with the tome.

'Gee, thanks,' I grunted.

'You're the professional, you get the book with the hard words,' she smiled.

We worked until dinner and afterwards we compared notes.

'Okay,' Lisa started 'my book confirms lots of the names and places. Kobylinsky at Tobolsk, the role of Yakovlev in moving the Romanovs and the journey to Tyumen, although it suggests the journey lasted longer, four or five days. The memoirs suggest just a couple of days. It's rather general. What about you?'

'Well, this more or less confirms the authenticity of the memoir. Names and places – it agrees even down to the texts of some of the telegrams, not necessarily word-for-word, but close enough to be translation differences from the Russian. It disagrees with your book, it reckons that the journey to Tyumen only took a couple of days. It was only just over a hundred miles and they were travelling about fourteen hours a day; that's averaging only about four miles an hour. With frequent changes of horses, they'd be travelling quicker than that, so that allows time for the delays he describes. It looks as if Edwin was really there, so tomorrow we continue on with account.'

The next morning dawned bright and mild, as Lisa and I met in the sitting room to continue our reading.

It was ninety minutes before Botkin declared himself fit to travel, by which time twilight was falling, but a bright moon would illuminate our journey. We raced along wildly with the bells that Krasnov's men had attached to the transport tinkling madly. A few miles from Tyumen we were met by the reinforcements I had sent for. It was in full darkness that we arrived at our destination. A railway engine with two carriages, one first class, the other second, waited at the station. I settled the royal party in their carriages and then headed for the telegraph office.

I again took over the office and settled at the key. The first telegram went to Goloshchekin in Ekaterinburg.

"Your detachments have the single goal of destroying my baggage. Did you know of this? I cannot but think you are being misled since they mock and belittle you in conversation. Do you guarantee the safety of the baggage? Remember Sverdlov and Vladimir Ilych stand behind us and keep us safe. I await your response.
Yakovlev"

The subsequent telegrams went to Sverdlov himself.

"I have only part of the baggage with me. I need to change route due to extreme circumstances. Attempts made by Ekaterinburg to destroy the baggage before I arrived. Baggage still imperilled by Ekaterinburg

118

detachments who have decided to attack us outside Ekaterinburg and massacre us if we do not hand over the baggage. With the exception of Goloshchekin, Ekaterinburg had but one goal: to destroy the baggage.
Yakovlev."

Within minutes I had a reply from Sverdlov.

"Perhaps you are too nervous? Are you exaggerating the dangers? Can old route be taken?
S"

It was becoming clear to me that passage through Ekaterinburg was just too fraught with danger. I recalled the map on which we had planned our route and a plan began to form in my head which would avoid totally the danger of Ekaterinburg.
I replied.

"Request permission to proceed to Omsk and seek further instructions there."
After a few minutes Sverdlov answered.

"Permission to proceed to Omsk. Telegraph when you arrive. Proceed with caution. Further instructions in Omsk.
S."

Sverdlov had agreed to my plan to outwit the extremists in Ekaterinburg and allow me to get Marie and her family to safety by a roundabout route, but first we had to get to Omsk. I gave instructions to the local railway officials then I joined Nicholas and his family in their carriage. I explained to Nicholas that on the grounds of safety we needed to change our route and we would be

119

setting off early in the morning. As I was leaving, Marie caught up with me outside. She hugged me close.

'Thank you for getting us here safely, Edwin.' She paused for a moment and her face became serious. 'If it was so dangerous for us, how will Alexei and my sisters get out of Tobolsk? We had you and Comrade Krasnov; they have no-one.'

'I don't think they're in danger Marie, it's your father that they want to get their hands on. This is about politics and power; I don't think for a minute that they want to wage war on women and children.'

She looked up at me and smiled.

'Thank you, Edwin. You are so good at reassuring me and allaying my fears. I feel so safe with you.'

I bent and kissed her, a long, lingering kiss. Suddenly, the opening door of the carriage cast a spear of light through the darkness and Marie and I jumped apart.

'Marie, you must come in. What are you doing out there?' the Tsaritsa called.

'It's alright Mama, I was just asking Commissar Yakovlev how he plans to reunite Alexei, Olga, Tatiana and Anastasia with us. I'm coming now.'

With a regretful look she turned and walked back to the carriage.

'It's really sweet. I hope they managed to get it together,' Lisa said with a glint in her eye.

'Very romantic, but we're talking about 1918 and she was an Imperial Grand Duchess; by the conventions of the times their relationship had already ventured into the scandalous. By today's standards I doubt they got past "first base".'

'Sometimes, Ian, you are a real spoilsport!'

'Yeah, that's what my ex-wife must have thought. Get back to the manuscript.'

It was still dark when the locomotive began to fire up its boiler. As the train prepared to leave Krasnov loomed out of the blackness.

'I can accompany you no further, my friend, but you and your charges are still in danger from those pricks in Ekaterinburg. I have ordered twenty of my best men to go with you, along with two heavy machine guns. They will protect you to the death – or answer to me,' he laughed. 'The rest of us will follow the railway east to Omsk.'

I divulged my plan to Krasnov.

'It might work, Yakovlev, in which case we may meet again along the way. In case we don't, good luck with your little princess.'

With a laugh he merged into the darkness and disappeared.

At five in the morning the train pulled out of the station, westwards towards Ekaterinburg. Twenty miles west of Tyumen, I called the train to a halt and had the carriages uncoupled. The unattached engine continued its journey westward whilst the carriages were hitched to a second engine I had arranged and headed back east to Tyumen, Omsk and safety.

I entered the first class carriage and spoke to the Tsar.

'Sir, I must ask you to extinguish all lights and pull down the blinds until we have passed back through Tyumen.'

'What is going on, Mr Etherington?'

'Sir, I have every reason to believe that you and your family would be in serious danger if we were to go via Ekaterinburg, I am afraid your family have few friends there. I am hoping that the engine that has continued westwards will fool our enemies long enough for

121

us to travel east as far as Omsk. From there we can make our way to Moscow by a safer route to the south. But for the ruse to work, we must go through as unobtrusively as possible.'

Then of course we must put out the lights. We are totally in your hands, young man.'

Within the hour we passed through Tyumen and were clear travelling east to Omsk and then Moscow. I stood on the platform at the rear of the Imperial family's coach and watched the scattered lights of Tyumen fade in to the darkness when I heard a rustle behind me and a hand slipped into mine. It was Marie.

Mama and Papa are asleep, I couldn't sleep. I hoped I would find you here.' She stepped close and slid into my arms. 'I feel so safe and complete when I am with you. I want this journey to last forever.'

Marie, all journeys must end, but I will always seek you out. I will get you and your parents to safety. Then I will go back for your brother and sisters. When that is done, I promise I will find you, if you want me to.'

With all my heart, Edwin. I owe you my life and I want to spend the rest of it repaying you.'

We kissed. I have no idea how long we spent standing there in each other's arms, but they were the best minutes of my life. Eventually, Marie broke away.

I must go back in before I am missed. Mama would not approve! I love you Edwin.'

122

Chapter 16

We had travelled about thirty miles when I felt the train slow and come to a halt. A group of horsemen blocked the track and had flagged the train down. I recognised the figure of Krasnov at their head, as had the guard in the engine, which is why we had stopped. I jumped down and he nudged his horse forward towards me. Leaning down from the saddle he spoke to me in low tones.

'You've been rumbled. Ekaterinburg has sent orders to Omsk, Kurgan and Chelyabinsk, along with god knows how many other cities, to arrest you and your charges and transport you to Ekaterinburg.'

'Thank you for the warning, Krasnov.'

'I will leave one man with the horses and bring the rest with you. We'll teach these Siberian arseholes. They'll never stand before real soldiers.'

'I appreciate your offer, my friend, but this battle will not be won by force; no matter how good your men are, we could never fight our way through. This is a battle that needs to be fought with guile and politics. Your mission has been completed, you must now go on as ordered,' I told him.

He reached down to offer me his hand.

'Good luck, may God go with you.'

I shook his hand and returned to the train with my mind in a whirl. If we really were blocked to the east and the south, what now?

The train rattled on for nearly four hours. Omsk was fast approaching. I made my way to the engine.

'Where is the next station?' I asked the driver.

123

Lyubinskaya, Commissar. It's about twenty miles from Omsk. We should be there in ten minutes or so.'

I want you to stop there. We'll uncouple the carriages and go on to Omsk without them.'

'If that's what you want comrade. No problem,' he agreed.

At Lyubinskaya station the carriages were shunted into a siding and I went into the Romanov's carriage to explain.

'I am going to leave you here with the guards, Sir. I will go on to Omsk to the telegraph and see what I can do to ensure that we can continue our journey unmolested.'

'Good luck, Mr Etherington, take care of yourself. We will await your return,' the Tsar said.

I called the sergeant in charge of the guard detail.

'Sergeant, I am going to go ahead with the engine. I want you to use your men to surround the carriages and keep everyone away. Until I return, you are responsible for the safety of my prisoners. Remember from whence my orders come and keep them safe.'

'I will sir.'

'Thank you sergeant, carry on.'

I climbed onto the engine and ordered the driver to make all speed to Omsk.

In less than twenty minutes the engine pulled into the station at Omsk. I hurried to take over the telegraph office and contact Sverdlov to find out the situation. It was not long before I received his reply.

"Return to Tyumen at once. The Ural Soviet agree to guarantee the safety of the baggage. Hand over all baggage to the Chairman of the Ural Regional Soviet. Your mission remains the same."

124

What was Sverdlov playing at? How could I guarantee the safety of my charges if I handed them over to Ekaterinburg? How could I get the Romanovs to Moscow if I handed them over to the Urals Soviet? It made no sense. I tapped out a message to Sverdlov.

"I must warn you again that the danger to the baggage, as both Omsk and Tyumen can confirm, is real. If the baggage is taken by the first route, I may not be able to retrieve it safely. The baggage will then be in danger."

There was a five minute wait before Sverdlov replied.

"Situation under control. Travel beyond Omsk not possible. Proceed as instructed."

I did not know what Sverdlov's plan was, but I appeared to have little option but to trust he really did have the local situation under the control of Moscow. However, I was unconvinced. I had a terrible feeling that I was taking the Tsar and Tsaritsa, and above all Marie, into extreme peril.

I arrived back at Lyubinskaya and went immediately to inform the imperial family of our change of plan.

"I am sorry, sir, the Omsk soviet fears we will head east to Japan and will not let us pass. We must return to Tyumen and go on through Ekaterinburg. I have been assured that the Urals Soviet has guaranteed our safety."

"Is it definitely settled that we go to Ekaterinburg?" Nicholas asked.

125

'I don't think we have any choice, Sir.'

'I would go anywhere but to the Urals,' Nicholas sighed. 'To judge by the papers, the workers there are bitterly hostile to me and my family.'

'I can only repeat, Sir, I do not think we have any alternative. I give you my word that I will do everything possible to keep you and your family safe.'

'Promise me, Etherington, if anything should happen to me, you will protect Marie.'

'I promise you, Sir, I will give my life before I let anything happen to your daughter.' A promise I meant, but was destined to be unable to keep.

It took the rest of the day and all night for the train to reach Ekaterinburg. Marie and I managed to snatch a few minutes together whenever we could, but it was all too little. Anxiety at what would happen when we reached Ekaterinburg was gnawing away at me. I could not escape the feeling that I was taking the woman I loved into extreme danger.

It was at 8.40 on the evening of Tuesday, 30th April that the train pulled into the station at Ekaterinburg. It was a bright, cloudless day, one that I would have enjoyed in other circumstances. A huge crowd of hundreds of workers greeted the train's arrival. They surged towards the train with cries of "Hang them here!" and "Spit in the faces of the filthy Romanovs". The Bolshevik sentries placed by the Urals Soviet made no attempt to keep the angry crowd away from the train.

'Stay inside,' I instructed the Tsar and his family. 'Whatever you do, do not raise the blinds or look out of the window.'

Jumping off the train I strode forward.

'Ring the train!' I ordered my guards. More loudly I shouted, 'Grab the machine guns.'

126

My words and the accompanying actions made the crowd back away in fear. For a while there was an uneasy standoff, then a convoy of open cars arrived containing Goloshchekin and a slight, fresh-faced young man who introduced himself as Comrade Beloborodov, the chairman of the Ural regional soviet.

'Comrade Beloborodov, I insist you allow me to continue with my prisoners to Moscow as per my orders.' I handed him the orders signed by Sverdlov and Lenin.

'I have been in communication with my old friend Comrade Sverdlov and we have made new arrangements.'

'You cannot possibly guarantee the safety of my prisoners; the behaviour of that mob and your inability to deal with it proves that.'

'I believe Comrade Sverdlov has instructed you to turn your prisoners over to me!' Beloborodov declared heatedly.

'Do not shout at me, Comrade. I represent the Central Executive Committee and you will respect my authority.'

'You have no authority, Comrade. Sverdlov has rescinded that. The Urals Soviet has control here and you have been declared a traitor to the revolution and your arrest has been ordered.'

'On whose authority?'

'On the authority of the Praesidium of the Urals Soviet.'

'My remit comes from the Central Committee, not a regional soviet. You exceed your authority. I insist that you allow me to continue my journey unhindered.'

'I will have you arrested and returned to Moscow in chains!' he threatened.

'Do that, I look forward to seeing your face when Comrade Lenin orders you to Moscow in the same state,' I countered.

127

By now the crowd had regrouped and was threatening to advance. Beloborodov ordered the train to be moved to a more secure location, a goods depot outside the town. I concurred as it seemed the best way to protect my charges.

When the train pulled into the goods yard, it was immediately surrounded by heavily armed troops from the Red Army. I countered by rousing my outnumbered troops to the alert. For three hours the stalemate dragged on, whilst Beloborodov brought in more heavily armed troops and heavy machine guns to reinforce the ring surrounding our train.

Beloborodov then stepped forward.

'Surrender the prisoners, Comrade Yakovlev, or my superior forces will storm the train and take them.'

'Edwin, what are you going to do? There are so many of them,' Marie whispered to me, as I looked out of the carriage window.

'I have no alternative, Marie, if I fight there is every chance that you could be hurt or even killed and there is no chance of us winning.' I looked deep into her wonderful blue eyes with my heart breaking.

'Comrade Beloborodov, I am prepared to surrender my prisoners to you, on condition that you guarantee their safety pending clarification from Moscow,' I called.

'I accept your terms, Yakovlev. Come out now.' I glanced at my watch, it was four in the afternoon, as I stepped down from the carriage. Beloborodov presented me with a document that formally transferred the Romanovs from my custody to that of the Urals Soviet and insisted that I sign.

Beloborodov then entered the carriage and informed Marie and her family that Moscow had ordered their detention until a trial could be arranged. They were, therefore, to go with him.

128

The Tsar was the first to leave the carriage. He was wearing a military greatcoat from which the epaulettes had been cut off. He was followed by the Tsaritsa and Marie wearing dark Persian lambs' wool coats and hats. Thus wrapped up, Marie was as pretty as a picture. She followed her parents into the first of the open cars. The last I saw of her was when she looked back at me as the cars pulled out of the yard, followed by a lorry loaded with heavily armed troops.

A Red Army officer approached me.

'Comrade, I have been instructed to place you under arrest. Will you please hand over your weapon and accompany me?'

'I have to go, Lisa. I've just remembered I have an appointment in town later this afternoon. Tell you what, I'll pick up a takeaway on my way back and we can continue with the manuscript then. Sorry, but it's a longstanding medical thing and I can't put it off.'

'Of course you have to go, Ian. I've plenty to get on with here and I promise I won't read on without you. It's tempting, but I'll wait for you.'

'Yeah, you do that. But make sure you keep the door locked whilst I'm out. There's been some sinister goings on and I want you to take care.'

'Okay Ian, I'll be careful and stay locked away until you get back.'

I left just after lunch. I quickly checked the wheel arches of the Saab and found a tracker attached to my car just like the one on Lisa's Mazda. It was dark by the time I got back to the house clutching Chinese takeaway in two bags. I locked the car and approached the door. Far from being locked, the door was ajar. What was Lisa playing at? I had told her to take care and keep the door locked and here it was open to all and sundry. I pushed open the door and was about to call out when I heard a muffled scream from upstairs.

Chapter 17

I rushed in through the door. I was about to throw myself up the stairs when the thought struck me that a weapon might be a good idea, just in case. I snatched the Webley revolver from the drawer and then took the stairs two at a time. There were sounds of a struggle emanating from Lisa's room. The sight that greeted me through the doorway stopped me dead. Lisa was lying on the bed on her back struggling. Her jeans and panties had been pulled down to her knees and kneeling above her a hard looking, rat-faced man in his thirties held a knife to her face whilst he struggled to undo his belt with the other. The butt of an automatic pistol peeked out from under his jacket. Despite the threat of the knife Lisa still squirmed in a vain attempt to extricate herself from under her assailant.

'Hold still!' the man snarled in a heavy eastern European accent. 'First we have a little fun; afterwards you tell me where the Tears of Christ are.'

'I don't know!' Lisa sobbed. 'Get off me!' Her assailant did not reply.

I raised the pistol then stopped and cursed myself for my stupidity. The gun was not loaded. By the time I got downstairs and loaded the pistol, Lisa would have been raped. There was no alternative. I hurled myself in a panicked dive at the man, the pistol flailing at his head. The heavy revolver struck him on the side of his head moments before my tackle drove him from the bed. I landed on top of the would-be rapist who, though dazed, was still gripping the wicked-looking knife. Fury surged through me as I thought of what might have happened if I had not been there. Rearing above him I smashed the gun down on his head with all my strength. Once, twice, three times the kilo of steel in my hand smashed down on his skull. I felt something crumple with the second blow, but it did not stop me delivering a third, even more massive, blow.

'Ian! Stop!'

Lisa's scream lifted the red mist before my eyes. I rolled off his limp body and was appalled to behold my handiwork. The left side of the attacker's skull was shattered, the six inch octagonal barrel of the revolver had left a crumpled indentation over an inch deep and as big as the palm of my hand from which blood oozed. It was also trickling from his ears. There was silence in the room except for the hideous, laboured breathing of the injured man that rasped from his throat. I retched dryly, horrified at what I had done. Then, after a final gurgling rattle there was just a terrible accusing silence.

'Ian...Ian are you alright?'

'He's dead,' I stammered and threw up.

'Good! The bastard tried to rape me. I hope he rots in hell.'

'...I killed him...I didn't have to... hit him so hard ...or as many times...I killed him.'

'Ian, look at me.'

I looked up at her from the floor. She had redressed herself and she took my face in her hands.

'You did what you had to do to protect me. He was armed, you had no choice,' she said firmly.

'I doubt the police will see it that way. We better call them.'

'No. Let's think about this for a minute. I'm not having you risking prison for manslaughter just because you tried to save me from a rapist and the system's concerned with his human rights.'

'We have to call the police, we can't just sit here with a dead body. Disposing of corpses is outside our skills set.'

132

'Mmmm,' she mused. 'Ian, what do you make of the tats on his neck?'

The random question threw me and I did not want to look closely at the man I had just killed. The very thought made me nauseous. I looked away.

'Ian, I need your help here, get a grip!' Lisa's voice was harsh and compelling

I forced myself to look.

'I don't know, it looks like Cyrillic, but I can't understand it.'

'Okay. Pass me his wallet and then use your handkerchief to pull out his gun. Don't leave any fingerprints,' she instructed.

I did as she asked.

'Is there anything notable about the gun?'

I peered at the squat automatic.

'Yes, it's got "Baikal, Made in Russia" stamped on the slide.'

'The wallet belongs to an Oleg Turganiev. It's concrete proof that this guy was Russian, and maybe the answer to our problem. Disposing of bodies might be outside our skills set, but I'll bet that someone we met recently has the skills.'

She left the room and came back with her phone. I was still sitting on the floor beside the man I had killed, my eyes glazed. I had always believed that to protect the ones I love I could kill without a second thought. I now found that killing was not that easy.

'Is that Ms Kuznetsova?....Lisa Mann here, was your offer of help real, because we have a problem?...A man has broken into my house and attempted to rape me, he's dead, Ian killed him defending me...If you really want to avoid bad press, I think it might involve you, his name was Oleg Turganiev according to his wallet, he's covered with Cyrillic tattoos and was carrying a Russian made firearm. If I called the police, it could cause problems for Ian and very bad publicity for Russia at this important time…I thought you might have a way to make the problem…go away…' There was a long pause. 'Yes, I understand; we'll be here. Thank you.'

Lisa crouched down and gently removed the revolver that I was still clutching in my right hand and helped me to my feet.

'Come on, Ian, we'll go downstairs, Ms Kuznetsova said she will be here in a couple of hours. We've got to wait for her.'

Still pale and sickened by what I had done, I allowed her to shepherd me downstairs. She settled me on the sofa then returned with a large glass of scotch.

'Drink this, you look terrible.'

I took a large gulp of the fiery liquid. The sensation of it burning down my throat to my stomach brought me round from my stupor.

'I'm sorry Lisa, I should be caring for you rather than going to pieces like this, it's rather unmanly.'

She knelt in front of me and gently took my hands in hers.

'No Ian, I'm okay, thanks to you. You did what you had to do; you didn't hesitate to throw yourself to my defence without a second thought, but it can't be easy to face the consequences of what you had to do.'

'That's just it, did I have to? Did I have to kill him?' I asked.

'Ian you're in shock. It was his choice; no-one invited him here armed to the teeth to attack me. He was still armed when you tackled him, he would have killed you without turning a hair. Kuznetsova knew the name; he's a known mafia thug. She said she would explain more when she got here.'

By the time Nadya Kuznetsova arrived I had recovered some composure. The Mercedes pulled on to the drive and she got out looking calm and elegant.

'Where is he?' she asked.

'Upstairs on the right, front room,' Lisa told her.

She went upstairs and returned a few minutes later.

'It's Turganiev. Explain to me what happened,' she asked.

We related the story briefly.

'You've done the world a favour, Ian,' she replied. 'It's a far better place for not having Turganiev in it. He is suspected of dozens of murders and multiple rapes in my country. It would not be inaccurate to describe him as a sadistic psychopath. Miss Mann is very lucky you arrived when you did, otherwise you would have found her dead, and her death would not have been quick or pleasant. This is precisely the sort of thing I was worried would happen. My government does not need stories in your press about attacks by the Russian mafia on innocent British women. Leave things to me. I have already booked you a hotel for tonight; when you return tomorrow morning, this problem will have... disappeared? Lisa, you need to pack a few things, I need to speak to Ian alone.'

Lisa left and Nadya sat down opposite me.

'I can see you are shaken by what has happened, Ian. It's not easy to take a life, no matter how justified, what you're feeling is what every good policeman or soldier feels. If you didn't you would be as bad as him. I have been there, Ian, and it never gets any easier,' she told me.

'How many...no, I'm sorry, I've no right to ask that.'

'I have not kept count Ian, but one is too many. Just know this, if you had not killed him, he would have killed both of you; even if you had wounded him, he would have still killed you. There is unfortunately only one way to deal with a mad dog. But your conscience will always trouble you. It is not supposed to be easy to kill - to deprive someone of life, even an animal like Turganiev, is a great responsibility. You will come to terms with it,

135

but you will never be comfortable with what you have had to do.'

'Thank you, Nadya, that makes me feel less of a wimp.'

'Any man who tackles an armed man with an unloaded pistol is no wimp. A fool maybe...'

I smiled slightly embarrassed.

'In the heat of the moment I forgot the gun wasn't loaded and we had locked the bullets away. They were World War One vintage, so they probably wouldn't have fired anyway.'

It was Nadya's turn to smile, then her face turned serious.

'You will need to watch Miss Mann closely. She too has been through an ordeal. Helping you has given her something else to concentrate on, but don't be surprised if there is a delayed reaction to what she has been through.'

I nodded; I had been thinking the same thing.

At that moment, Lisa returned carrying a holdall and a small suitcase.

'I threw a few of your things into a case too, Ian. Where do you want us to go?' she asked Nadya, who responded by naming an expensive hotel about twenty miles away.

'The bill has already been paid,' she said. 'Consider it my thanks for helping to avoid a scandal.'

'We'll take my car,' Lisa stated.

'No, I'll drive,' I said.

'I don't think so; you've just drunk enough whisky to anaesthetise a horse.'

'My bad, I forgot that. Take the Saab anyway, it's more comfortable.'

'I'll remain here and meet my cleaners.' Nadya stated. 'I now have your cell phone number, I will ring you in the morning when everything is tidied up here.'

'Thank you Nadya,' said Lisa. 'I didn't know if you would help, but you've been as good as your word.'

'Not all diplomats are liars,' Nadya smiled.

'Not all diplomats are FSB or RSF trained,' I countered.

Nadya was suddenly serious.

'Do be careful. Now you must realise that I was not exaggerating the danger. It doesn't matter whether you are looking for the Tears or not, or even whether you know where they are, as long as people think you do, you are in great danger. Do not underestimate the threat, take every precaution.'

We thanked Nadya again for her assistance and Lisa drove us off towards the hotel.

Nadya had done us proud. After we registered we were shown to two well appointed, comfortable rooms. I carried Lisa's holdall into her room. As soon as we were alone she turned to me.

'Ian, thank you for...' Then she dissolved into tears. '....you saved me from...if it hadn't been for you, I'd.....'

I held her to me and she sobbed into my chest. For five long minutes she shook and cried into my shoulder. Suddenly she looked up and kissed me, I felt her tongue slip between my lips. I pulled her closer and responded hungrily.

'NO!' my brain screamed.

I broke away.

'Lisa, we can't...'

She took my hand and pulled me towards the bed.

'Ian, I can't be alone tonight...not after...stay with me, please.'

I held her by her shoulders at arms' length.

'Lisa, this isn't right. You're in shock. In the morning, we would both regret it. I'll stay with you, I won't leave you alone, but that's it, nothing more.'

I lay on the bed and held her in my arms, as she snuggled close to me and I held her until she fell asleep.

I lay there for a long time wondering, 'If only...' until I too dozed off to sleep.

Chapter 18

The next day dawned bright. I was awoken by the light that streamed in through the curtains. Lisa was still curled up in the crook of my arm, blonde hair spread over her face and across the pillow. Very gently, I extricated my arm and got off the bed. I was heading for the door when I heard her voice.

'Ian?'

'It's okay, I'm just going back to my room to get a shower.'

'Come here and sit down.' She patted the bed.

I did as she asked.

'Ian, about last night...thank you. I don't know what came over me,' she looked abashed. 'It wasn't fair on you. I'd never cheat on James, I just...I was...confused.'

'You just desperately needed comfort, you were frightened and in delayed shock; I'm not surprised after what nearly happened. You weren't yourself.'

'No, but you were; the perfect gentleman and a good friend.'

'I couldn't take advantage of you like that,' I said. 'But I was tempted!' I added with a grin. 'Look, let's forget it happened; I'll go take a shower and meet you for breakfast.'

I was sitting in the dining room half an hour later when Lisa sat down beside me.

'I brought the manuscript. I thought we could read on over breakfast, whilst we wait for the all-clear from Nadya.'

'Yes, that was quick thinking last night to call her, I'm glad one of us was thinking straight.'

'Oh yeah, I was really making good decisions last night.'

'Let's just agree neither of us exactly covered ourselves in glory last night and move on.'

'Oh no, you really came through when I needed you. You almost certainly saved my life last night and my....honour? I'll never be able to repay you.'

'There's nothing to repay, you would have done same for me.'

'Yep, next time you're in danger of being raped, I'll be there to save you!' she smiled.

She placed the manuscript between us and turned to the right page.

I spent the next week under arrest. I was questioned repeatedly and forced to explain my actions over and over. Believing I had the full support of Moscow, I stuck to my story of obeying orders. Eventually Beloborodov was forced to release me, but only on condition that I signed a paper admitting that my instructions were confused and the intention had always been to turn the Romanovs over to the Urals Soviet. I signed because I was no good to Marie or her family as long as I remained incarcerated.

I was driven into Ekaterinburg along Voznesensky Prospekt, the low hills and dark pine forest receded behind me and the further I went along the road, the more opulent the houses and mansions became. The pale blue of the washed out sky was besmirched by dark clouds of smoke emanating from the factories. In Voznesensky Square I blustered my way into Goloshchokin's office. He looked up from his desk.

'How can I help you, comrade?'

'I demand to see the Romanov family. My orders from Comrades Sverdlov and Lenin make it clear that I am responsible for their welfare. It is also imperative that

140

the family be reunited with the members they left behind in Tobolsk as soon as possible.'

'My understanding is that you have signed over responsibility for your charges to the Ural Soviet. The matter is no longer your concern. Go back to Moscow, comrade.'

'I cannot see Comrade Lenin being quite so forgiving about me abandoning my duties. Until I receive orders to the contrary, I will remain here and expect to have access to the Romanovs on a frequent basis, as my papers demand.'

'We will try to accommodate you, Comrade. I will pass your request on to Comrade Beloborodov and the Ural Soviet in due course.'

'Don't get me wrong, Goloshchokin, that was not a request, it was a demand. I will be contacting Comrade Sverdlov, so that my position and authority can be made clear to you,' I said, with steely determination.

'Give Yacob Mihailovitch my best wishes. Tell him that Philip Isaevich still remembers the bad old days in Turukhansk.'

It was his subtle way of informing me that he had more history and sway with Sverdlov than I did. My anxiety for the safety of the Imperial family and particularly Marie rose to a whole new level.

'We will let you know when the Soviet authorises you to visit. Let my office where they may contact you.'

I left his office and walked past the Ipatiev House, which now bore the sinister name of the House of Special Purpose. At number 49 Voznesensky Prospekt, it was one of the grandest houses in the town. On a hillside, the house rose to three stories of whitewash plastered brick and stone. The ornate entrance was largely hidden by the surrounding palisade and at the rear of the house I could just make out a first floor balcony above the newly *erected wall. A guard stood at the entrance and the side windows were all firmly shuttered. I leant on the wall, knowing that Marie was just feet away in the house, but I could get no nearer to her.*

From the dining room window we saw Nadya's Mercedes pull up in the carpark. Two minutes later she joined us at our table, ordering coffee from the waitress.

'Your house is all clear now. My team has finished.'

'Thank you Nadya,' I said.

'I told you last night, I'm grateful for the opportunity to avoid the bad publicity.'

'Nevertheless, we're grateful,' Lisa added. 'I know I was pretty doubtful about your intentions, but I was wrong. I'd like to apologise.'

'No apologies necessary, Lisa,' the Russian said. 'Look, the intruder from last night has known confederates.' She put two photographs on the table and pointed to the first, a short bald man with a moon-face. 'That is Vitali Zhabin.' Then she moved on to the second, which showed two men. She indicated the first man, a shaven-headed, broad-faced muscleman. 'Dmitri Bukhalo, quite obviously the muscle. A deeply dangerous man.' Then she pointed at the other man, a lean silver-haired man with a pointed face. 'Feodor Markin, he's the brains behind the group. He's the right-hand man of this character – Leonid Polunin.' She placed on the table a third photograph of a tall, handsome man in his forties, dressed in an Armani suit. 'Polunin has his fingers in many pies all over Europe, most of them very illegal pies. He is totally ruthless and has been fixated with finding the Tears of Christ for the past ten years. It's Polunin you can thank for your visit last night.'

'You think these are the people who believe we know where the Tears are?' I asked.

142

'Almost certainly. If you see any of these men, run, run like mad. These are very ruthless thugs who will go to any lengths to get what they want. There will probably be a temporary lull for a few days at least. They will not know what happened to Turganiev. As far as they know, he has just fallen off the grid. For the time being they will wait for him to resurface, but eventually they will lose patience and move themselves.'

'Are we safe to go back to the house?' Lisa asked.

'The odd visit may be alright, but I would not recommend you stay there, nor would I stay in your house, Ian,' Nadya replied.

'This is bloody ridiculous!' I exploded. 'We don't have the bloody diamonds and we have no idea where they are. We haven't even been looking for the blasted things!'

'It's not a matter of reality, but perception, Ian. They think you are looking for them and may know where they are. It is that perception that will affect how Polunin will respond. To be honest, the best thing you can do is to find the Tears and sell them, give them to a museum or whatever. Then Polunin will have no reason to pursue you.'

'So, the only way we'll be safe is to find the Tears?' Lisa asked.

'That would be my advice.'

'And if we can't find them?' I enquired.

'I don't think you can afford to fail, Ian. If you don't find the Tears, you may never be safe.'

'Great! Were the tracking devices on our cars put there by Polunin?' I asked.

'Tracking devices?' Nadya frowned. 'Show me.'

I took her outside and showed her the tracker lodged in the wheel arch of the Saab.

'I cannot be certain, but I doubt that was done by Polunin. That tracker is one of the latest GPS trackers, it's state of the art. They have only recently come into service with our security forces. I doubt Polunin has access to them just yet,' she said.

'So you're telling us there's a second person or group involved?' Lisa asked.

'It looks like it. You must be very careful. I had someone check the old Cheka files, everything concerning Yakovlev has recently been removed from the archive. You almost certainly have competition for the Tears, and you cannot afford to come second!' She glanced at her watch. 'I must go. Take care, please.' Nadya climbed into her Mercedes and drove off in a spray of gravel.

'Fucking great!' Lisa swore. 'Not only do we have the Russian Mafia after us, there's an unknown second group involved too and possibly even a third. What have we got ourselves in to, Ian?'

'Look, I suggest we check out and go back to your place to get our stuff. Then we should head out somewhere anonymous to decide what to do next.'

I drove to Lisa's and pulled on to the drive, parking alongside the Mazda.

'Go and grab our cases,' I told Lisa. Whilst she was in the house I pulled the tracker from the wheel arch and carefully laid it under the Mazda. Whoever was tracking us would now think both cars were at the house. Lisa came out a few minutes later with our cases and I told her what I had done.

'So, we can take the Saab and no-one will know where we've gone?' she asked.

'That's the idea.'

'Where do we go?'

'I'd suggest some anonymous motel where we can't be traced,' I responded.

We drove to a motel to few miles from the house and booked in, paying cash for two rooms for the next two nights. That way there was no record of us using our bank cards, just in case we could be traced that way. We met in Lisa's room and settled to read the manuscript in earnest. The sooner we reached the end, the sooner we might find where the Tears could be and get our lives back.

Chapter 19

Sequestered in Lisa's room, we got out the manuscript and began to read.

It was another week before I received permission to visit the Ipatiev House. By that time the remaining family members had been transported to Ekaterinburg by river on board the steamship, Rus. Marie would now be reunited with her brother and sisters. I presented my authorisation at the main gate, where I had to wait until the Commandant was summoned. Avdeyev was slightly built, with brown hair and a small moustache. Despite his reputation as a drunk, he was sober on this occasion.

'Why do you bother us comrade?' he asked in a surly manner.

'I thought my papers made that clear. I am to inspect the conditions under which the prisoners are held on behalf of Moscow. I will want to speak to each member of the family separately.'

Avdeyev looked at me with annoyance, but led the way into the house. The Imperial family was imprisoned on the first floor. The Tsar and Tsaritsa shared a room with the Tsarevitch Alexei; the four Grand Duchesses shared a second room and the family had access to a dining room and a sitting room that was split into two by an archway.

I settled myself into a chair in the dining room as the former Tsar came in. I stood and he held out his hand for me to shake.

'It is good to see you Etherington. I was worried about you, but I cannot get any information out of these damn Bolsheviks.'

'Are you and your family being well treated, Sir?'

'Avdeyev is a drunk,' he said with distaste, 'but he is not too bad. His deputy Moshkin is a brute. He does his best to encourage the guards to humiliate us at every opportunity and I am fairly sure he is stealing from our belongings.'

'I am sorry, Sir. I will do my best to get him brought under control.'

'Do you have any news about our onwards transportation?'

'No, Sir, I am afraid you are stuck here until pressure from Moscow can be brought on the Urals Soviet. However, I am working on alternate plans, but there is some way to go. How are your family?'

'Olga, Tatiana and Anastasia have been very quiet since their arrival. Alexei is much better and Marie is Marie, as always. Unfortunately, my wife is unwell. I have been told you wish to speak to them all, but I would be grateful if you would leave my wife to rest and excuse the two younger children.'

'As you wish, Sir. If it would be easier, I would be happy to interview the two Grand Duchesses together, if they are still weary from their journey, then I will see the Grand Duchess Maria.' I held my breath, hoping he would not suggest my seeing all three grand duchesses together.

'Certainly. I will send Olga and Tatiana in. They are unaware of your identity, we do not get enough privacy here for me to be able to tell then safely.'

'Thank you, Sir. Is there anything that you need?'

'Some more reading matter…and some fresh eggs would be welcome.'

I stood up.

'I will see what I can do, Sir.'

'I will ask Olga and Tatiana to come in.'

With that the Tsar left, shoulders hunched and head bowed. I watched him as he shuffled out quite amazed at how much he seemed to have aged in just a matter of days.

Moments later the two Grand Duchesses came in, the 'big two' as Marie referred to them. Both appeared quiet and subdued. I was shocked, especially by the appearance of the Grand Duchess Olga, who had been an attractive twenty-two year old when I had last seen her, but now looked like a middle-aged woman. Her red-rimmed eyes had a haunted look. They were distant and unresponsive to my questions, responding monosyllabically. After a few minutes I was forced to give in and ask them to send their sister in.

Marie came into the room, closing the door behind her. She flew into my arms and kissed me passionately.

'Edwin, I was so worried, I thought those brutes had harmed you, when we could get no news of you.'

'I am fine, Marie. I was well treated whilst I was locked up, which was only for a week. The rest of the time I was trying to get permission to see you.'

'It is so wonderful to see you again.' She kissed me again. I held her close, holding her so tight I feared she would break. The kiss was long and lingering. Eventually we broke apart, breathless.

'I told you they've got it bad,' Lisa grinned.

'Yeah, yeah. Life's just one big romance story,' I said. 'Until your wife pisses off and marries another man.'

'Ian…'

'No, it's alright Lisa. I'm just a bit bitter and twisted.'

'With good cause, Ian, anyone would be upset by what's happening to you.'

'I shouldn't have said anything, forget it.'

'I won't forget it. You need to talk about it. You can't bottle it up, Ian.'

'Look, Lisa, can we talk about it later? I'm not ready to deal with this now. It's taking me all my time to keep it behind the wall I've built in my mind.'

'Okay, Ian, but we WILL talk.'

'Let's just get back to the story can we?'

Marie, I must speak with you, if we take too long, it might be difficult for me to get back in to see you. Is everything alright here?'

'No, Edwin, it is not,' she shook her head sadly. 'Who would think that after fourteen months of imprisonment we would be treated like this? They are not saying anything, but there were problems with Olga and Tatiana on the way here. Anastasia told me they were assaulted and 'touched' by the soldiers that brought them here. They were locked in a cabin on the Rus and Anastasia says she could hear their screams.'

'I don't want to appear indelicate, Marie, but are we talking about rape here?' I asked with cold steel in my voice.

'I don't think so, Edwin, but I think they were roughly handled and perhaps forced to do things they did not want to. What brave men the Bolsheviks have on their side.'

'I will see that the matter is dealt with, I promise, Marie.'

'Then there are the guards here. The ones on the landing take deliberate pleasure in humiliating my sisters and me with crude comments, especially when we have to

149

pass them to get to the lavatory to relieve ourselves. There is one who will not even allow us to close the door!'

My blood boiled to think of these refined and sheltered young women being treated in this way.

'Don't worry, Marie, I will put a stop to that before I leave this building. I will not have you treated in such a demeaning manner.'

'Thank you, Edwin, I knew I could count on you.'

Then she was in my arms and we kissed again. At length we broke apart.

'Marie, I have to go, but I will be back as often as they let me. I will find a way to get you and your family out of here, I promise.'

'I know you will, Edwin, come back soon.'

'I will.' I stood up and turned to leave the room when Marie's voice halted me.

'Edwin, take care, I love you.'

'I love you too, Marie, and I will get you out of here.'

'I told you,' Lisa crowed. 'Oops, my bad. I didn't mean to disturb you.'

I stormed into Avdeyev's office, he was just handing over to Moshkin. I fixed him with an angry glare.

'Who commanded the transportation detail for the Romanov children?' I demanded.

'Khokhyrakov guarded them with a detachment of Letts. Why?'

'Where is he now?'

'I don't know, probably down at the docks awaiting orders. What's it to you?'

'I'll ask the questions, Avdeyev. And I give the instructions. The Romanov family is to be treated with

150

respect. You will remove the guards who have been on duty on the landing and replace them with more civilised members of your detachment. You will also keep that ape under control.' I stated, nodding to Moshkin.

Moshkin started to stand.

'Sit down, comrade. Unless you want me to start an in-depth investigation into the missing belongings of my prisoners.'

Moshkin looked shaken, but sneered, 'You can prove nothing.'

'I can damn well prove theft. I have a full inventory of the baggage moved with the Romanovs; perhaps we should audit those possessions?' Moshkin looked defeated. 'You will return everything you have stolen and ensure that your men do so too. If you fail, or there is any repetition, I will see that a full enquiry is launched.'

'You cannot come in here telling me what to do!' Avdeyev shouted.

I slapped my warrant on his desk and said softly and menacingly, 'Oh but I can; read that. If there is any more abuse of the prisoners, I will not only have you shot, I will command the firing squad personally.'

It was a bluff, I did not know how much sway my warrant now possessed, but Avdeyev was not to know that.

'As you wish, Comrade; I will ensure that the guard detail is changed.'

'Do that and remember, I will be back regularly to check!'

'Are you sure this is all accurate, Ian?' Lisa asked.

'I'm no expert, but it does fit in with the facts that I know. I read *The File on the Tsar* years ago. I remember there being something in that about how

151

poorly the Romanovs were treated by Avdeyev and the guards.'

'*The file on the Tsar?*' Lisa questioned.

'The book I mentioned the other day, written by two journalists in the 80s,' I responded.

'OK. What happened next?'

'There's only one way to find out. Read on.'

I made my way down to the docks. After a few enquiries, I found Khokhryakov sitting in a bar. He was watching his men, a rough looking bunch, who looked like the sweepings from the local prison. They were a mixture of Czech and Hungarian prisoners of war with just the occasional man from the Baltic to whom the term Lett more accurately applied. I walked up to his table and again produced the useless warrant.

'Outside!' I commanded.

The tall man rose questioningly and followed me outside. As the door closed, I grabbed him by the front of his tunic and slammed him against the wall. I punched him hard in the face and blood spurted from his nose.

'Comrade Lenin gave me orders personally to ensure the safety of the Romanov family, yet you allowed the grand duchesses to be assaulted by your so-called men. What is your excuse, Khokhryakov?'

'I couldn't control them. I tried, but they simply wouldn't obey orders,' he whined.

I pushed him away in disgust and he sprawled on the ground. I turned and stormed off. I was still in a rage when I entered Goloshchekin's office.

'I want Khokhryakov and that rabble he commands transferred immediately to the front, to the most intense fighting on at the front.'

He looked up at me from his desk.

'What the hell is going on?'

Khokhyrakov was so ineffectual that he allowed the Romanov women to be mistreated whilst he was transporting them. I doubt Comrade Lenin will be impressed by the behaviour of your men. Do you know what this could do if word were to get out to the allies? The damage that would be done? I demand that you take action and post this scum to a place where they might atone for their crimes.'

Goloshchekin looked shocked at my news.

'That is a disgrace, Comrade. You are right to bring it to my attention. I have no love for the Romanovs. Personally, I would put the whole pack on trial for crimes against the People, but I cannot condone such behaviour towards young women, we must maintain order and law. There is some fierce fighting against a White counterattack to the south; they will be dispatched as reinforcements at once.'

'Write the orders and I'll deliver them personally.'

Golshchokin scribbled the order and slid it across the desk to me. I picked it up and folded it before slipping it into my inside pocket. Then I turned and left without another word. I returned to the docks. Khokhyrakov was still sitting morosely in the same bar. He greeted me sullenly.

'What do you want now?'

'Your orders.' I said, throwing the paper on to the table in front of him. He picked it up and read it and the colour drained from his face.

'This...this is a death sentence for me and my men.'

'That scum you lead will find the Whites a more difficult proposition than some helpless young women. You can all learn what being a soldier really is - the hard way. If you survive, it will improve their moral fibre and

153

might even teach you some leadership skills. You leave immediately. Go and get your men ready.'

I left him sitting there and walked out into the afternoon sun.

'Go multi-Great Uncle Edwin,' Lisa chanted. 'It didn't pay to piss him off did it?'

'He definitely had an interesting way of dealing with the problem. He was certainly a man of action,' I said.

Chapter 20

At one o'clock we broke for lunch and collected sandwiches and bottles of Coke from the nearby town. The story was really heating up now and neither of us wanted to leave the narrative of the manuscript for too long. Within fifty minutes we were returning to our task, when I noticed a voicemail on my mobile. I listened to the message.

'Hi, Ian, it's Josh here. Where are you? I tried your house, there's no-one there and you're not answering your mobile. Give me a ring, I've made a major breakthrough in the Yakovlev-Lachrymae mystery.'

I looked at Lisa.

'Ring him and see what he's found.'

I dialled his number, putting him on speaker so that Lisa could listen in. Josh's voice came tinnily through the speaker.

'Hi Ian. I'm glad you got back to me. Look, I found a document that throws a whole new light on the Yakovlev issue.'

'It's hard to explain over the phone. Where are you? I'll come over and show you tomorrow. I'm sure it will answer all your questions.'

I looked at Lisa questioningly. She nodded in agreement.

'Look, Josh, you must keep this to yourself, Lisa and I have been subjected to some unwanted attention because of this research and we've had to go somewhere incogito. We're at the King's Motel on the A140 outside Earl Stonham.'

'Well, this sounds very James Bond! I'll be with you about eleven tomorrow. See you then.'

We settled in Lisa's room and recommenced reading.

In the light of the Tsar's request, I arranged for nuns from a convent just outside the town to deliver fresh eggs twice a week to the Imperial Family at the Ipatiev House. It was three days before I got permission to visit again. This time however, it proved impossible for me to see Marie alone for more than a few seconds. All I could do was tell her that the abusers of her sisters had been dealt with, before we were interrupted by the arrival of the Tsar and Tsaritsa. All the time I was talking to her parents, Marie was casting longing glances at me, looks I could not return for fear that her parents would notice. I left the house depressed and upset by my inability to hold Marie or even speak to her. I walked morosely along Voznesensky Prospekt when a man collided with me as I crossed the road. I was about to complain at his clumsiness when I felt something being thrust into my hand. Keeping a straight face, I strode on along the street until I came to an alley. I slipped into it and unrolled the roll of paper that I had been passed. At once I recognised the hand-written scrawl, the message came from Bruce-Lockhart. It read:

'Etherington, Matushka says that we should meet as we have much in common.' Scrawled on the back was an address and a time, 19.30.

I arrived promptly and found the door unlocked. Entering the house I found a blonde man in his forties awaiting me in the gloomy room.

'Etherington? My name is Stephen Alley, we have a mutual friend, C.'

I shook the offered hand.

'What's the plan? I presume that's why you're here, a new plan.'

156

'Correct. I've been here for a week, working on a new plan. I've a team of four agents, Hill, Hitching, Michelson and MacLaren. Like you, we all speak Russian like natives and can pass as locals. I understand you know MacLaren.'

'MacLaren's wife is my cousin. I know Malcolm well. He certainly could pass as Russian.'

'Right, over the past week my group has straggled into Ekaterinburg singly and we are now awaiting our instructions.'

'What's the plan?'

'We take the Family north to Murmansk. Hitching has obtained the necessary motor transport for us to whisk the Romanov's away. We'll use the back roads out of here, some of the gradients are a little steep, but I think it can be done.'

'How do you think we're going to get them out of the house?' I asked.

'I'm still working on that. We'll meet again when I have the details sorted out. In the meantime, my men and I need to keep our heads down, the Cheka are rather active. I want you to meet with Armistead, he's a trouble-shooter for the Hudson's Bay Company. He'll act as go-between until we're ready. For now, you must go about your normal business.'

For the next few days I did precisely that, pestering Beloborodov for permission to visit the Romanovs on a regular basis, sending telegrams to Sverdlov urging him to use his influence to get the Family released to me for transportation on to Moscow and freedom, and making what arrangements I could to make life in the Ipatiev House more bearable for my darling Marie and her family. On the third day I was approached by Armistead as I sat eating a meal in an inn. He introduced himself and then instructed me to meet with Alley that evening

157

at the same address as before. When I arrived he was already waiting for me.

'Come in, Etherington. Sit. I am afraid we've hit a snag. We have the essentials of a plan to get the Romanovs out, but we need finance to make it happen. I need money to enlist the necessary local help to break them out, and then more for bribes so we can spirit them away. The only problem is that His Majesty's Government seem reluctant to provide the cash. Without it, our hands are tied and there will be no rescue.'

I thought for a moment and something Marie had said came back to me. We had been talking of the Romanovs' life once I got them out of Russia and she indicated that they still had a considerable amount of royal jewellery secreted away.

'Leave it with me. I'll meet you here at the same time tomorrow,' I said.

'Taking up bank robbery, old man?'

'Never mind where I get the finance as long as I get it.'

'Fine. I'll meet you here tomorrow.'

The next day I had permission to visit the Ipatiev House again. At eleven o'clock I presented myself at the house and again informed them that I wanted to interview members of the Imperial Family. Once again, I was ensconced in the dining room and I jumped to my feet as the Tsar came in.

'Sit down, young man,' he said. 'Thank you for the eggs and books you arranged.'

'It was a pleasure, Sir. How are your family?'

'Alexei is getting stronger and went outside yesterday. Olga and Tatiana seem rather withdrawn, but I cannot find out the nature of their problem. Anastasia is bored with being cooped up here and Marie, is her usual self ....as you know,' he said with a glint in his eye. 'It's

158

my wife who worries me, she seems so depressed and lifeless; worst of all I am able to do nothing about it.'

I'm sorry to hear that, sir. I too have a problem. The British Secret Service has sent a team to get you out of here and away to safety in Murmansk. They have a plan that I'm not yet privy to, but don't have the finances to execute their mission.'

The Tsar regarded me appraisingly.

'Marie told you about the jewels,' he stated. "What do you need?"

'Yes sir, I know about the jewels. I think a few thousand roubles should answer their need for now.'

'When will we know of this plan?'

'As soon as I do, sir.'

He nodded and stood up.

'Wait here.'

With that he left the room and for ten minutes I waited. Then the door opened and Marie came in. She flew to me and hugged me, turning her face up to be kissed. It was several long minutes before we broke apart.

'Papa said to give you these,' she said, placing three small diamonds into the palm of my hand. 'He said that you had a plan for us to escape.'

'Not my plan, there are other British agents working on it. I know no details as yet.'

'He also asked me to give you these for safe keeping,' she said, handing me a small red velvet bag. I opened the bag and emptied out two perfect matching blue diamonds that scintillated in the morning sunlight coming through the window. They're called the Tears of Christ. They're uniquely valuable but very unlucky. Ill fortune has always dogged those who possessed them. Personally, I am glad to see them go, maybe our luck will change, but I don't want their curse to fall on you, Edwin.'

159

'It's fine, Marie, I'm not superstitious. I don't believe in fate or luck, either good or bad. They're just diamonds. I'll keep them safe for you, until you need them. How are things here now?'

The guards are much better behaved now, thanks to you. One of them is quite sweet. There is no need to get jealous though, Edwin. He is kind and funny, but he does not have a place in my heart like you do.'

I held her in my arms again.

'Marie, you are my one true love. If I live to be a hundred, I could never feel for another woman what I feel for you.'

We kissed again, a kiss that seemed to go on forever, until we were disturbed by a knock at the door and a moment later Anastasia poked her head round the door.

'Marie, Mama wants you in the sitting room.'

'That was close,' I said, as the head disappeared. 'If she had come straight in, we would have been caught in a rather compromising position.'

'It was deliberate. Nastya knows about us. I had to tell someone and Olga and Tatyana would never approve or understand. Nastya has always been the sister I confided in.'

'Tell her that her delay in coming in was very diplomatic and thank her for me.'

Marie laughed and her blue eyes sparkled.

'I will tell her. But I must go Edwin. Will I see you soon?'

'As soon as I can make it, my love.'

She gave me one last longing kiss and then she was gone.

That evening I delivered the smaller diamonds to Alley. He appraised them carefully.

'Well, cash would have been better, but these will do. I am sure that Hill will have contacts that can turn these into cold hard cash.'

'When will your plan be complete?'

'Any day now, just as soon as Hill converts these diamonds into cash.' 'And when do you plan to tell me?'

'Look, old man, you are the most vulnerable of all of us, going in and out of the Ipatiev House. It only seems sensible that we keep you in the dark until the last minute in case you are rumbled.'

I did not like his answer, but I could see his point. It was just that I was so desperate to get Marie out of that house.

'Bad business with the Grand Duke Michael,' Alley drawled.

'What?'

'There are rumours that he was murdered near Perm three days ago. All the information I can get seems to imply that the rumours are true. If they're prepared to shoot the Tsar's brother, we must assume that the Imperial Family are in the utmost peril and act as soon as possible.'

'But Lenin and Sverdlov would never countenance it, Lenin in particular.'

'In case you haven't noticed, the local Bolsheviks don't seem to be fully in tune with the wishes of Moscow. Besides, I wouldn't trust that little weasel Sverdlov as far as I could throw him. No, we must move as soon as possible.'

Certainly the news of the execution of Grand Duke Michael made my blood run cold. Time was running out. I had to get Marie and her family out of that prison; before it was too late.

I visited the house again a few days later, but once again, I had no opportunity to be alone with Marie,

161

despite the best efforts of Anastasia, who tried several times to engineer a situation where we could have time together

My next visit was on Thursday 27th June, Marie's nineteenth birthday. I smuggled in a birthday cake for her and seized the opportunity to see her alone in the dining room.

'Thank you for the cake, Edwin,' she said.

'Marie, before anything else, you must tell your father that it's tonight. Alley's plan to break you out takes place tonight. You must all be dressed and ready to go at all times tonight.'

'Oh Edwin, tonight, on my birthday we will finally be free. That is the best present you could have given me.'

She embraced me and we fell into a deep lingering kiss. Then the door burst open.

Beloborodov and Goloshchekin stood in the doorway with a shocked Tsaritsa.

'Marie!' the Tsaritsa barked.

'Comrade Commissar, what is the meaning of this?' Beloborodov enquired.

'No wonder you were always so interested in the welfare of the prisoners,' Avdeyev put in snidely from the rear of the group.

'You need to leave, now, Comrade,' Goloshchekin's tone brooked no dissent. 'I will be informing Comrade Sverdlov of the behaviour of his "Special Commissar". Guard!'

The guard from the landing bustled in.

'Escort Comrade Yakovlev from the building at once. Avdeyev, Yakovlev is to be accorded no further access to this building.'

The guard took my arm and pulled me from the room. I caught one last glimpse of Marie's tear-filled blue

162

eyes as I was escorted out. As the door closed behind me I heard the Tsaritsa's voice.

'Maria, you bring shame on yourself and your family by such scandalous behaviour. We will speak of this later, in private.'

The guard was friendly as he led me to the door.

'I don't blame you Comrade, she's a good looking girl,' he said with a wink, 'but you should not have got yourself caught. A pity, I wouldn't have turned her down.'

As the door of the Ipatiev House closed on me, I realised I had burned my bridges. I had to get Marie out tonight, or I might never see her again.

'Is that true?' Lisa asked. 'Were they really caught like that?'

'I don't know for sure. According to the internet, there were rumours of the Grand Duchess Maria being involved in some indiscretion with a guard. But to the best of my recollection he was a young guard called Skorokhodov. There does seem to have been a cool relationship between Maria and her mother and elder sisters after the alleged incident. But it's mostly surmise and rumour, there's little in the way of checkable fact,' I said.

'So this fits in with what little is known?'

'It seems to, but the confirmed historical record is vague, to say the least.'

With that we turned once more to the memoir.

Chapter 21

Miserably I made my way to the prearranged meeting with Alley.

'What is the plan then?' I asked. 'It had better work because I am persona non grata at the House.' I did not explain why.

Alley laid out a hand-drawn plan of the House on the table.

'With you, we have fifteen men. We will break up into three groups of five. The groups will enter here, here and here,' he tapped the map. 'Each group will move independently to the rooms where the Imperial Family is held.'

My heart sank as I saw what could be my last chance of rescuing Marie disappear.

'If you follow that plan, I doubt there'll be any survivors to get to the Imperial Family. Who the hell drew this plan?'

'One of my local agents, a monarchist officer. Why?'

'What did he do, draw it from outside the wall? Because he's missed the machine gun nest on the balcony, here, and on the ground floor, here. As well as that, there are well-armed guards, here, here, here and here! This isn't a rescue mission, it's a suicide mission.'

'Bugger! Are you sure?'

'I've seen them with my own eyes.'

'So what you're telling me is this place is bristling with weapons. It's impregnable!'

'Not impregnable, but close to it.'

'Damn. We'll have to abort. There's no way we can get them out of that bloody house. We'll have to bide our time. Stay on the alert and try to break them out whenever they are moved. They can't keep them in there forever.'

'There's no way to let the Tsar know the rescue is aborted, he and his family will be waiting all night in vain,' I said. 'And Marie will think I have abandoned her,' I added silently.

'That's unfortunate. Is there any way you can re-establish contact?'

'Not first hand. I was barred by Beloborodov and Goloshchekin, they gave Avdeyev strict instructions. There might be a guard I can get to pass messages, especially if you can supply some bribe money.'

'I've rented a room opposite the House, I suggest you base yourself there.'

It was two days before I managed to engineer a meeting with the guard. It was not hard to play the heart-broken Romeo separated from his Juliet. The guard was sympathetic and agreed to carry letters to and from Marie, for a considerable fee. I slid a letter across the table to him. He looked at it blankly, it was in English.

'My Darling Marie,

I am so sorry that the event planned for the night of your birthday failed to materialise, there were organisational difficulties. How are things there, my love? I hope you were not scolded too severely by your mother after we were found together. It breaks my heart to be able to walk the other side of the palisade wall from you and not be able to see or speak to you. I am working on another way for us to be together and I will not rest until we are reunited.

All my love.
E. "

'What's this?'

'It's in a foreign language in case it falls into Goloshchekin's hands, or if the former Tsaritsa should see it.'

He grunted, clearly unhappy, but after the exchange of some more roubles, he thrust the letter into his pocket and agreed to meet me the next night, should Marie reply.

Seleznov, the guard, did not make the rendezvous until the night after. He had bad news. Avdeyev had been summarily replaced, as had all of the interior guards. The new Commandant was Yakov Yurovsky, an officer of the Urals Cheka with a history of extremism. He had brought in his own internal guards, a group of Letts, who were as militant as their commander. There was some slightly reassuring news. Seleznov was now on duty in the compound where the Romanovs exercised each day and for an increased fee, he agreed to try to continue to get messages to and from Marie.

Two days passed and there was nothing. I decided to try a plea to Goloshchekin and went to his office, only to find that he had gone to Moscow to consult with Sverdlov and was not expected back for a week. Another two days passed before Seleznov brought a reply.

"My Dearest E,

My heart leapt with happiness when I received your letter. I have given Papa your message and assured him that you still have our interests in mind. Things are difficult for me here. Mama is still furious with me and is ignoring me. Olga and Tatiana were scandalised to hear about us and have been ostracising me too. Thank God for

166

Nastya and Papa. Nastya has been a tower of strength and Papa has been understanding. You might not have royal blood, but I told you, Papa approves of you. I hope I can see you soon, my love. I miss you and cannot wait until we can be together.

Your Marie"

I arranged to meet him the following evening with my reply.

I spent the day surveying the Ipatiev House from my window, straining to see if I could get a glimpse of Marie. That evening I handed Seleznov a brief note to pass on. He had refused to take a full letter, as he had had problems in managing to collect Marie's reply unobserved. He wanted a smaller scrap of paper that would be easier to secrete and pass to Marie. My message read:

"Darling Marie,

I am still working on your behalf. Every day without you is an eternity of emptiness. I miss you my love, do not despair, we will be together soon.

All my love

E"

Seleznov promised to meet me as soon as he had a reply and told me to be at our rendezvous each night at eight o'clock, as he did not know when he would be able to get the message to her or pick up the reply from her.

I heard nothing for the next two days, but in that time Goloshchekin had returned from Moscow. Again, I went to see him to try to engineer my readmission to the Ipatiev House, but he refused to even see me. Instead

167

he sent a junior officer with a message that he had his instructions from Sverdlov and the Romanov family were no longer of concern to me. That in itself concerned me. What was Sverdlov planning in conjunction with the Ural Soviet? Had he abandoned the agreement with Britain? Certainly, he had always seemed to be a reluctant participant in the rescue mission. I became more worried than ever about Marie's safety.

I passed the next day in a state of anxiety before Seleznov appeared at the rendezvous with my reply from Marie.

"My Dearest E,

I was so happy to hear from you, I was afraid that the change of guards would mean I would no longer get your letters. I am well, though Mama and the Big Two are still very cold to me. I am worried about Papa, he seems so depressed. Come for us soon, my love, I long to see you.

Ever your Marie "

It was clear that our rescue attempt was going nowhere fast. In desperation I sent a coded telegraph to Bruce-Lockhart asking for pressure to be brought to bear to free Marie's family. The reply was for us to sit tight and await events. He hinted that game changing events were imminent in the next few weeks, but there was no further detail.

That night I sat down to pen a reply to Marie; I had to try to keep up her spirits and those of her family.

Dearest Marie,

I am afraid there is no news to report, though I have not given up on you or your family. Trust in me and tell your father to do the same. I am hopeful that something will happen soon that will change your situation and allow us to be reunited. My love for you is stronger than ever. Remember that I will never give up on you.

Your

E"

I was not to know it, but that was to be the last contact I had with Marie.

My legs were stiff from sitting for so long and I stood to stretch. I walked over to the window and looked out. A dark four-wheel-drive was pulling into the almost empty car park. I idly watched it stop and saw two men get out. The driver was a large shaven-headed man, from this angle I couldn't see his face. The passenger was also shaven-headed and wearing a black leather jacket. Something about them looked familiar. As one turned to speak to the other, I caught sight of his face and recognised one of the thugs in the Ford that had chased us a few days before.

'Fuck! It's them, the guys from the Ford. How in Christ's name did they find us? Grab your stuff. Anything that's not to hand leave!'

I ran to my adjacent room and snatched up my holdall. Lisa was already outside her room. I glanced at the indicator on the lift. The elevator was descending in response to a summons from the ground floor.

'The fire escape, quick!' I instructed.

We flew down the three flights of stairs to a ground floor passage that linked the reception area with the dining room and kitchen. I peered cautiously through the circular glass window set into the fire door. I could hear the man's south London accent as he distracted the receptionist.

'Shit, one's stayed in reception while other's gone up to get us! This way, let's go.'

I led her at the run through the dining room into the deserted kitchen beyond. The kitchen door was unlocked and we burst out into the open air. I looked franticly around and noted that we had to pass the SUV to get to the Saab in the secluded corner we had parked in. As we passed the big vehicle I noticed that the doors had been left unlocked.

'Here,' I said throwing the Saab keys to Lisa, 'take my bag and start the car.'

'What about you?' Lisa called over her shoulder.

'I don't fancy another car chase, especially against this beast, the Saab will never outrun it. It can't be seen from reception, so I'm going to try to immobilise it.'

I opened the driver's door and was disappointed to see that the keys were not in the ignition. The easiest way to delay our opponents would be to drive off in their car. Hot-wiring a car was well outside my abilities, so that was not an option. I pulled the bonnet release handle, low on the bulk head beside the door. I ran round and lifted the bonnet. I glanced underneath find what I wanted. An angry shout sounded and I quickly let the bonnet fall. The two men were sprinting towards me from reception at a good pace. I turned to run, but at my age, I doubted I could reach the Saab before they caught me.

With a roar, the Saab pulled up alongside me with Lisa at the wheel. I wrenched open the door and threw myself inside.

'Go!' I shouted.

Lisa needed no second telling and the Saab turned tightly and headed for the exit. I looked through the rear window to see one man pull a pistol from under his coat and start to raise it.

'Gun!' I said and ducked down, but the man in the leather jacket slapped down his partner's hand and gestured towards the SUV.

'They'll soon catch us in that,' Lisa stated.

'Only if they can start it,' I grinned holding up a fuse in my hand. 'The fuse for the fuel pump, they won't be going far without that!'

Lisa laughed and drove on rapidly.

'Where to?' she asked.

'We need another bolthole. You pick.'

Lisa drove for thirty-five minutes to a village ten miles from the house, where she pulled in to the car park of an inn.

'We can stay here,' she said.

'You go in and book us in, I'll move the car in case anyone sees it.'

I drove the Saab out of the car park and parked it in a quiet residential street a few hundred yards away. By the time I had returned to the inn, Lisa had arranged rooms.

'I've got us rooms, Dad,' she said loudly.

I caught on quickly, but wasn't sure what names she had used.

'Lead on then, love,' I told her.

Once in our room, Lisa told me she had booked us in as Ian and Liz Peters, a father and daughter.

'How the hell did those thugs find us?' I asked.

'I don't know, but I think we'll be safe here for now.'

There was something niggling at the back of my mind, but try as I might, I couldn't put it into words.'

'We've really got to solve this, Ian. It's getting far too scary.' Lisa said. 'We need to finish this memoir and get this sorted.' She laid the papers on the bed and began to read.

There was no message from Marie the next evening. That night, as I lay in my bed I could hear the distant sounds of heavy guns as the White army closed on Ekaterinburg. Rumours were flying around that the Reds were planning to withdraw from the city. If that was to be the case, then the chaos of their retreat could present the opportunity we needed to free the Imperial Family.

All the next day the sounds of the fighting drew closer and there was an air of panic about the city. I met with Alley to finalise the plans to swoop and free Marie and her family. Although there was no news from Marie, I was in better spirits than I had been for weeks. A wave of optimism washed over me, I was sure that Marie and I would soon be on our way to freedom.

I was awakened by a muffled volley of gunshots. I rolled over in confusion and checked my watch; it was two fifteen in the morning. Three or four ragged volleys followed and then silence. My first instinct was that the Whites had reached the city, then my blood ran cold as I realised the shooting was coming from the House opposite. I hurriedly dressed, in time to hear further volleys followed by five or six single shots. By that time I was out of the door and running towards the Ipatiev House. I was immediately halted by three guards with fixed bayonets.

'No-one is to approach the house Comrade.'

'Let me through, I am Special Commissar Yakovlev, I am the representative of the Central Committee. I insisted you allow me to pass.'

'I am sorry Comrade. My orders are clear, no-one gets near the house.

At that moment a woman's scream sounded shrilly from behind the house, only to be abruptly cut off. I turned from the guards and began to run to the road that bordered the rear of the house. Once again I was

172

prevented from getting through by a cordon of implacable guards. I tried to push my way past them, but I was forcibly restrained by three of them. Pinned and unable to move I could do nothing but listen to the noise of motor engines as fading into the night.

'There's nothing to be done, Comrade,' a sergeant said to me as I was released. 'Whatever has happened in there is over and done with now. There is no point in getting yourself arrested, that won't help anyone. Go home.'

I returned to my room, hoping against hope that I was wrong and Marie would be alright. In my heart I knew that I had lost my one true love, but my mind was not ready to accept it. It was a long night.

As soon as it was light I went in search of Seleznov. I found him at breakfast at our usual meeting place.

'Seleznov, what happened last night?'

'You really do not want to know, Comrade. I am afraid your lady is dead and her whole family with her.'

I suddenly felt empty as my worst fears were realised.

'What happened?'

'It would be no kindness to tell you, my friend. It is better you remember her as she was.'

'Tell me. I have to know.'

'As you wish. I saw nothing personally, we were all sent to guard the exterior of the building. But I spoke to one of the Letts who was inside. At about two this morning, the Romanovs and their servants were taken to the basement having been told that they were to be moved. Yurovsky and that drunken bastard Ermakov led a group of Letts, who entered the room and opened fire from the doorway. From what I was told, the powder smoke was so dense that they couldn't see their targets

173

and ricochets were flying around like hail. They were forced to leave the room to let the smoke clear. Then they went back and finished the job.'

'No-one survived, you are sure?'

'Comrade, the former Tsar and his wife were killed at once, many of the others were only wounded, which is why they had to go back in. I hear the girls were hard to kill. The bullets bounced off their chests and Ermakov could not even finish them off with a bayonet. It is rumoured that their bodices were filled with jewels.'

I felt as if iced water were running through my veins. Then and there I swore that I would bring retribution upon Marie's killers. My mind rebelled at the idea, but I simply had to know.

'How did Marie die?'

'Are you sure that you want to know?'

'I don't want to know, but I have to. Please, tell me.'

'From what I have been told, your lady tried to escape, she was beating on a locked door calling out "Edwin," whatever that means. She was cut down by a bullet in the leg. She and her youngest sister were still alive when the shooting was stopped. When they went back in they shot your lady in the head and her sister was finished off with a bayonet.'

'Thank you for telling me.'

'I am afraid it's not over yet. As they were carrying the bodies out to the lorry, your lady came to and sat up screaming. The shot must have only grazed her head. One of the Letts tried to bayonet her, when that failed he smashed her face in with his rifle butt to silence her.'

Chapter 22

Lisa looked up with tears trickling down her cheeks.

'Is that how they died? Did Marie really die in that terrible way?

For a moment I could not reply - I too was affected by the gruesome death of the young woman we had come to know through the manuscript.

'I'm afraid so,' I said, thickly. 'As far as I know, it's accepted that Marie was shot in the thigh and collapsed, only to be shot in the head later. One of the younger grand duchesses supposedly survived the massacre and had to be finished off later. Some sources say it was Maria, others it was Anastasia, there are suggestions it could have been both.'

'But for her to die like that...It's horrible. Poor Edwin!' Lisa's voice was choked with raw emotion.

'Yes, I know, it's almost like losing someone you know and it was a nasty way to die. But one thing I learned a long time about history, you don't allow yourself to identify too much with the characters.'

'But I can identify, Ian,' she said. 'They were in love...I liked Marie and...I cannot begin to understand what Edwin must have felt.'

'I know, it's hard, even for a hardened old sod like me. But we have to read on, we've got limited time to get to the bottom of this.'

'Slave driver!' she sniffed and wiped away a tear.

I ran from the room and vomited in the street outside. Marie was dead and had suffered such a terrible death, seeing her parents and sisters murdered and then to survive, only to be beaten to death by a drunken thug.

The vision of her beautiful face battered and bloody filled my consciousness and the world spun. I vomited again.

'I told you it would be better if you didn't know, Comrade. I am sorry for the loss of your lady. She was always pleasant and kind to me and she didn't deserve that.'

'What happened to the bodies?' I asked. The least I could do for Marie now was to ensure that she got a decent burial, but even that was to be denied her.

'No-one knows. The Letts are very tight-lipped about it. The rumour is the bodies were burned and the remains disposed of in a disused mine shaft.'

'Which of those bastards killed her?' I demanded angrily.

'If your thoughts are moving towards revenge, my friend, then forget about it. Leave this place and never come back. Don't get yourself killed seeking vengeance; she would not have wanted that.'

'I need to know.'

'Alright, but this is only barrack room gossip remember. It was that drunken oaf Ermakov who shot her in the leg initially. He tried to bayonet her and her younger sister, without much success, so it was Yurovsky, who tried to finish her off by shooting her in the head. There are various stories about her end, some say it was Ermakov, others blame a Lett called Soames. I reckon it was probably both of them.'

I committed the three names to memory. They would pay for their crimes.

'You can't tell me that Yurovsky did this on his own authority.'

'Oh no, Comrade. Comrade Goloshchekin was seen there a little later to supervise the removal of the bodies. Yurovsky's orders must have come from him.'

176

*Silently I added Goloshchekin's name to my list,
and if he was involved, then he must have had Sverdlov's
orders or at least his acquiescence. Thus another name
was added to my list.*

'Good for Edwin, I hope he got the bastards,'
Lisa interjected.

'I'm afraid not, Yurovsky certainly lived on; I
think he died in the late 1930s. Sverdlov died soon after
the Romanovs, but I thought his cause of death was 'flu
not Edwin related. I'm afraid you're going to be
disappointed,' I said.

'Well I hope he gets some of them. If ever
anyone deserved to die, it's those bastards. At least they'll
all be dead by now; I hope they rot in hell!'

'Take it easy, it was a long time ago,' I said, but
there was no reasoning with Lisa. She was a young woman
in love, who identified so closely with another young
woman in love, the murdered grand duchess. For Lisa,
this was no longer simple historical research, this was
personal.

'Let's see if he gets his revenge,' she said.

*I returned to my room feeling detached and
empty. Alley was waiting for me there.*

'What's happening?' he asked.

*'It's over,' I replied in a monotone. 'They're all
dead. They were murdered last night, all of them.'*

'Are you sure?'

*'I heard the shooting myself and the details have
just been confirmed for me by one of the guards. They
were all shot in the basement early this morning and the
bodies moved out of town and hidden.'*

*'Fuck! That's that then. They reckon that the
Whites will be here within a week. Since the mission's
over, I suggest we all get out of here. I'll report in to*

177

Bruce-Lockhart and then we'll withdraw. Do you want to come with us?'

I shook my head.

'No. I've got business to attend to here.'

'Business? Your mission is over, old man.'

'I've got something to attend to. I'll make my own way out of here,' I said stubbornly.

'Your choice, but I think you're making a mistake.'

'If I am, it's my bloody mistake, so leave me to it!' I snapped.

'Take it easy, old chap. I meant no harm.'

'I'm sorry. I'm rather upset. I got to know the Imperial Family quite well. What happened to them is deeply upsetting.'

'Well, you know your own mind best. But be warned, the wise man said "Revenge is a dish best eaten cold." If you're on a mission of vengeance, I quite understand, the murdering scum deserve everything they get, but there's no point in acting rashly and getting yourself killed too. I'll leave you a car, so you can make you own way out of town. Perhaps we'll see you around.'

He left me sitting there, my blood like ice; I was filled with a cold resolve, Marie would be avenged. I sat staring out of the window until it began to get dark; I don't know how many hours it was. I didn't move or eat; I just sat there empty and desolate. As darkness fell I went out, hunting. It took some time before I tracked down Soames. He was sitting drunkenly in a tavern drinking with several other Lettish guards. I ordered food and forced myself to eat, knowing that I had to, if I was to keep up my strength for the task ahead. The stew tasted like sawdust in my dry mouth and swallowing was an effort, but I forced it down despite my nausea.

178

Soames was a large brutal-looking man with a square face and cropped hair. He was boasting to his comrades in a low voice about his feats the previous night.

'When we unloaded the bodies I stuck my hand up the German bitch's skirt and fingered her. I can die a happy man,' he boasted.

I was filled with disgust and fury, but hid it.

'A drink for the brave soldiers!' I ordered in a drunken voice, throwing a handful of coins on the bar.

The Letts were quick to take up my offer. I kept plying them with drink until they stood up shakily to make their way back to barracks. I caught Soames by the arm.

'Comrade, please walk with me and tell me more of what happened. I have to report back to Moscow tomorrow and the more information I can gather, the better.' He looked at me a little suspiciously, but allowed himself to be separated from the others. Looking at him, I realised he was not as drunk as the others. Walking slowly, I let the others draw well ahead. Passing a narrow alley, I suddenly pulled him off balance and spun him into the darkness. He hit the wall hard and staggered; before he could recover I thrust my pistol into his face.

'Not a sound, you worthless piece of shit. You're not dealing with unarmed women and children now.'

At gunpoint I shepherded him out to the edge of town. The moon had come out from behind the clouds and the terrified look in his eyes gave me a certain satisfaction. Now he was feeling just a little of what Marie had felt before she died. He turned towards me, now totally sober.

'Comrade,' he pleaded, 'why are...'

I shot him twice in the head and used my foot to roll the body into a ditch.

'One!' I said.

179

'Yessss!' Lisa hissed. 'That's one of the bastards got their just desserts. I'm glad that there was some justice.'

'I'm glad to see you are so invested in the story,' I smiled. 'But you do realise that your multi-great Uncle Edwin is basically a vigilante? Judge, jury and executioner, all in one.'

'Well, there was hardly any chance of getting justice for Marie's murder in Bolshevik Russia. What option did Edwin have?' Lisa retorted.

'I'm just pointing out that Edwin has a darkish side. And I'm not saying I blame him. I might have made similar decisions myself in the circumstances.'

'Come on,' Lisa demanded. 'Let's see if he gets any of the other murderers.'

I returned to my room; I did not sleep, but sat in my chair waiting for morning. As dawn broke, I could see the chaos outside in the street as the Bolsheviks began to prepare to abandon the town. I took myself down to Goloshchekin's headquarters and found a good vantage point from which to await my chance.

Two hours passed before I saw activity in Goloshchekin's office. Through the window I could see the vague outline of a figure moving hurriedly round the office.

'He's grabbing whatever evidence he can before he runs away,' I thought to myself. 'Well it's not going to be quite that easy Comrade Goloshchekin!'

A car pulled up by the door, the driver clearly waiting for someone. I drew the pistol and checked the loaded cylinder. The car was only a few feet from the door; I would not get more than one shot. The doorway was thirty yards away, well within the range of the Webley, but it would take a good shot. I was a good shot.

180

I raised the pistol and waited. A guard stepped forward and opened the door of the car. The door of the building opened and Goloshchekin bustled out. I gently squeezed the trigger. The hammer raised and the sights were locked on the centre of his chest. Goloshchekin had reached the car. I squeezed the trigger a fraction more and felt the hammer drop.

Click.

There was no roar from the gun, just the dry click as the hammer struck the bullet without detonating the primer in the fat .455 bullet. Desperately I squeezed the trigger twice more. The gun roared twice and the recoil made it buck in my hand, but Goloshchekin was safe in the car which rapidly pulled away. I had missed. The guard swung his rifle from his shoulder, looking for where the shots had originated from. Carefully, I backed away from my hiding place and hurriedly departed. I cursed my luck. Six bullets in the cylinder, a hundred in the box from which I had loaded it, yet the one inert round had been the one under the hammer. I cursed and made my way back to my room to regroup.

I had missed my chance with Goloshchekin, for now, but there were others on my list. Ermakov and Yurovsky. They directly had Marie's blood on their hands. They too had to pay. I searched for Yurovsky in vain. His unit had moved out of town to join the main Red army that was still falling back to the west. In the confusion it was impossible to tell where he might be. In fact the chaos was so great I doubted if he knew where he was. He would have to wait. That left Ermakov.

Chapter 23

We were both feeling rather stale and decided to take a stroll in the afternoon sun before returning to the manuscript. As we walked, we discussed the situation.

'Well we're getting towards the end of the story, but we've only got one mention of the Tears. There's nothing about what happened to them,' Lisa commented.

'Yes, that's a major problem. We're running out of time. We need to find those bloody diamonds if we're to dig ourselves out of the shit we appear to have got ourselves into,' I said. 'How do I let you drag me into these things?' I grinned to take the sting out of my words.

'I'm sorry, Ian. I did not mean to get you into another mess.'

'Hey, I embarked on this quite willingly and there no way either of us could have known where this was going to lead when we set out. I've been pursuing this as much as you. It was through me asking Josh to research that we came up on people's radar. So it's my fault not yours.'

After stretching our legs, we resumed reading.

It took me two days to track down his address. When I arrived there he was gone. His wife and son were still there, but fearing the retribution of the advancing Whites, Ermakov had gone into hiding. His son was sick with German measles and his wife had stayed to look after him. I questioned them thoroughly, but it was apparent that they had no idea of his whereabouts. He had abandoned his family and taken off with his tail between his legs.

It was no use remaining in Ekaterinburg once the Whites took over. My guise as Special Commissar Yakovlev would be a dangerous hindrance. Even if I persuaded them that I was really a British officer, there would certainly be other British officers attached to them and I would be ordered back to Britain. I had things to do before I was ready to go back to England.

I moved out of Ekaterinburg, travelling amongst the scattered units of the Red Army in search of either Yurovsky or Ermakov. I remember little of that time; it felt almost as if it was happening to someone else. My grief for Marie dominated my life. It was there when I awoke, it pursued me through the day and haunted me in my sleep. Several months went by and my crusade seemed to be doomed to failure. Reluctantly, I postponed my reckoning with them and turned my thoughts towards Moscow.

The car carried me north-west, away from the Urals and the unhappy memories it held. It took me some time to navigate the chaos and get back to Moscow. There was one person whose location I did know – Sverdlov – the spider at the centre of the web; the man whose duplicity had cost the Imperial Family their lives and robbed me of Marie. That is why I had returned to Moscow.

I held my grief in check and began to coolly plan how I might exact retribution on him.

For nearly a month I watched the Kremlin from afar, plotting how I might get to Sverdlov. It was not an easy goal for he seldom appeared in public. If I was to get to him, it would have to be in the well-guarded confines of the Kremlin.

Sverdlov, the betrayer, the inside man! Now I knew what had been niggling at me.

'The bastard!' I declared.

Lisa looked at me quizzically.

'I thought historians were not supposed to get emotionally involved,' she said.

'It's not the story, the traitor, the inside man. I know how they've been tracking us. It's Josh! He knew we were going to Colchester and we were run off the road. We told him we had the memoir and low and behold, your house is burgled. Then he is the only person we tell where we are and those goons turned up. The bastard's sold us out. When I get my hands on him...' I tailed off.

'It all fits,' Lisa said. 'He's been manipulating us, he clearly got a better offer and he's been selling us out. Someone bought him off. Presumably our friends in the Russian Mafia.'

'If he's responsible for the attack on you, I'll break his fucking neck...'

'This is getting us nowhere. We know now that we'll get no help from Josh, so it's all down to us. I suggest we get back to the story.'

As it was, I decided on the simplest approach. One night at a quarter to twelve, I presented myself at the entrance I had used all those months ago in a different world. Proffering the documentation I still possessed from both Lenin and Sverdlov, I told the guard commander that I had been ordered to present my report to Sverdlov in person. The officer consulted a list.

'You are not on my list, comrade,' he stated.

He tried to telephone through to Sverdlov's aide, but as I had calculated, could get no reply at that time of night. A typical apparatchik, he seemed in a quandary, not daring to phone Sverdlov himself, but reluctant to

184

take the responsibility of allowing me admission. I decided to push him and use his indecision to my advantage.

'Fine, I'll go back home to bed and wait until you have all the paperwork in the right order. I hope you can explain to Comrade Sverdlov why he will be wasting his time waiting for me in vain. What is your name comrade? I'm not going to carry the can for this and Sverdlov will blame someone.'

The indecision in his eyes increased. He was afraid to take responsibility, reluctant to offend me, someone who apparently had connections in high places, and fearful of Sverdlov. Then he broke.

'Very well comrade Yakovlev. I can see from your papers that you are engaged in matters of state. Please step inside.'

Once again I was searched and I was relieved of my trusty revolver.

'One of my men will accompany you to Comrade Sverdlov's quarters.'

I had not counted on that. I thought I would be able to bluff my way through and be free to execute my plan. Now there was an unforeseen complication. We climbed the service stairs past the first floor, an area that was mainly offices and quite deserted at this time of night. I stopped suddenly and the guard, caught unawares, turned towards me only to be caught in the midriff by the punch I threw. As he doubled over, expelling all the air from his lungs, I brought my knee up hard into his face. He reeled back with his eyes glazed and I followed up with a massive blow that caught him in the throat. He went down clutching his throat and turning blue as he struggled to draw breath through his damaged airway. Within moments he was unconscious, perhaps dead. I dragged him into an empty office and used his military belts to tie him.

185

Now I was free to deal with Sverdlov. I carefully navigated his darkened office and knocked on the door of his bedroom.

'Come in,' a sleepy voice said.

I knocked again.

'Come in,' louder this time.

I knocked a third time.

'I said come...never mind.' I heard the sound of bedsprings and then movement from within the room. The door opened and a tousle-headed Sverdlov looked out.

'What is it?'

I gave him no time to respond. Grabbing him by the throat I pushed him back into the room and closed the door. Unable to cry out, Sverdlov's eyes bulged with disbelief as he recognised me.

'Yes, you remember me, don't you, you bastard?' I spat. 'I'm the man you used for a fool and betrayed. You arranged the murder of the Romanovs didn't you?'

The fear in his eyes told me the answer.

'I loved Maria Romanova,' I stated, and watched the fear turn to terror as he realised what my words meant.

Still gripping his throat, I pushed him back until the back of his legs caught on the bed and he fell back across it. He struggled as I pressed the pillow down on his face. His arms and legs thrashed then slowly went limp. I arranged his body on the bed and covered him as though he were asleep.

Leaving the Kremlin presented no real difficulty; the guard system had been set up to keep people out, not in. As I had calculated, the guard had changed at midnight and it was a different officer who returned my pistol and bade me goodnight.

It was announced the next morning that Yakov Mihailevich Sverdlov, the Chairman of the Central

186

Executive Committee of the Congress of Soviets of the SFSR, had died in his sleep of the influenza that was sweeping Moscow. Whether this was seriously believed, or whether it was a cover to avoid admitting he had been killed in the well-guarded Kremlin, I could not tell.

I considered going back to the Urals in search of the remaining killers but in the chaos of the civil war there, I doubted I would have had any more luck than I had the previous year. I hung around Moscow because I had nowhere else to go. A month after Sverdlov's death, quite by chance I met Alley in the street.

'Etherington?' he asked, 'is that really you?'

'Hello, Alley,' I said weakly.

'Good god man, you look as if you've aged ten years. Why are you still in Russia?'

'I told you, I still have things to do.'

'You are a wanted man here. If you remain, you'll be signing your own death warrant. C has sent out orders that you are to be arrested and smuggled out of Russia for your own good. Jesus Christ, man, if you are captured by the Cheka, then we're all at risk. We've got enough problems with the aftermath of Bruce-Lockhart's failed attempt to kill Lenin, if you were captured it would be catastrophic.'

I thought for a while; finding Ermakov and Yurovsky was like finding a needle in a haystack. I wanted to wreak revenge upon them, but the chances were slim and in the meantime I was endangering my fellow agents and the interests of my country. For the first time in a long time thoughts of my family penetrated the grief that dominated my mind. I had abandoned my sister Libby to look after little Daisy and I did not even know if my brother Thomas had survived the war to help her.

'What do you propose?' I asked.

187

It's time for you to go home, my friend. We can smuggle you out through the Black Sea and then through Romania or Bulgaria and on to the Med.'

You're right; it's time I went home

The narrative stopped abruptly in mid-sentence. The remainder of the page had been torn off and the subsequent pages removed. The one remaining page was largely blank except for a neatly written message:

I have removed the last pages of Edwin's story because I am not sure that the Tears of Christ should ever be recovered. Emily, or those who come after you, if you have the desire, you will need to search.

Ad occidentem castrum ante arborem Poenum metalli pyxidis sepultus est.

Chapter 24

'What the…?' Lisa exclaimed.

'It looks like your multi-great aunt has set us yet another riddle to solve,' I said.

'But what does it say?'

'Mmm. It's Latin, but it's a bloody long time since I did any Latin. I can recognise the words west, tree and buried, but that's all.'

'Hang on, I'll put it through Google Translate,' Lisa said, tapping away on her laptop. There was a brief pause before she read.

'To the west of the castle, before the Carthaginian tree the metal box is buried.'

'Great, that makes a lot of sense,' I commented.

'Well there are the ruins of a castle on the heath, about a mile away from the house. It could be to do with that.'

'And I'll bet there are lots of trees on the heath, too!'

'Yes, but why's that a problem…oh! It could be any number of them.'

'Uhuh. And what the bloody hell is a Carthaginian tree?' I asked.

'I wish I knew. But we do have one thing to help us,' Lisa grinned.

'Go on,' I prompted.

'METAL box?…Come on, Ian, think!'

'I give in, just tell me.'

'The metal detector in the attic! I bet that's why Aunt Emily had it. The coins we came across, she probably found whilst she was searching for the box.'

'Presumably, a box she didn't find.'

'Yes, she'd have reunited the end with the main story if she had,' Lisa added.

'Okay. Why don't we go to this heath and see what the lie of the land is.'

'Come on, we'll pick up the Mazda en route,' Lisa said.

'No way, we take the Saab, there's still a tracker on the Mazda. We don't want to tip our hand to whoever's keeping tabs on us.'

We climbed into my car and Lisa directed me to the heath. While I drove, she described how the heath had been the grounds of a large late 17th century stately home. It had been bequeathed by its last owner to the local council, but that had been in the great depression and there were no funds for its repair and upkeep, consequently the council had the house demolished. As we drove on to the heath, I saw that it was a large area of open countryside that was thickly wooded in parts. I estimated that the parkland covered about two square miles. In dismay I looked around.

'I hope we can come up with something that'll refine our search area, or we could be here forever,' I stated.

'It is rather large, isn't it?' Lisa replied.

'Even if the castle is our starting point, the heath must stretch over a mile to the west. We have to find the other marker that defines our search.'

I pulled up in the car park and Lisa led me to the nearby remains of a mediaeval castle. The stone walls stood ten to twelve feet high and formed a small square. This was presumably the keep of the small castle. Squinting at the sun to orientate myself, I looked to the west for the "Carthaginian tree". There were at least five trees in a, more or less, westerly direction. There were two oak trees, a willow, a sycamore and a cedar tree, the latter being one of several that were dotted around the heath.

Lisa looked at the trees.

'Marvellous, which of those is the Carthaginian tree?' she asked.

I said nothing.

'Ian?'

'Hang on, I've got an idea,' I said excitedly. 'Get out your iPhone and Google Carthage.'

She did as I asked, frowning in puzzlement.

'Okay. Carthage, an ancient empire in north Africa, rivals to the Romans, who defeated them in the Punic Wars.'

'What does it say about the origins of Carthage?'

'Er...Founded by the Phoenicians in the ninth century B.C. Supposedly the name meant new Tyre.'

'That'll do it,' I said smiling.

'What? Ian, you are the most infuriating man! Tell me!'

'Poenum means Cathaginian, but could also be Phoenician.'

'SO WHAT?'

'Alright, I'll stop teasing you. Phoenicia was the area we now call Lebanon, and that tree is a Cedar of Lebanon.'

'So, the box, presumably containing the last pages, is buried between here and that tree?' Lisa asked.

'Well...It could be, but I'd have thought that Aunt Emily would have found it with the metal detector. There's only one real way to check.'

'We collect the metal detector and give it a try?'

'You got it,' I said.

It only took a few minutes to drive to the house. I parked a few hundred yards down the road and we warily approached the house on foot. After the events of last night, we could not be too careful. Every precaution had to be taken. Our wariness proved to be unnecessary; there was no sign of anyone. Whilst Lisa headed up to the attic, I checked the rest of the house. Nadya's cleaners had done a good job, there was no sign of what had happened in Lisa room. Lisa arrived, brandishing the metal detector.

'It's surprisingly light,' she said. 'The battery's charged too, so we can use it now.'

Back on the heath, I assessed the twenty yards of rough grass that separated the castle ruins from the cedar tree. Fortunately, the late afternoon had turned cloudy and chilly and the heath was deserted. I calculated that we needed to cover a strip some fifty feet long by twelve feet wide. Six hundred square feet to scan.

'Do you want me to do this?' I asked.

'Have you done it before?'

'No, but I've seen it done.'

'Okay,' Lisa consented.

'You stand there, you're my marker.'

I walked in a straight line from Lisa's left to the tree, sweeping the detector in a three foot arc in front of me. There were no responses, so I repeated the search pattern as I walked back to finish at Lisa's right. I then got her to move six feet to her right and we repeated the process. There were only two responses and I marked each with a rag brought from the car for that purpose.

'Here,' Lisa handed me a trowel she had picked up from the garden.

I looked around to check there were no witnesses, I wasn't sure of the legality of treasure-hunting in a public park. Taking the trowel, I began to dig beneath the first marker. I removed the turf over a six inch square hole and began to scrape away. Four inches down I found it — a rusty six inch nail. I rescanned the hole with the metal detector with no further response. I moved on to the second marker. The hole I dug there contained a rather battered Roman coin.

'At least we know where Aunt Emily got her collection,' Lisa commented dejectedly. 'What do we do now, there's clearly nothing here between the castle and the cedar. So where do we go from here?'

'I don't know. This was our best bet. It's getting dark, so we can't do too much more tonight.'

I sat on the ruin of a low wall and looked around. Could I have been mistaken in my interpretation?

'Can I borrow your iPhone?' I asked Lisa.

'Sure.' She handed it to me and I began to take photographs of the views from the castle that we could then examine at our leisure tonight.

It was getting on towards twilight, so we returned to the inn for a meal. Both of us were rather depressed after the initial excitement at decoding Libby's message had evaporated. Conversation was desultory and we retired to our separate rooms early. For some reason, the mental barriers I had erected around the remarriage of my ex-wife had crumbled. I could not drive the idea of Jane, the woman I still loved, married to someone else. Since our divorce, I had reluctantly come to accept the end of our marriage, but the idea of her marrying that bombastic prat, Simon, cut me to the core. It seemed pathetic, but the last vestige of our thirty year marriage was her bearing of my name – now even that was to go. I didn't begrudge her chance at happiness, but I did envy her. Ironic for a historian, I was stuck in the past. I was trapped, frozen in time and unable, or maybe unwilling, to move on. The emptiness of my life was a stark contrast to Jane's new life. I didn't want to spend the rest of my life alone, but I couldn't see me with anyone else. At my age meeting new people, especially women, wasn't easy.

All of the images I had tried to keep from my mind flooded back. I spent the night going round in mental circles. I lay in bed and tossed and turned, but sleep would not come. Eventually, I gave up trying to sleep and I turned to Lisa's laptop that I had borrowed. Maybe if I could occupy my mind, then I could escape from the problem that haunted me. A vague recollection from my school days was niggling at the back of my mind. A few minutes' searching on the internet confirmed what I suspected. I turned to the pictures of the heath that I had uploaded earlier. I examined each one carefully for clues that we might have missed. Zooming in, I examined the detail of each photograph and there it was. In the corner of the third photograph, I thought I could make out one particular feature, which if I was right, might help us to resolve the riddle. With a sense of renewed hope, I returned to bed and this time I slept.

Chapter 25

I awoke the next morning to the insistent ringing of my phone. I groaned and fumbled for the mobile.

'Yes?'

'Come on sleepyhead. I've been awake for ages,' Lisa's cheerful voice trilled.

'Uh…sorry. It wasn't a good night. What time is it?'

'It's eight o'clock and we've got half a heath to metal detect.'

'You're far too cheerful,' I complained.

'Yeah, I spoke to James last night and he's going to be home soon. It always cheers me up when he's coming home.'

'I don't want to bring you down, but that's all the more reason for us to get this resolved. Having James back in the country makes him vulnerable. He could be used to get at you, unless he's going to join us in virtual hiding.'

'I hadn't thought of that. That's worrying.'

'But I do have some good news for you. I think I may have found another starting point for our search.'

'What?'

'Give me ten minutes to shower and I'll show you,' I said.

Almost exactly ten minutes later, an eager Lisa was knocking on my door. When I opened it, she looked me up and down.

'Jesus, you look like crap. I haven't seen you look this bad since Jane walked out on you.'

'Yeah, you remember those mental barriers I was building to cope with her forthcoming wedding? Well, they rather fell down last night.'

She looked concerned.

'This has really hit you hard hasn't it, Ian?'

'It's rather pathetic, but yes, it's really got to me,' I confessed.

'It's hardly surprising. You guys were together a long time. I remember Mum found it difficult when Dad remarried, even though she was in a new relationship herself. So, it's perfectly understandable.' She gave me a hug. 'I know you'll try to defend her, but I hate her for what she has done to you.'

'You're right, I will try to defend her. She spent years being unhappy with me. She deserves the chance to be happy.'

'But it leaves you feeling…left out?…Lonely?'

She had hit the nail on the head.

'I can't do this right now. Can we change the subject?' I asked. 'I was looking at the photographs I took last night and I think I've come up with something.'

'What?' she asked.

'I need to show you, rather than tell you. I might be wrong and the only way to be sure is to go over it on the ground.'

'You're going to make me wait until after breakfast, aren't you?' she complained.

'I'm afraid so.'

'Poohead'

'To change the subject, I've been thinking about Josh Ryan. I don't think he's working with the Russian mafia. He may have sold them information, but I think he's working for himself. Those guys at the motel weren't Russian, they were Londoners. I somehow don't see the Russians sub-contracting. Either Josh is working for those Cockney thugs, or they're working for him.'

Lisa looked at me thoughtfully.

196

'They're probably in it together. I can't see how an academic from Suffolk would have the connections to employ people like that at a moment's notice, but that doesn't explain how he knew them at all.'

'I'd still like to find a way to fix that treacherous little bastard.' I commented.

'I've got an idea,' Lisa smiled, 'but you made me wait, so I'll tell you about it later!'

Forty minutes later we were back at the heath. Once again, it was overcast and chilly. As before, the heath was deserted. We parked the car and I led Lisa to the west side of the ruined castle. With our backs to the low walls I scanned the landscape from the Cedar tree we had previously investigated to the north. I was right.

'Look!' I pointed to the north-west. 'What do you see?'

'Not much, there's a bit of a bump, nothing special,' she replied.

'That's what I'm talking about. That low sort of platform, there.' I pointed to a raised area some two hundred yards away. It rose some five feet above the level of the surrounding ground.

'I think that's the remains of an earlier motte,' I said.

'What's a motte?'

'An early type of castle, consisting of a wooden tower on a raised artificial mound and a living compound, a bailey, beside it. I think that is the remains of a demolished motte. I think there's a clue in the Latin. I looked it up, it didn't use the term *castellum* for castle, it used *castra*, which can mean castle but also camp or fort. It's a more appropriate term to use for an earthwork.'

'How the hell do you know that?' she asked.

'A misspent youth. I spent too many holidays when I was at school and university on archaeological digs. I remembered that places ending in *cester, caster* and *eter* were originally Roman forts, from the Latin *castra*,' I told her.

Lisa's eyes searched to the west of the mound.

'There's a cedar tree only twenty yards or so away from the mound. Do you think that is our search area?'

'I do.'

'Come on, then. Let's get the metal detector from the car and find out.'

We collected the detector and trowel and began to follow a similar search pattern to the previous day. Sweeping the detector in a three foot arc, I walked back and forth between the motte and the tree. Each time the machine registered a response, we marked the spot with a piece of paper weighted down by a stone. By the time we had finished the survey, we had six markers.

Lisa began to dig with the trowel at the first site. She had only dug a few inches, when our treasure was uncovered – the ring-pull from a drink can. The next two hits were no more successful. The fourth hole went down over a foot, without finding anything made of metal.

'This is hopeless,' Lisa said, dusting the dirty from her hands. 'There's nothing here and I'm ruining my nails.'

'Keep going,' I said. 'The contact was quite strong, if I remember rightly. That implies something bigger than a ring-pull. It could also be deepish. Want me to dig?'

'I can manage,' she replied indignantly. 'You don't have to be a man to dig.'

'Okay, okay. I'm not going to argue gender politics. You can keep on digging, providing you stop whinging about your nails.'

She grinned up at me.

'Do you really think I'm such an airhead?' she asked. 'I only put that in to wind you up.'

'I refuse to answer on the grounds it may incriminate me.' She laughed and recommenced digging. She hollowed out an area eighteen inches deep by eighteen inches square. It took her nearly fifteen minutes, before the tip of the trowel hit something with a hollow metallic sound.

'Got it,' she crowed.

Another five minutes scraping and she lifted an iron casket from the hole. The box was about six inches by nine and painted with green enamel paint. The seams were sealed with wax to make it watertight. We kicked the soil back into the hole and replaced the turf, before adjourning to the car with our booty.

'How do we get it open?' Lisa asked.

'I've some tools in the back,' I replied and went to the boot to return with a tyre lever. I used the end of the lever to scrape away the wax and then hammered it into the gap that was exposed. I twisted the lever and pried at the lid until, with a grating screech, it gave way and sprung open. Lisa looked inside and then picked out some sheets of paper – the missing end of the story. She smoothed out the old paper and held it so we could both read.

...I have responsibilities there', I said.

So it was that I found myself in the port of Ragusa. I remembered the town from the visit with my family before the war, when it had been part of the Austrian Empire. Now it was in the newly formed Kingdom of Serbs, Croats and Slovenes. The early summer sun warmed my back as I walked through the streets of the Old Town whilst waiting for my ship.

Rummaging for my wallet in my case, I felt two hard lumps at the bottom. Frowning, I pulled out the velvet bag containing the two blue diamonds that Marie had given me - the Tears of Christ. I hadn't seen them

199

since Marie had put them in my hand. Tears filled my eyes as I remembered her words.

"Ill-fortune has always dogged those who possessed them."

How true she had been.? It was then that my own response to her ran through my mind.

"I'm not superstitious. I don't believe in fate or luck, either good or bad. They're just diamonds and I'll keep them safe for you, until you need them."

I could not have been more wrong. They were not just diamonds; they were the harbingers of ill-fortune. They had cost me my Marie. I had promised to keep them for her, it was a promise I could not keep. Valuable or not, I felt that the stones should not be allowed to bring tragedy to anyone else, but at the same time, I could not throw away what Marie had entrusted to me. Nevertheless, as I walked around the town walls, the temptation to hurl the ill-fated gems into the sea was great. With the diamonds in my pocket, I roamed the Old Town pondering what I should do. Close to the wall in the south-east corner of the Old Town, I passed the ruins of an old church and out of curiosity came down from the wall for a closer look.

"What happened to the church.?" I asked a passing old man.

"It was destroyed in the Great Earthquake," he replied. I spoke to him in Russian, his reply was in Serbo-Croat, a language similar enough to allow mutual comprehension.

"How long has it been a ruin.?"

"Ever since the earthquake," he replied.

"When was the earthquake.?" I persisted.

"Three hundred years ago," the old man responded. "They should have rebuilt the Santa Maria church," he muttered, as he walked off.

200

Santa Maria's church – the name reverberated in my head. Where could be more fitting to leave the diamonds given me by Marie? They might be worth a fortune, but I didn't want them. To leave them in a church bearing her name just seemed right.

I climbed over the debris into the nave of the church, all the time looking around me. The southern walls of the nave and chancel were still standing at nearly full height; the northern ones had suffered greater damage. I walked around the church, examining the ruins. In the nave, marble plaques were dotted around the walls. I began to examine the epitaphs of those long dead people left there by those who loved them. One in particular caught my eye. It was slightly above head height and the black engraved lettering had weathered almost to the colour of the marble. The plaque read:

VICINO A QUESTO LUOGO SI TROVA IL
CORPO DI
MARIA ANTONIA DRZIC
AMATA FIGLIA DI LUKA DRIZIC
CONSIGLIERE DI QUESTA CITTA
MDLXV
MDLXXXV

Translated it read: "Near this spot lies the body of Maria Antonia Drzic, beloved daughter of Luka Drzic, councillor of this city. 1565 to 1585".

This Maria, like my Maria, had died all too soon. My eyes filled with tears when I thought of her and what I had lost. It all seemed so fitting, to leave Maria's diamonds in the care of this other Maria. The mortar of the stone beside the plaque had crumbled, allowing me to work the stone loose and slide the Tears of Christ into the void behind the plaque before replacing the stone. A far

201

as I was concerned, the Tears of Christ could stay there for all eternity, where they would bring no more tragedy and misfortune.

Two days later, as I was about to leave, I returned to the church. There I did what I had needed to do for the past year. Under the memorial to Maria Držic, I left a single red rose for my Marie. As her body had been denied proper burial, there was nowhere for me to leave a symbol of my love for her, so I left it there, at the memorial to this other Maria. It was little enough, but it was the best I could do. I prayed that one day, I might be able to pay my respects at the real grave of the woman I loved.

Post scriptum.

I made my way back to Britain, to find to my joy that Thomas had indeed survived the war and won a good Military Cross in the process. Libby, my sister, had grown into a charming and refined young woman and even my little sister Daisy was growing up fast.

I wrote the original part of this memoir as a way of coming to terms with the events in Russia in 1918. However, I find myself still haunted by the fate of Marie and her family. I have felt myself disconnected from the life all around me. The ghosts of the past still live with me in the present. I cannot but feel that I let Marie down, there should have been more I could have done to save her. Most of all, I feel that she cannot rest peacefully whilst her death remains unavenged. My contacts in Russia inform me that both Yurovsky and Ermakov survived the civil war and still live in Ekaterinburg, or as it is now ironically renamed Sverdlovsk. More and more I find myself drawn back to Russia and fulfilling the oath I took. Libby is nearing thirty and Daisy nearly twenty, my duty to them is done. It is time to return to Russia and complete my duty to Marie, or die trying.

P.P.S.

Libby, I have left you this memoir to try to explain everything. To the best of my knowledge, the Tears of Christ remain where I left them. If you wish to search for them, I think Marie would have approved, but I hope that you will leave them I would hate for the ill-fortune attached to them to befall you.

Your loving brother,

Edwin

Chapter 26

'It's so sad, he went back to Russia and that's the last trace of him. Did he get Yurovsky and Ermakov? I wonder what happened to him?' Lisa asked.

'Nothing good, I'm afraid. I did some homework,' I replied. 'If Edwin carried on using the identity of Yakovlev, there are records of Yakovlev being executed for treason in 1938 during Stalin's Great Purge. Yurovsky died a few months before; allegedly from a peptic ulcer, but if the Soviets lied about the death of Sverdlov, they could have lied about Yurovsky. Maybe Edwin did get him.'

'I hope so. What about the others on his list?'

'No,' I answered, 'Goloshchekin died in 1941 and Ermakov in 1952. Edwin certainly failed there.'

'It's so sad,' she said again. 'But we did get to the end of the story and the Tears of Christ. Just one thing, where's Ragusa, I've never heard of it. It doesn't sound very Croatian or Serbian.'

'This one I do know,' I said. 'Ragusa is the old name for Dubrovnik, I went on holiday there with Ja..' My voice faltered as I remembered the time when my ex-wife and I were happy together. I forced the memory from my mind. 'If we want to get the diamonds, we have to travel to Croatia.'

'Road trip!' Lisa said excitedly, then as she saw the worry in my face, she stopped. 'What?'

'I just want to make sure that's what you really want. Maybe we'd be best to let Nadya's people know we've found the location of the Tears and bale out, leaving them to it.'

'It's not like you to be superstitious, Ian.'

'It's not superstition, Lisa. After what happened the other night…'

'I see your point, Ian, but would that stop Polunin and co?'

'Well, he'd have nothing to gain in terms of the diamonds, but if he blamed us for putting them out of his reach…'

'So we're damned if we do and damned if we don't,' she said. I nodded. 'So I say we go for it. Once we have the stones, it puts us in the driving seat, we can dictate the agenda.'

'What do you propose? Give one diamond to the Russian government and the other to Polunin and let then slug it out?'

'Now there's an idea,' she smiled. 'But if you think we should duck out now, then I'm with you. I owe you too much to push you into something dangerous if you're unwilling. I'll phone Nadya and tell her what we've found.'

'No. You're right, there's no telling how Polunin might react. It would be nice to hand it all over to Nadya, but I don't think we can. Like it or not, I think we've got no option but to see it through,' I said.

'There's one option we've both discounted, we could just tell Polunin,' Lisa said.

'But…'

'But I'm damned if I'm going to give him what he wants after what Turganiev tried to do to me.'

'I'm with you there. We're agreed, we carry on. So we need to book flights to Dubrovnik.'

'Let's go back to the house, we can use the internet there to book and I have to pick up my passport anyway.'

'Okay.'

We drove back to the house. As I turned the corner into the lane, I could see smoke rising. Not a heavy pall of smoke as yet, but a thin grey mist.

'Lisa, dial 999!'

'Uh?' Lisa looked up from where she was rereading Edwin's final instalment.

'Look!' I said nodding ahead urgently. 'Fire. I think it's your place.'

I pulled on to the drive and could now see through the broken kitchen window. Smoke was rising through the broken glass and beyond I could see the flickering light of flames.

'Give me your keys.' I said grabbing the fire extinguisher from the car.

Lisa handed them over. 'Ian, you'll never put it out with that!'

I grabbed the hose that was lying coiled in the garden and turned on the outside tap it was coupled to. I began to play the jet of water through the window onto the fire beyond.

'Lisa, take over here, I'll go inside and see what I can do.'

'There's an extinguisher in the hall, behind the door. Be careful, Ian.'

I ran into the house, picking up the larger extinguisher as I ran. Kicking open the kitchen door I quickly assessed the situation. The wooden cupboards along the outside wall were ablaze and the flames were beginning to get a purchase on the wooden beams that ran up to and along the ceiling. Once they fully caught alight, there would be no stopping them. I coughed in the smoke, then called out to Lisa.

'Aim the hose at the ceiling beams. You've got to stop them from catching fire!'

'Okay. The fire brigade's on its way, if we can stop it spreading, they should be able to save the house.'

With Lisa's water jet playing on the ceiling beam, a steady rain fell on the flames on the cupboard below; not enough to extinguish it, but it was stopping the spread of the fire to the ceiling. I used the powder extinguisher from the car to put out the flames that were creeping up the wall beam and then turned to the larger extinguisher. "Always aim at the base of the fire." The instructions from the health and safety training at work echoed through my mind. I squeezed the handle and aimed the resulting jet of water at the hottest part of the fire where the flames were licking up the cupboards. The water had some effect, but it ran out before the fire was out. I crossed to the broken window.

'Lisa, pass the hose in to me.'

'Okay. There's another fire extinguisher in the study, I'll get it.'

I played the jet of water at the hungry flames that continued to climb from the cupboards. I was containing the fire, but was making little inroad into putting it out. Lisa arrived with another fire extinguisher.

'Aim it at that cupboard,' I instructed.

'You do it, there's another extinguisher upstairs, I'll get it.'

'No! I don't want you trapped upstairs if it spreads. Here!' I thrust the hose into her hands and snatched the new extinguisher. This time the powerful jet of water began to have an effect. In the distance I could hear the faint sound of a siren. The fire brigade were close. The flames were still not out when the extinguisher ran dry, but there was a heavy crunching on the gravel outside as the fire engine pulled up. Two firemen ran into the kitchen trailing a heavy hose. As the water coursed through it, it bucked and twisted like a snake. Then the fire-fighter opened the valve and a high pressure torrent of water spewed from the nozzle. In less than a couple of minutes, the fire was out.

'You were lucky,' the sub-officer in charge of the engine said. 'If you had arrived any later, the fire would have really got hold. Old places like this can go up like tinder. All the same, it was a damned fool thing to try to put it out yourselves. You should have waited for us.'

I tried to look abashed, but Lisa looked at him challengingly.

'You said it yourself, I could have lost the entire house if we hadn't contained the fire. I'd have lost everything. I don't think this is lucky,' she said staring around at the twisted burned out cupboards and soot-stained wall panels. 'How did it start?'

'The broken glass on the floor over there, looks like a bottle.' He picked the base off the floor and sniffed it. 'White spirit!' he exclaimed. 'Along with the broken window, I'd say we're talking arson. It can't have happened much before you arrived. The police will need to be informed, it's probably vandals.'

'We're about to go abroad, will they need us?' Lisa asked, fluttering her eyelashes helplessly. I struggled to hold back a laugh at her blatant attempt at male manipulation.

'No, Miss, you can give a statement when you get back. We'll make sure the place is secure for you and we'll let the police in if necessary.'

We collected Lisa's passport and headed out to the cars. Under the windscreen wiper of Lisa's Mazda was a folded piece of paper. I tugged it out and opened it. Scrawled on it were just eight words —"Property first, people next. You have been warned." I silently showed it to Lisa.

'Bring your car too,' I said. 'I've an idea that we could use the tracker on it to our advantage.'

Lisa followed me to my house to pick up my passport. We used the internet there confirm travel arrangements to Dubrovnik and find a hotel for two nights whilst we were there.

That night we stayed anonymously in a small local hotel. The next morning I knocked at Lisa's room. She came to the door whilst speaking on her mobile phone. I only caught the end of the conversation.

'…are you sure? It's really good of you to help, this goes beyond your brief…Well, yes it is fitting…Yes I've got the address. Thanks again. Bye.'

I looked at Lisa questioningly, but she merely smiled at me.

'Wait and see,' she said. 'You've made me wait for you to explain, now it's my turn.'

Mystified, I just shrugged.

'Come on, let's go.'

We set off for the Channel Tunnel. At Lisa's request, I drove.

'Ian, have you got Josh's number?'

'Yeah, it's in my phone, but why do you want that treacherous bastard?'

'Payback! I have a plan that will fix him once and for always.'

'What?'

She simply smiled enigmatically.

'Okay, okay. Here.' I passed her my phone.

'Right, I'm putting it on speakerphone. Don't say anything other than to confirm you're here.'

She dialled the number. At the third ring, I heard Josh's voice.

'Hello, Ian?'

'No, it's Lisa, Ian's driving.'

'Are you alright? You had gone from your hotel without checking out when I got there.'

'Mmm. We had a bit of trouble, but it's okay now. We've got the end of the story; we know where the Tears are.' I looked at her sharply, but she ignored me. 'We're having a lot of trouble with some characters who seem to be searching for the Tears as well. We're having to go to ground at a friend's place in London. We won't be there until about ten tonight, but if you meet us there, we'll tell you what we've got and you can fill us in on your findings. Make sure we can see you when you arrive, after everything that's been happening, we're naturally a bit paranoid…' She went on to give him an address in London that I had never heard of. When she hung up looking at her with confusion.

'What are you up to, Lisa?' I asked.

'Just a bit of disinformation. If it works, it will resolve the problem of Josh for good,' she said.

'And you're not going to tell me the rest, are you?'

'Wait until tomorrow and see if it worked.'

'Tease!'

Taking Lisa's sports car was part of my plan. We would park it in Belgium to distract any pursuers, whilst we flew out of Brussels to Dubrovnik. We left Lisa's car in Ieper, a town I knew well, and caught a train to Brussels. Now anyone looking for us would be looking nearly a thousand miles to the north-west of where we were.

From Brussels we used cash to buy airline tickets to Dubrovnik, landing there in the late afternoon. We found an hotel in the Stari Grad – the old town, enclosed by the historic walls again paying in cash. It would be next to impossible to trace us. We were both somewhat jaded and decided not to go searching for the ruined church that night.

Dubrovnik was the town of steps. We walked along the Stradun, the main street, a wide pedestrian road where the limestone pavement had been polished to the finish of marble. The city was built on a grid plan and the streets that ran at right angles rose in steep flights of steps on both sides of the broad street.

It was pleasantly warm, a welcome change from the weather at home and we sat outside a pavement café and ate. Lisa's eyes nearly popped out of her head when the two biggest pizzas I had ever seen arrived at the table.

'That's ridiculous,' she commented. 'I'll never eat all that.'

She was wrong, huge though the pizzas were, the base was thin and light. We talked about our plans for the next day and before we realised, the pizzas were gone.

'I can't believe I ate all that,' Lisa stated. 'I won't fit in my jeans tomorrow.'

'It was good though, wasn't it?'

'Mmmm. It was yummy,' she replied. 'What time is it, Ian? I've lost all track of time since you made me turn off my mobile phone.'

'It's about nine. I'm sorry about the mobile, but I think we could be traced if they were on, at least that's what happens on TV. Better to be safe than sorry.'

'I know you're right, but not having my mobile feels like losing an arm!' she declared. I smiled and slid a small packet across the table to her. She frowned in puzzlement, but I motioned for her to open it. She tore open the wrapping to reveal a prepaid international sim card.

'I knew you couldn't go cold-turkey and not have a phone, so I bought you that. Now you can have all the advantages of your phone and internet, but you can't be picked up by GPS, as to all intents and purposes, you're a different phone.'

'Thanks, Ian. It still seems strange not to be able to get texts or calls, but this will do for now.' She disassembled her iPhone and slid in the new card. 'Now, where is this church we're looking for?'

I spread a town map on the table.

'It's on the other side of town. This is the Stradun, here. If we follow it down to the Sponza Palace, then take the road that goes up past the cathedral, we should find it between the cathedral and the walls. It's about half a mile, mostly flights of steps going upwards,' I told her.

'I'm shattered, we've been up since dawn. I'm glad we don't have to tackle all those steps tonight,' she said.

We returned to our hotel and arranged to meet for breakfast the following morning. Considering how badly I had slept the past few nights, I slept pretty well. At eight the next morning, I was awakened by the alarm on my watch. I showered and shaved, before dressing and tapping at Lisa's door. She answered the door, looking attractive as usual, but there was a tired look around her eyes.

'Come in, Ian. I just need to finish my make up, you don't want to see the dark circles under my eyes.'

I sat on her bed and watched her applying her make-up. In five minutes she was her usual spectacular self.

She had turned on the television, leaving Sky News muted in the background. Lisa looked up with a gurgle of laughter. I looked at the screen too late to catch the breaking news that was scrolling across the bottom of the screen.

'What?' I demanded. She pointed to the screen. I looked at the words flowing across the bottom of the picture. "Three armed intruders arrested at the Russian consulate."

She turned up the sound in time for us to catch the well-groomed presenter say, 'Breaking news. Police have reported that three armed intruders are under arrest after breaking into a Russian consular building last night. Reports are coming in that the intruders were apprehended by Russian security forces and handed over to the Metropolitan Police. As yet there is no indication as to what the intruders wanted...In Paris...' The voice moved on to a new story.

'Bye, bye Josh!' Lisa waggled her fingers.

'Okay, Lisa, you've had your fun and paid me back for being enigmatic. Now what the fuck is going on?'

'Well, I had this idea, if we could get Josh and his two mates picked up by the police in possession of guns, they'd be off our backs for about seven years. So I phoned Nadia and explained the problem. I hoped she had a contact in the Met that we could use. She wasn't happy about leaving unarmed coppers facing armed thugs – I hadn't thought of that. But she quite liked the idea of helping to deal with Josh – it made us safer and caused her less problems. So she suggested an address we could lure him to, it was an annex building of the Consulate that wasn't much used. We figured that if I told him we were arriving late, he'd bring his posse to get there first and ambush us when we arrived. Technically, it is Russian territory, so she could use her own people to arrest them once they broke in. She could then hand them over to our police. I should image that at this very moment Josh and his mates are in a police station somewhere being sweated by Special Branch.'

'You are amazing, Lisa. I always said I wouldn't want to get on the wrong side of you,' I told her.

'Yeah, well, payback's a bitch. I don't appreciate having men with guns come after me or my friends. And I really don't like someone trying to take me for a fool!'

I turned off the television and shook my head in wonder.

'You are unbelievable. Come on, let's go get something to eat.'

We left the hotel and went to a pavement café, where we ordered croissants, orange juice and coffee. Suitably sustained, we set out to find the ruined Santa Maria church. We had decided over breakfast that the easiest way to find the church would not be from the ground, but to do what Edwin had done; walk the city walls and find it from there.

The day was warm and sunny. Pretty soon I had worked up a fair sweat climbing flights of steps and towers as we circumnavigated the walls. We reached the walls that ran along the craggy cliffs on the seaward side of the town. From there we could look down on the orange pantiled roofs of the town. From our vantage point we could see a void in the buildings to our left.

'Is that a ruin from the war in the nineties, or is it our church?' Lisa asked.

'I'm not sure from here. But the signs we saw last night showed every shell strike when the town was besieged in the war of independence and this was beyond the range of the Serbian artillery. All the damage was done in the centre and eastern parts of the town.'

We drew closer and could see that there was a fairly large space in between the buildings, where weed infested ruins lay in a chaotic tumble. None of the ruins looked much like a church.

Chapter 27

I looked down from the walls and scoured the jumble of walls amongst the ruins. It had been many years since I had done any archaeology, but I thought I could recognise the outline of a church when I saw one. I could make out walls, windows, stairs and doorways, but none of the walls that I could see even had the correct east-west orientation.

'This is useless,' I told Lisa. 'Maybe we need to go down there and look at the ruins on the ground. I can't see anything from here that could be interpreted as a church. I wonder if these ruins really do date from the War of Independence.'

'I don't see how going down there will help; if you can't make out the plan of the building from up here, you'll never do it from ground level. I mean it's a bit like looking at it on Google Earth from up here,' Lisa objected.

'You're right, of course. I was just grasping at straws. If we can't make out a church from here, we'll never do it on the ground,' I admitted. 'So, now what?'

'Google Earth! Of course!' Lisa exclaimed pulling out her iPhone. She tapped away to bring up a satellite view of the Old Town. She moved the map and then spread her thumb and forefinger across the screen to expand the image. 'We're here.' She pointed to the image. 'But there's a ruin over here too. It should be about a hundred meters that way.' She nodded further along the wall.

'Okay, let's give it a try.'

We walked along the wall for a few minutes, then Lisa stopped and pointed.

'Look, there. Those are ruins, they're a bit further in from the walls, but they match what we're looking for.'

I looked at these latest ruins. The building was certainly on an east-west alignment and vaguely cruciform in outline. There were short, vaulted transepts that crossed the main building, two thirds of the way long its length.

'This looks far more like it,' I told Lisa. 'Look, you've got the nave there and the chancel is here – that's where the altar would be. Then you've got the two transepts crossing it.'

'The ruins look older than those other ones somehow,' Lisa said.

'You're right. Look at the foliage and weeds. In the other ruins, there were few weeds growing along the top of the walls, the ground was covered in tall weeds and a few bushes. Here the flora is much more established. That tree is growing in what was the inside of the building, but to judge from its size, it's considerably more than twenty years old. It looks like we might have found the Santa Maria church. How do we get down there?'

Lisa consulted the map we had been given when we paid to go up on to the walls, it showed all the entrances and exits, but not much else.

'It looks like there's a way off the walls a bit further along,' she said.

We walked for another few hundred meters and found a tower where a flight of steps took us down from the wall. A few minutes' walk and we had reached the church ruins. The site was surrounded by a chain-link fence. There was a gateway through the fence. I pushed it and was surprised to find it was unlocked. I beckoned Lisa through.

'I don't know if we're allowed through here, so let's get going, whilst the going's good,' I said.

We hurried into the nave area of the church, where we began to search the walls for the memorial to Maria Drzic. In the near century since Edwin had left the Tears of Christ here, the sun and rain had further eroded the plaques. Many had weathered so badly that they were no longer legible. For a few minutes we frantically scoured the memorials.

'Got it!' Lisa called excitedly. 'Maria Drzic. It's here.

I looked at the plaque she was pointing at. The weather had bleached all colour out of the inscription. The incised letters were now the same colour as the surrounding marble, making it difficult to read. I traced the lettering with my fingers. Lisa was right, it read:

VICINO A QUESTO LUOGO SI TROVA IL
CORPO DI
MARIA ANTONIA DRZIC.....

Lisa began to feel around the plaque with her fingers. 'Fuck it. I'm not tall enough, you'll have to search for the loose stone,' she declared. 'Why do I have to be so bloody short?'

'I thought you said it was an advantage being short,' I reminded her.

'That was then, this is now and it's a bloody inconvenience. So stop being so superior and take over here,' she snapped.

'Okay, okay. I'll be good and stop winding you up.'

I started to feel round the edge of the marble. The mortar round the memorial was crumbling in several places now, but I soon found the stone that Edwin had described removing. I wiggled the stone loose and reached inside.

'Yuk!' I declared.

'What?'

'Cobwebs.' I held up my fingers.

'Ewww!' Lisa wrinkled her nose.

I wiped my fingers clean on the seat of my jeans and reached inside again. I felt around with my fingertips until I touched the degraded velvet of the bag. As I eased it from the niche it disintegrated. I threw the remains aside and reached in for a third time to emerge with one brilliant blue diamond that scintillated in the morning sun.

'It's beautiful,' Lisa said in awe.

'Here.' I held it out to her. 'You hang on to it whilst I get the other one. I groped around in the hole and found the second diamond at the back of the recess, where it had rolled. I held it out in the palm of my hand and Lisa placed its partner alongside it.

'They're perfectly matched,' Lisa said.

'Što ti radiš ovdje?' An angry voice called out from behind me.

I quickly thrust the diamonds into my pocket and turned to face the newcomer. He was a short, red faced man in his fifties, who was gesticulating wildly towards the gate. Lisa stepped toward the man with a smile.

'I'm sorry, we don't speak Croatian. Do you speak English?' she asked. The man looked blank.

'Engleski,' she translated. The sight of Lisa seemed to drain the aggression from the man. 'I think he wants to know what we're doing here,' she said.

'Play dumb,' I advised.

' To je privatna. Morate otići,' the man said.

'I think that's something to do with private. We should leave,' Lisa said. 'Sorry,' she said to the man and when he looked blank, she followed up with one of her few words of Croatian, 'Oprostite.'

The man nodded and shepherded us out of the site. Lisa and I walked off down the road arm in arm.

At a nearby cafe, we ordered coffee and surreptitiously examined what we had found. A thought occurred to Lisa.

'Ian, how are we going to get them back into the UK? We can hardly go through customs with fifty million pounds worth of diamonds. I can't see them believing we just found them!' she said.

'I hadn't thought of that,' I replied. 'Give me a couple of minutes to think.'

We drank our coffee in silence, whilst I racked my brain. An idea occured to me, but I wasn't sure how viable it was.

'I've an idea. I don't know if it will work but...'

'But what?' Lisa demanded.

'We need to go to the beach.'

'The beach? Ian, stop being so cryptic!'

'Okay, we need to go to the beach to look for stones. I'll explain when we get there.'

We paid the waiter and made our way out to the harbour. Standing on the harbour mole, I pointed across at the beach outside town.

'That's where we need to go,' I said.

We walked past the restaurants that lined the quayside, fighting our way through the crowds who were disembarking from a cruise ship for a day trip. We walked uphill to the main gate, past the two pike-wielding guards stationed there in renaissance dress for the tourists. We crossed the drawbridge and walked up hill along the road that followed the coast. Half a mile outside town, we came to the beach that lay at the foot of some cliffs. Descending the steps, we walked across the beach that was a mixture of sand and shingle.

'Okay, are you ready to tell me what we're doing?' Lisa asked.

'Yep. Look at the cliff we've just come down. It's made of a sort of soft limestone. If we can find a piece the right size, we could sort of hollow it out and hide the diamonds inside.'

I walked among the early season sunbathers, searching for the right piece of rock. It didn't take too long before I found one. It was slightly bigger than my two fists together and water had eroded a deep hollow in one side. I showed it to Lisa.

'If we make the hole bigger, we could put the stones inside and seal them in with something like fibreglass,' I told her. Then, clutching the stone, I led her back into town.

It took a long time to find a hardware store and even longer to find a motor accessory shop to buy fibreglass, but by mid afternoon we had everything we needed. I used the hammer and chisel we had bought to enlarge the hollow and smoothed the ragged hole with a file. Then I wrapped the diamonds with paper and sealed them into the hole with the fibreglass and finished it all off with a layer of sand to disguise the filler. I then left the whole thing on the balcony outside my room to harden.

Early the next morning we set off to the airport with the stone safely packed in Lisa's hand luggage. By early afternoon we had landed in Brussels and passed through customs without any problems. By evening we were back in Ypres.

'What do we do now?' Lisa asked, as we sat having dinner outside a restaurant in the main square.

'We pick up your car and spend tomorrow looking round the battlefields, just to confuse anyone tracking us. We'll head for home late tomorrow night.'

'Okay, if you think it will work. I do like it here,' Lisa replied.

'Yes, they did a pretty good job of reconstructing the town. It's hard to believe that there wasn't a building left standing at the end of the First World War.' I nodded to the cloth hall on the other side of the square. 'That was destroyed right down to the ground floor, except for the tower and even that was gutted.'

'They've done a really good job of rebuilding, it's a pity Britain didn't do as well after World War Two. I mean have you been to Coventry?' Lisa exclaimed.

When we had eaten, I took Lisa up to the Menin Gate to witness the Last Post ceremony that took place there every evening. As usual, the haunting notes of the bugle call sent shivers down my spine as we stood there, dwarfed by the high walls of the gate that were inscribed with the names of the missing from the Salient. At the end of the silence, Lisa walked to the wall and began to read some of the names.

'I can't believe there are so many names. Did all these men simply disappear?'

'They don't know where they are buried, but there are thousands of graves listed as unkown,' I told her.

'How many names are there here?' she asked.

'Over fifty thousand, but there are another thirty-five thousand comemorated at Tyne Cot, I'll show you tomorrow,' I informed her.

With the ceremony over, we strolled back to our hotel and after a couple of drinks in the bar, retired to our rooms for the night.

Chapter 28

After breakfast the next day, we picked up the Mazda and I gave Lisa the whistle-stop tour of the Ypres Salient. We took in all the highlights, like Tyne Cot, the biggest British military cemetery in the world; the muddy trenches preserved at Sanctuary Wood and the grave of John Condon, who allegedly was only fourteen when he died for King and Country. The latter in particular affected Lisa.

'Those bastards really didn't give a toss, did they?' she ranted. 'For fuck's sake, he was fourteen, there's no way he could have passed for nineteen!'

'Remember, recruiting sergeants were paid a bounty for each recruit they signed up,' I reminded her.

'That makes it worse. Christ, he was only a kid. It's crime as much as the assassination of the Tsarevich Alexei.'

'Come on, I've got one more thing to show you before we go back home. It's a bit out of the way but...'

I drove the Mazda and headed out along the narrow country roads south of Ypres. It took us nearly half an hour before we climbed up onto Messines Ridge. I pulled the sports car in beside what appeared to be a tree covered knoll.

'What is it?' Lisa asked.

'Wecome to Spanbroekmolen,' I said. 'When the British army captured this ridge in the summer of 1917, they dug twenty-one mines under strong points on the ridge and blew them just before the attack started. This was the biggest. Come on.'

I led her from the car along the path that crossed the large earth bank, continuing my guided tour.

'This was the largest planned explosion in history, until the atomic bomb in World War Two. Ninety-one thousand pounds of explosive. The explosion was heard in London and the ground shook in the south of England. This is what it did.'

At that precise moment we topped the bank and Lisa was amazed to see the ninety feet wide, forty feet deep crater filled with water. We followed the path round the crater.

'From what I read, Edwin's brother Thomas was involved in the attack on this ridge. He would have seen this explosion.'

We sat on a bench in quiet contemplation.

'It's hard to believe what happened here all those years ago. I mean, it's so peaceful now.'

'Yep, it's called the Pool of Peace. It's owned by Toc H an international christian organisation.'

'And there were twenty-one explosions like this?'

'No, this was the largest. And only nineteen were set off. For some reason two were left; they decided not to use them and the army subsequently lost them.'

'Lost? How the fuck do you lose an underground tunnel full of tons of explosive?' Lisa asked in amazement. 'I'll bet the Belgians loved that!'

'I don't really know. I suppose the mapping and recording was off. There'd have been few landmarks to go by and no GPS,' I said.

'Hey!' Lisa exclaimed. 'They're not still down there, are they?'

'One exploded in a thunder storm in the 1950s, but the only casualty was a cow. The other's never been found.'

Lisa looked around as if expecting a cataclysmic explosion at any moment.

'You mean it's till under here?'

I laughed.

'You're quite safe. To the best of my knowledge, it's supposed to be at the other end of the ridge, miles away.'

'You rat, you were deliberately winding me up!' Lisa declared. She got up and walked to the pool's edge, looking down into the water. Suddenly, a tall figure wearing a black leather jacket, jeans and a black ski mask emerged from the trees. He pointed a large black automatic pistol at me.

'The Tears of Christ. Give,' he demanded in an eastern european accent, holding out his left hand.

'We don't have them,' I lied.

He raised the pistol threateningly. I saw Lisa look to my left, signalling with her eyes and gesturing slightly with her head. I edged in that direction. Clearly Lisa had some sort of plan. Now the angle formed between Lisa and our assailant and myself was greater than forty-five degrees. He was finding it difficult to cover us both with his gun. His eyes flicked back and forth between us and he seemed on the point of stepping back so he could watch us simultaneously, which was not what Lisa wanted.

'The diamonds are in the car,' I said quickly, gesturing extravagantly towards the car, away from Lisa. He automatically glanced in that direction, turning his head away from Lisa for a second. Quickly, she stepped in, swinging her shoulder bag like an athlete throwing the hammer. The bag smashed into the side of his face with a satisfying thump. Stunned, the man was knocked from his feet and sprawled on the ground, losing his grip on the pistol. I quickly leapt forward and kicked the gun hard so that it skittered across the ground and splashed into the pool.

'Come on,' Lisa yelled and ran towards the car with me close on her heels.

Behind the Mazda stood a dark coloured Ford. As we ran towards the car I stooped and picked up a thin twig from the ground. Lisa leapt into the driving seat and started the engine, but I knelt at the nearside front tyre of the Ford. Twisting off the dust cap, I pushed the twig hard into the valve and was rewarded with a hiss of escaping air. With the twig lodged there, the tyre continued to deflate as I jumped into the passenger seat of the Mazda beside Lisa. The masked man was just appearing at the head of the path from the pool.

'Go!' I instructed.

The sportscar accellerated away as I saw the gunman running unsteadily towards his car. He jumped into the driving seat and started the engine and roared after us. Lisa threw the Madza into the first bend and the nimble sportscar gripped the road and continued to increase its speed. I looked through the rear window to see the Ford wallow round the corner and veer sharply to the left as the flat tyre offered no traction and the wheel rim dug into the road surface. With difficulty, the driver managed to control the vehicle and was forced to pull up and watch us drive away. He would be going nowhere until he had changed the tyre, by which time we would be well away.

'Quick thinking back there,' Lisa complimented me. 'I'd have never thought of the tyre.'

'I've read too many thriller novels over the years. At least I learned something. It was nothing compared to your Margaret Thatcher impression,' I laughed. 'What the hell have you got in that bag?'

Lisa passed over her bag. There was certainly a heavy weight in the bottom. I reached in to find the rock in which we had hidden the Tears.

'Jeez, that must have been like being hit with a medieval mace. You're a dangerous person when roused.'

'You don't know the half of it,' Lisa laughed. 'I had to keep the rock somewhere, I couldn't leave it in the car. It had been a bloody nuisance all day pulling on my shoulder. I just thought it might as well do some good.'

225

'It certainly did that,' I smiled.

'Who do you think that was, Ian?'

'I haven't got a clue. He was Russian or something similar, but with the number of Russians caught up in this, it could have been anyone – except Nadya,' I added.

'Because he didn't have the boobs,' Lisa interjected with mock disgust. 'You're are all the same. Put you in a life-threatening situation where guns are being waved around and you can still think of nothing but boobs. Men!'

'Guilty as charged,' I laughed. 'You know what they say, when a man stops noticing things like that, it's because he's dead.'

Lisa shook her head in mock sadness.

'What do we do now?' Lisa asked. 'Do we carry on sightseeing?'

'No, I think we should head back towards the Channel Tunnel. It's a bit too risky to stay around here after that. Remember there's a bug on the car, we can be followed.'

'Let's take it off and ditch it,' Lisa suggested.

'Leave it until we get back to England. It'll be easier for us to disappear then. If we fall off their radar here, it'd be too easy for them to pick us up at the Tunnel terminal when we get back.'

'Good idea. But it's a pity, I'd have liked to have seen more. There's a horrible fascination about this place and it's all so sad. Will you show it to me another time, Ian?'

'Gladly, Lisa.' I could think of little that I would have enjoyed more than having the excuse to spend more time with Lisa, guiding her round the Belgian battlefields.

We set off for Calais, Lisa driving at speed, but staying just within the speed limit. We did not want trouble with the French police whilst carrying forty million pounds worth of diamonds to which we had no legal claim.

Chapter 29

We caught the late afternoon shuttle back to Folkestone. As Lisa had driven the continental leg, I was taking my turn at driving the Mazda.

'I know you've been suffering from withdrawal symptoms,' I told her. 'You can put your own sim card in now.'

Lisa quickly pulled her iPhone from her bag and switched it on and inserted her original card. Almost immediately it chirped to indicate a waiting text message. With studied concentration, Lisa tapped at the screen.

'That's strange,' she said. 'James' dad wants me to phone him.'

She scrolled through her contacts and selected a number.

'Hello, Roy, it's Lisa...' There was a pause then I saw the colour drain from Lisa's face, almost as if someone had opened a tap and her eyes filled with tears. 'What happened...?' Her voice rose an octave. 'How is he...?. When did this happen...?I'm just outside Folkestone, I'll be with you in an hour.'

For a moment, she just sat there, stunned, a single tear trickling down her cheek.

'James... James has had an accident in Budapest. He...he's in hospital with multiple injuries. His dad...says he's in a...a serious condition.' She buried her face in her hands.

There was a motorway exit just a few hundred yards further on, I turned off and immediately pulled over. I put my arm around her and pulled her to me. For a minute or two, she wept into my shoulder; then she pulled away. She composed herself, using her fingers to wipe away the wetness from her cheeks.

'I need to go to his parents' place, it's near Hastings. Will you come with me, Ian?'

'Of course, whatever you want,' I told her.

She tapped the address into the satnav to guide me and I drove as if all the devils of hell were after us.

'Ian, you don't think...You don't think his accident is to do with me?' she asked in a small voice.

'I don't know, we haven't enough to go on. It'll do no good to speculate until we know more.'

It didn't take as long as I expected to get to James' parents' house. I pulled on to the drive of a large, three-storey, detached Victorian red-brick house and got out as Lisa flew to the door. A tall, good-looking man of my own age answered the door; his face was grey and taught with strain. Lisa hugged him.

'Roy, this is Ian. He's been helping me with the house. Ian, this is Roy, James' father,' she introduced us.

We shook hands and he invited us in.

'I'm sorry to hear about your son,' I said. Roy nodded in response, unable to find words at that moment.

'Roy, what happened?' Lisa asked.

'I don't know much, there was a phone call from his company just after mid-day. Apparently, it happened late last night. He was the victim of a hit and run driver. This car just swerved off the road, mounted the pavement and then drove off. The police are searching for the car. He was taken to hospital. I phoned, but I can't get much sense out of the hospital. Sarah's away at her sister's in York, she'll be back first thing tomorrow. We've booked a flight to Budapest tomorrow evening.

'What flight?' Lisa asked. 'I'm coming with you.'

Roy gave a weak smile.

229

'I booked you a ticket after you phoned. I knew you'd want to be there. I'll make a room up for you. Will you be staying too, Ian?'

'No, you've got enough on your plate,' Lisa said. 'Ian and I will book into that hotel my dad and step-mum stayed at last year. If you hear anything about James, you will let me know, won't you, Roy?'.

'Of course, Lisa, I'll phone you straight away.'

We stayed about an hour and Lisa phoned the hotel to book us rooms for the night.

'Ian, you take the Mazda back to Suffolk tomorrow, I can't leave you stranded. I'll ring you when I get back from Hungary.'

'You won't, you'll phone me as soon as you find out anything. You were there for me when Jane left, it's my turn to reciprocate,' I told her.

'I think James got hurt because of the Tears. You remember what the note said – first property, people next,' she said. 'It's all my fault. I should have listened.'

'You don't know that, so don't start beating yourself up. Accidents do happen. Some of the driving in Eastern Europe leaves a lot to be desired.'

'Could we take a detour please, Ian?'

'Sure, where do you want to go?'

'There's a place up on the cliffs, overlooking the sea. It's where James proposed. I just need to sit there and think for a while. I know it sounds silly, but it'll make me feel closer to him,' she said.

'You've got it, and it isn't silly.'

'Thanks, Ian.'

She directed me up a winding lane that led up to the cliffs, some hundred feet above the sea. The view was impressive. At her instruction, I pulled over into a cliff top car park. Lisa got out of the car and sat on a bench deep in thought, thinking of a much happier time. I looked around the car park. It was quite large and would probably have held a couple of hundred cars. The cliff edge overlooking the sea was about twenty yards from the car park. People were kept away from the edge by a fence that ran half way between the parking area and the cliff. At the other end of the car park a second exit led on to a lane that wound along the cliff top.

'Ian, will you walk with me?' Lisa asked.

'Sure, kid.'

I put my arm around her shoulder and we walked in silence along the fence that lined the cliff. When we reached the far side of the car park, Lisa stopped.

'That wasn't there when we came up here last year,' she said.

She indicated a striped steel pole six feet long and four feet from the ground that barred the other exit. The barrier linked two huge sandstone boulders that had clearly been part of a recent landslide that had come down from the hill and blocked the road. The boulder on the landward side was close up against the solid rock face that climbed ten feet above the entrance. Though the landslide had been largely cleared, except for a covering of gritty sand, the road had been closed because the slide had taken out the safety barrier that guarded the drop and had collapsed the edge of the cliff, so that the verge beside the road now crumbled into the edge of a sheer drop into the sea.

'We came up this way,' she said. 'We couldn't do that now… Oh, Ian, what will I do if I lose him? I couldn't take that.'

'You're not going to lose him, Lisa.' I hugged her close. 'It'll be alright, you'll see. Go to James tomorrow and stay with him, you'll feel better.'

Lisa nodded and we sat on the rocks in silence, whilst she faced the fears that haunted her.

It was beginning to get dark by the time we came down off the cliffs. Lisa had regained more composure, though it was clear that she was still blaming herself for what had happened to James, thinking it was some sort of reprisal. We grabbed a burger in a fast-food outlet, though Lisa did not manage more than a few bites. Afterwards we returned to our hotel. I took the rock containing the Tears of Christ to Lisa's room. If she were leaving the country for Hungary the next day, she would need somewhere safe to store them until her return. With a tyre lever taken from the Mazda, I chipped and pried away at the disguised fibreglass until I had freed the stones. I wiped off the powered filler and handed them to Lisa, but she refused them and put them into the pocket of my jacket.

'You hang on to them, Ian. I'm flying out to Budapest tomorrow, so I can't take them. If they're responsible for what's happened to James, I don't want them. I'll come and see you when I get back and we can decide what we're going to do with them.'

At that point she was interrupted by the insistent trilling of her mobile phone. She picked it up and answered it. I knew instantly what it was; the devastated look on her face left little room for doubt. Tears coursed down her cheeks as she struggled to remain in control.

'Thank you for phoning, Roy. Will you be okay?'

Once she had hung up, the brave façade imploded. She sat on the bed with her face in her hands.

'James...' she sobbed. 'James died...an hour ago... Oh God!'

I sat beside her and put an arm round her.

'Lisa, I'm so sorry,' I said inadequately. I knew that no words of mine would be able to ease her pain. This time there was nothing I could say to her that would make it better.

She curled up on the bed in a foetal position and her body shook with wracking sobs. Rarely have I felt quite so useless. I lay down beside her and reached for her hand. She turned to me and buried her face in my chest. I hugged her tightly to me as if I could physically ward off her pain with my body.

'It's…all…my…fault,' she sobbed into my chest broken-heartedly. 'James…died…because… I…wouldn't leave things alone…fucking diamonds!'

I made soothing noises and hugged her even closer. Her tears soaked through my shirt and I could feel the moisture trickle across my torso. For half an hour she wept. I held her, until exhausted, she wept herself to sleep. I kissed the top of her head and I too cried for her loss.

The morning dawned bright and clear. I awoke stiff, tired and haggard, but compared to Lisa I looked good. Her face was ashen, with smudged runnels of mascara streaking her cheeks and puffy, red-rimmed eyes peered out through the tangle of blonde hair. I left her to shower and try to repair some of the damage. When she joined me for breakfast, her hair was scraped back into a ponytail and she wore no make-up, save some reapplied mascara but her face was still deathly pale and her eyes were still red and swollen from crying. She managed to consume nothing but a cup of coffee.

'I ought to go and see James' parents,' she said mechanically. 'Will you come with me, Ian? I don't think I can do this alone.'

'Of course I will. When do you want to go?'

'Straight away. I need to get this over as soon as possible. I just don't know what I'm going to say.'

Lisa slid into the driving seat of the Mazda and started the engine. She unclipped the fabric roof and stowed it adeptly behind us.

'Sorry, Ian, I need some sunshine at the moment, everything else seems so dark,' she explained.

As we pulled away from the hotel car park, I saw a black Land Rover Discovery pull out behind us.

'Have we got company?' I asked Lisa, turning in my seat.

She glanced in her mirror before replying.

'I'm not sure, I can't see who's inside. Hang on!'

She swung the car left at the next junction. The Land Rover followed. At the next set of traffic lights, the Discovery pulled up alongside us. I looked up at the windows and saw two familiar faces looking down at us. I locked eyes with Feodor Markin in the rear seat. He slowly nodded at me and gave a knowing smile. I could see the bulk of Dmitri Bukhalo in the driver's seat. From the front seat the round faced Vitali Zhabin waggled a nickel-plated automatic pistol and indicated that we should get out of the car. The shadowy figure beside Feodor Markin, I could only imagine was the last of the four, Leonid Polunin.

Without waiting for the lights to change, Lisa floored the accelerator. With its tyres screeching and smoking, the Mazda shot off as if it were the start of a Formula One race. The engine roared as the car fishtailed away, establishing a gap between the cars.

With the Discovery trailing in our wake, I looked across at Lisa. Her pale face was a stony mask, her lips were compressed into a thin line and there was a look of steely determination in her bloodshot eyes.

'Those are the fucking bastards who killed James,' she spat, as she stamped the throttle to the floor.

The Mazda accelerated away faster still with its engine screaming. I glanced at the rev counter, which even between gear changes never dropped out of the red zone. The manual says that the Mazda does nought to sixty in just over seven seconds – it seemed a lot quicker than that! The Discovery failed to match our speed as the gap lengthened. Lisa swung right into a country lane and then seemed to slow, she was constantly glancing in her mirror. I turned round in my seat and saw the Land Rover make the turn into the lane. Again Lisa stepped on the gas and the Mazda surged forward. The lane was narrow with intermittent passing places, I prayed that we didn't meet anyone coming the other way. I had survived one high speed crash last year, but that had been in a heavy BMW; I didn't fancy my chances of survival in Lisa's toy car.

The nimble Mazda swung round the twisting road, holding tight to the curves and bends. Some way behind us I could see the Land Rover wallowing around, clearly finding it difficult to match the Mazda's speed and agility on the winding road.

Lisa was staring ahead, lost in concentration, gripping the wheel with white knuckles. I was about to ask her what she planned to do, but thought better of it, not wanting to disturb her concentration at this speed. As the Mazda reached a cross roads, Lisa again slowed; it seemed almost as if she were trying to entice the Russians to follow us, rather than lose them.

The Mazda continued to fly along the narrow country roads of the Downs. Bracing myself against the dashboard, I could only admire Lisa's handling of the car as it hurtled round corners and bends. I had to give her credit, the girl could drive. The wind whipped past us because of the open top. As we reached a straight section of road, I looked behind me and could see the Land Rover some four hundred yards behind us. At the next junction, Lisa slid the car into a right turn. For a moment the wheels locked and the car began to drift towards the ditch that lined the road. Lisa eased off the brakes at once and expertly steered us out of the skid, then dropping down a gear zoomed away faster than ever. The road was now climbing rapidly.

'Lisa, take it easy, you'll kill us both or crash and those thugs back there will catch us.' I had to shout because the wind was carrying my voice away. Lisa's only response was to step on the gas even harder.

'I know what I'm doing, Ian,' she said impassively. There was something in her eyes that almost scared me. The road continued to climb and a crash barrier was all that was between us and an increasingly virtiginous sheer drop into the sea. I kept silent, I really did not want to spoil her concentration on a road like this at this speed. The road forked and to my dismay, Lisa took the road that continued along the coast. A few hundred yards in along the road a red and white plastic road sign declaring - 'Road Closed' - blocked the way. Without hesitation, Lisa ploughed right through the sign, smashing the plastic into smithereens.

'Lisa, what the hell are you doing?' I yelled. 'The road's closed, we're trapped.'

'I know what I'm doing!' she repeated. 'It's okay, trust me.'

I did trust her, but I was scared all the same.

Now Lisa eased off the gas and concentrated on simply maintaining our lead over the pursuing Russians. Nevertheless, the Mazda was travelling at nearly seventy miles an hour. Rapidly approaching was a blind left-hand bend; at this speed, we'd never make it.

I had underestimated Lisa. The engine screamed as she dropped down a gear and stood on the brakes. As we turned into the bend, Lisa changed down again, slowing us enough to take the bend. The bend carried us though more than ninety degrees, before spitting us out twenty yards from the blocked entrance into the cliff top car park. Lisa hit the throttle hard. We were travelling at more than fifty as Lisa aimed the car directly at the barrier. The two huge sandstone boulders hurtled at us. The steel pole that connected them seemed as if it was going to catch us at windscreen height. With a yell of fear I instinctively ducked below the level of the dashboard.

Chapter 30

There was an explosive bang as my wing mirror smashed against the rock, then to my surprise we were through. The barrier must have passed millimeters above the top of the windscreen. Had the top been up, it would have been torn off. Lisa breaked sharply and spun the steering wheel to the right. The car skidded to a halt broadside on to the barrier. Ten seconds later the Land Rover appeared around the bend, far too fast to stop before the boulders and barrier. Things seemed to go into slow motion. I could see the look of horror on the faces of Bukhalo and Zhabin. Collision at their speed with the tons of solid rock that the boulders represented would be fatal. I could see Bukhalo's thuggish face break into a scream as he stamped on the brakes and wrenched the wheel to the right away from the rock face.

With a tremendous rending crash, the Land Rover ploughed obliquely into the seaward boulder. There was a the sound of tortured metal as the Discovery bounced off the rock and slewed off the road and toppled over the cliff.

I tore my horrified gaze away from the sight and looked at Lisa. She sat there with the same determined expression she had shown since we first saw the mobsters. It was then I realised that this had been her plan since they had begun to chase us. Her lip curled as she said again,

'Those bastards killed James!'

I didn't know whether she was trying to justify what had happened to herself or me.

She pushed open her door and got out. She walked round the car and examined the smashed wing mirror.

'Fuck, I'm going to need a new wing mirror! That won't come cheap.'

'Lisa, is that all you've got to say? Four men just died there.' I said.

'I knew I could get my car through there,' she said, 'and there was no way that beast of a Land Rover could get through. I thought they'd smash into the rocks, I never thought they'd go over the cliff...But I'm not sorry. They're the ones that killed James, or had it done.'

She thrust her hands into her pockets and began to walk back towards where the Land Rover had disappeared. I climbed out of the car and on shaking legs started to follow her. I caught up with her at the wire that fenced off the cliff. She was standing there gripping the wire and staring down. The car remains of the Land Rover were not visible, but I knew that like me she was imagining the sight at the foot of the cliff.

'Are you okay?' I asked her.

'I didn't set out to kill them, Ian,' she said softly, 'but I can't say I regret it. I didn't have a real plan...I thought they'd smash their car up and we'd get away...I thought they'd probably survive, though I didn't care if they didn't.'

Before I could reply, there was the sound of a car crossing the car park at speed. It slammed to a halt ten feet from us and Pavel got out. He looked as we had seen him before, except for a large bruise on the left side of his face.

'Very clever, I'm impressed,' he said. 'I would never have thought of that as a plan. You did well. But now you give me the Tears!'

'We haven't got them,' I lied.

Pavel's reponse was to pull a large automatic pistol from a shoulder holster under his jacket.

'No games,' he told me. 'Unless you hand over the diamonds, I will shoot the girl!'

That left me with no alternative, I was beaten. I reached into my pocket and pulled out the diamonds. Keeping the gun trained on me with his right hand, Pavel held out his left and I put the diamonds into it. For a moment he looked at them wonderously, then he dropped them into his jacket pocket.

'So much for the patriot,' I said. 'Were you working for them all along? What are you going to do now, sell the diamonds?'

'The Tears belong to Russia. They will be returned there. I would not work with scum like Polunin, who brings disgrace on my country.'

'I see the bruise on your face. You were the one in Belgium, weren't you? So this was an FSB operation all along, Nadya played us,' I stated.

'Nadya, pah! That bitch thinks she is so clever, but she is nothing but a pretty face, she got where she is on her back! A woman like that could never be promoted to her level otherwise. No, I have a higher loyalty than the materialist principles of the FSB. My loyalty is to Mother Russia. You got lucky in Belgium, but it would have been better for you if I had taken the diamonds then. Now it is more...complicated.'

'Okay. You've got the Tears, so we'll be on our way,' I ventured.

'He's not going to let us go just like that. Are you, Pavel?' Lisa spoke for the first time, her voice calm. 'You can't afford to let us go. Can you? What happens? Do we take a dive off the cliff like Polunin?'

I could not believe how calm she sounded. I had been hoping against vain hope that he would just let us go. As my former wife could testify, self-delusion was one of my strong suits. Then it dawned upon me. I thought back to the time when Jane had left me and I realised that Lisa didn't care if she lived or died. I recognised the signs, I knew what it was like to feel you had nothing left to lose.

'That's the idea, Miss Mann. You have seen me; though I have only contempt for the FSB, I do not want them hunting me for the rest of my life. Now step over there.' He gestured with the gun towards the boulders and the unfenced edge of the cliff.

'You don't scare me,' she told him, her pale face steely with determination. 'My stupidity in chasing those diamonds cost me the best thing in my life. There's nothing you can do that's worse. Go on, end my pain, please.'

'Fuck that,' I declared. 'I'm not going to take a header off that cliff to make things easier for you, Pavel.'

'Then I will shoot you now, West.' He raised the pistol. My eyes darted around helplessly. He was too far away to jump him and there were no other options. I braced myself for the shock of the bullet.

There was the crack of a pistol. A detached part of my brain was surprised to hear it, I had expected the bullet to travel faster than sound. I stood there wondering whether it was the shock that made me feel nothing. I looked down – had Pavel missed?

Then I saw Pavel stagger, a confused look on his face. He tried to raise the pistol, but a second shot rang out and a puff of red mist sprayed from his head as his knees buckled and he crumpled to the ground. For a moment I was at a loss, then I saw Nadya step from behind the boulder by the entrance.

'Are you both alright?' she asked, barely sparing Pavel's body a glance.

'Yes, thanks to you. It seems we are in your debt again,' I said shakily.

Nadya looked pointedly at Lisa. I immediately got her message.

'Lisa, are you okay?' I asked her.

Lisa stood there as if she had been frozen, her face even paler and her eyes staring fixedly and brimming with tears.

'Lisa, come back. You're scaring me more than Pavel did.' I wrapped an arm around her shoulders.

'How do I live without him?' she whispered. 'I can't do it.'

'Yes, you can,' I told her. 'You take it one day at a time. Of all people, I know what it's like. You told me when I lost Jane, it gets easier,' I said inadequately.

'But it's my fault. James died because of me. My single-mindedness and arrogance got him killed. How do I live with that?'

'You don't have to,' Nadya put in. 'I'm sorry for your loss, Lisa, but you must not blame yourself...'

'That's the problem, I do,' Lisa interrupted.

'No you're not to blame!' Nadya told her sternly. 'I heard of your fiancé's death last night. I had some of my colleagues in Budapest up all night checking into it. I too feared Polunin was behind it, but it was an accident, a simple, terrible accident. You had nothing to do with it, Lisa. It would have happened, whether you and Ian had been involved with the Tears or not. James' death was nothing more than random, malevolent chance, it was just coincidence.'

Lisa looked at her with tears streaming down her cheeks.

'You mean, it's not my fault?' she asked in a voice thick with emotion.

'It was no more your fault than it's your fault when it rains. It was nothing you did and there was nothing you could do. Grieve for your fiancé but don't blame yourself.'

Nadya bent and removed something from Pavel's jacket pocket.

'Here, these are yours,' she said holding out the Tears of Christ.

241

Lisa took them and for a moment just stood staring at them in her hand. She walked to the wire fence near the cliff top. She simply stood, gripping the wire fence and staring out to sea, giving full rein to her grief.

'It really was an accident?' I asked Nadya quietly.

'Of course not.' Nadya said scornfully. 'It has the hallmark of Polunin all over it, but she does not need to bear that cross for the rest of her life. It is much better for her to believe that her fiancé's death had nothing to do with her. What she is going through is difficult enough; if a white lie can make it easier for her, then so much the better.'

'Thank you, Nadya. You didn't have to do that, your compassion does you credit.'

There was a sad look in her eyes.

'I know what she is going through, guilt is a terrible thing. My husband was an army officer. He was off duty when he was killed by a suicide bomber five years ago...our three year old son was with him. If I had been there I would have read the signs and saved them, but I was late, they were waiting for me.'

'I'm sorry, Nadya,' I said softly.

'I don't tell you to get sympathy, but so you understand why I lied to Lisa. Now go to her, she needs you now more than ever.'

I walked over to Lisa and put my arm round her and she turned and allowed me to hug her. She looked past me at the Russian with her face streaked with tears and mascara.

'Thank you, Nadya. For taking the trouble to find out about what happened to James. It doesn't make me feel any better, nothing could do that, but I don't have to blame myself any more.'

'How long have you known that Pavel had his own agenda?' I asked, nodding towards the body on the ground.

'I knew something was wrong when you showed me the tracker on your car. I told you, it was the latest type, it has only just come into service with us and I recognised it as being one of ours. I couldn't have told you at the time, you'd never have trusted me. I remembered Pavel's outburst at your house and did a thorough check on him. He was associated with an ultra-nationalist paramilitary group. Their views are almost Nazi. He thought that the retrieval of the diamonds would be a propaganda coup for them. What he didn't know was that the group was secretly financed by Polunin – he was not cleared for that level of information. He was so bitter that he had been put on my team; as you heard, he did not like a woman being promoted over him.'

'So, Pavel thought he was really working for this nationalist group, when all the time he was working for Polunin?' Lisa enquired.

'Exactly. Everything he sent back to his political friends ended up with Polunin. I tapped into the trackers on your cars and activated the GPS on Pavel's car. Together they led me here, and just in time.'

'What happens now, Nadya?' I asked.

'Polunin is dead, and good riddance. Without the diamonds, Pavel's nationalist friends will fade into obscurity. If you would give me a hand with Pavel's body, you can be on your way. I have people nearby who will help clear up the mess. I would be grateful if you would mention what has happened here to no-one.'

'We owe you that much and a lot more. As far as we are concerned, we saw nothing,' I agreed.

'Does that apply to you too?' she asked Lisa.

Lisa said nothing, and merely nodded her agreement.

I helped Nadya lift Pavel into the boot of his car and she got in and drove away with a wave. Lisa still stood at the fence looking out to sea, a haunted look on her face. She opened her hand and looked at the diamonds.

'They're so beautiful, but have caused so much pain. Edwin had them and he lost Marie. Marie and the Tsar had them and they lost their lives. Now I have them and I've lost James,' she said. 'I think Marie was right, they're cursed. I don't want them to cause anyone else to feel like I do now.'

She drew back her arm and, as hard as she could, she hurled them out over the cliff edge towards the sea. The brilliant blue stones sparked and scintillated in the sun as they disappeared towards the sea a hundred feet below.

For a moment I stared in disbelief as forty million pounds plummeted into the English Channel; but Lisa was right, beautiful though they were, the world was probably better off without the diamonds. I didn't know if they were cursed, but seven people had lost their lives in the past few days because of them. At least now no-one else would.

I turned to Lisa.

'Come on, kid,' I told her and shepherded her gently into the passenger seat of the Mazda. With tears in her dark blue eyes, Lisa turned to me.

'Ian, take me away from here,' she said.

Epilogue

Three months after I had stood next to Lisa at James' funeral, I stood beside her in the Peter and Paul fortress in St Petersburg. Liv, our literary agent had been impressed with our writing of the story of Edwin and the Romanovs. Now the advance she had got from a publisher was paying for our trip. In the past few months I had seen a lot of Lisa, as she struggled to come to terms with the loss of James, I had been so wrapped up in helping her that Jane's wedding day came and went unnoticed. Lisa still had a long way to go, but I was relieved to see some of her old *joie de vivre* beginning to return. This pilgrimage was her idea.

The taxi from our hotel had crossed the bridge on to Rabbit Island and through the gateway into the star-shaped fortress. We had disembarked in the central car park, where Lisa attracted some attention from the Russian army cadets who were visiting the fort. I looked round to take in the neo-classical buildings of the Mint, then turned to follow Lisa. She led the way towards the Saint Peter and Paul Cathedral. The church was unlike any we had seen in Russia. Baroque in style, the building was yellow coloured and instead of the typical onion-domed towers, the cathedral had a delicate gilded spire that rose four hundred feet above the city. After the heat of the day, the ornate interior was pleasantly cool. The sight took my breath away. The domed roof was supported by columns of what seemed to be marble and an elaborate chandelier hung down. The walls were richly decorated and gilded.

We walked through the mausoleum of the Tsars. We passed the heavy polished marble tombs of

Peter the Great and Catherine the Great with their gilt orthodox crosses on top and double-headed eagles at the corners, and the enormous tomb of Alexander II, carved from a single block of green jasper. Then we arrived at the St Catherine Chapel, a side chapel, where the bones of Nicholas II and his family and servants had been interred in 1998. As we looked in through the entrance, we could see the flower covered stone altar to our left. On the wall immediately in front of us were the memorials to Nicholas and Alexandra, to their left those of the Grand Duchesses Olga and Tatiana were placed. To the right were the memorials to the younger daughters. A single teardrop trickled down Lisa's cheek as she looked at the gold cyrillic lettering that translated as:

Her
Imperial Highness
Grand Duchess
Maria Nicholaevna
Born
At Peterhof
1899 June 14th/June 26th
Killed
At Ekaterinburg
1918 July 4th/17th

Lisa reached into her bag and extracted a single red rose that she laid at the foot of Maria's memorial. The card attached bore a simple message:

'For Marie,
With eternal love,
Edwin'

She stood, head bowed for a moment, then duty done, she turned and we walked away together.

Author's Note

The story of the fate of the Russian Imperial Family took place much as described here. Vasily Yakovlev did really exist, though there is no evidence of him being a British agent. Neverthless, he is one of the more enigmatic characters in history. He really did address Nicholas as 'Your Majesty' and he did try to take the Romanovs to safety via a route that avoided Ekaterinburg. After the deaths of Nicholas, Alexandra and the children, he fought against the communist 'Reds' for the 'Whites' in the civil war — strange behaviour for a Special Commissar of the All Russian Central Executive Committee of the Communist Party.

The Grand Duchess Maria Nicholaevna has always had the reputation of being the most attractive of the Romanov sisters in both appearance and character. With fair hair and large blue eyes, known in the family as Marie's saucers, she is often described as a true Russian beauty. It is said that she was sweet natured and caring, wanting nothing more than to marry and have lots of children.

Although not academic, Maria was a talented artist — interestingly she drew and painted left-handed, whilst writing with her right hand. She was blessed with a memory for faces that was extraordinary. Of all the Tsar's children, she was least comfortable with her rank. Having simple tastes, she enjoyed the company of ordinary people and knew all of the servants and guards of the palace by name. In captivity, Maria was the most resilient of the family, even Yurovsky, the eventual murderer of her family reported *'She did not behave at all like her elder sisters. Her sincere, modest character was very attractive to the men, and she spent most of her time flirting with them.'* One of her guards recalled, *'Marie Nicholaevna seemed the most pleasant... If she had been well fed and if they had let her stay outside, she would have been a true Russian beauty ... When Marie Nicholaevna smiled, her eyes shone with such brilliance that it was a pleasure to see... Her laughter was so gay and infectious that one derived pleasure from playing and joking with her.'*

Nevertheless, Maria was spirited, on one occasion telling off the guards of the Ipatiev House for their crudity. Certainly, Maria did seem popular with the guards, one in particular, Ivan Skorokhodov, smuggled a cake into the house for her nineteenth birthday and was dismissed after being found in a compromising (though probably relatively innocent) position with the Grand Duchess, which resulted in Maria being ostracised by her mother and older sister in the last days of her life. Even in those last fateful days in the Ipatiev House, Maria remained optimistic that the family would be allowed to go to live in England, where she would marry and have the children she so desired. That all came to an end in the cellar of the House of Special Purpose in the early hours of 17th July 1918, a fate Maria truly did not deserve.

For those who wish to delve more deeply into the events of this period, I can thoroughly recommend *The fate of the Romanovs* by Greg King and Penny Wilson, a work I found particularly helpful and interesting.

For nearly eighty years the actual fate of the Romanovs was uncertain, with all sorts of rumours about survivors. At various times Maria, Alexei, Tatiana and of course Anastasia were thought by some to have survived. Alas, there was no happy ending for any of the Imperial Family. In 1991 the skeletal remains of Nicholas, Alexandra and three of their daughters (and their servants) were disinterred close to a dirt road in a forest near Ekaterinburg. DNA comparison with living relatives, including the Duke of Edinburgh, later confirmed the identities, but the Tsarevich Alexei and one of the younger daughters were absent. Russian scientists claimed the missing daughter was Maria, American scientists claimed that it was Anastasia. The remains were buried with full honours in the St Peter and Paul Cathedral in St Petersburg on 17th July 1998, eighty years to the day after they were murdered. Speculation that there might have been survivors was crushed by the discovery of two partly cremated skeletons in 2007, not far from the original burial site. Two years later DNA testing showed these to be the remains of the missing children, one is certainly Alexei, though the debate about whether the female remains are those of Maria or Anastasia is ongoing. At the time of writing, the remains of the last two children have still not been reunited with the rest of the Imperial Family.

Stuart Allison
Suffolk 2012

Printed in Great Britain
by Amazon.co.uk, Ltd.,
Marston Gate.